# Stick-Up Girl

# Stick-Up Girl

*Zari*

*www.urbanbooks.net*

Urban Books, LLC
300 Farmingdale Road, N.Y.-Route 109
Farmingdale, NY 11735



ISBN 13: 978-1-64556-762-2
EBOOK ISBN: 978-1-64556-764-6

First Trade Paperback Printing March 2026
Printed in the United States of America

10 9 8 7 6 5 4 3 2 1



Distributed by Kensington Publishing Corp.
Submit Orders to:
Customer Service
400 Hahn Road
Westminster, MD 21157-4627
Phone: 1-800-733-3000
Fax: 1-800-659-2436

The authorized representative in the EU for product safety and compliance
Is eucomply OU, Parnu mnt 139b-14, Apt 123
Tallinn, Berlin 11317, hello@eucompliancepartner.com

# Chapter One

Deneisha Lewis sat patiently in the lobby of The Riverfront Hyatt Regency in Jacksonville, Florida. She had been invited to a meeting of the top drug dealers in the city. Sean Collins called the sit-down. He controlled a substantial piece of the market in Northeast Florida and South Georgia. As she sat there, wondering what the meeting was about, she took a moment to reflect on how she got there.

It really began the day she was released from the Cobb County Adult Detention Center after serving a year for shoplifting. Deneisha, who everybody called Neisha, was born in New York, where she lived for fourteen years with her mother and two brothers. She was the middle child. Her mother cheated on her husband. The affair didn't last long, but the result was a baby girl.

Her husband found out about the affair, so when her younger brother was born, he insisted on DNA testing for not only that child but also for Deneisha and her older brother as well. The boys were his children. Deneisha was not. He left her that same day.

Deneisha had always felt like her mother blamed her and not the affair for her husband leaving her. Maybe it was because she looked just like the man she cheated with, a fact that she never let Deneisha forget.

"You look just like your no-good daddy. Smell like him too."

After her husband left her and desperate to fill the void, she tried to replace the good man she had, but she ended up with one no-good man after another. The last no-good man took an interest in 14-year-old Deneisha, and one day, when her mother wasn't around, he cornered Deneisha and felt her up.

When her mother got home, Deneisha told her what happened. She immediately called her man into the room and confronted him about it. He didn't deny what he had done, but he blamed it on Deneisha.

"You see how she walks around here dressed—half-naked."

"I do not."

"Yes, you do. Don't lie. When you ain't around, that's what she does. Flirting with me, trying to tempt me."

"He's lying, Mommy."

"No, I'm not. Tell the truth!" he shouted. "She damn near was begging for it."

"You're a fuckin' liar!" Deneisha shouted and took a swing at him. Her mother grabbed her hand before she made contact.

"You need to watch your mouth, little girl, and show some respect for me and my house. If you can't, maybe your fast ass needs to go and find somewhere where you can act grown since you think you already are."

Deneisha was hurt that her mother took his side over her own. She called her aunt, who lived in Atlanta. She was actually her mother's aunt, but she had always been Aunt Carlitha to Deneisha.

"Your mama never did have good sense when it came to men. She messed around and ran off the only good man she ever had. Damn shame. It's gonna happen again, especially now that he thinks she's on his side. He can do whatever he wants with you, and if you say anything, he'll just call you a liar, and she'll believe him."

"What should I do?"

"Your mama ain't gonna like this," she paused and giggled. "Maybe she will, but I think you should come down here and live with me before that man does something vile to you."

"You serious?"

"I sure am. I got plenty of room, and this place is better than that dump she got y'all living in."

"She's gonna say no."

"She there right now?"

"She's in her room."

"Put her on the phone. I'll talk to her."

"Hold on," Deneisha said excitedly and rushed off to hand her mother the phone.

To her surprise, her mother agreed, and by the end of the school year, she had moved to Atlanta and started school in the fall. There, she met her two best friends, Brianna Commer, who everybody called Breezy, and Court. Her real name was Courtney Fields, and although the three of them were so different, they became the very best of friends.

Courtney was the good girl of the three. Don't get me wrong. She liked to hang out with her girls and have fun, and she got into her share of trouble, but she knew where her lines were and didn't cross them. Brianna was the wild child. She was usually the reason they got into trouble. Deneisha was somewhere in the middle. Since none of them came from affluent families, their desire to look fashionable and wear the latest clothes led them to shoplifting. And they were good at it . . . until the day they weren't. Brianna got caught, got arrested, and since the items were valued at more than $500, she was charged with a felony and was sentenced to two years in the Fulton County Jail.

That was the day that Courtney quit the shoplifting life. She had seen an old 1959 musical comedy called *Never Steal Anything Small* with James Cagney. She didn't watch the whole movie, only the title, "*Never Steal Anything Small.*" It stuck with her, and she vowed never to steal anything small ever again. The next day, she began looking for a job.

"If I stick my toe back in the game, it's gonna be for real money. Not no nickel-and-dime shit," Courtney told Deneisha that day and announced that she had an interview at the grocery store down the street from their apartment.

Unfortunately, that wasn't the path Deneisha chose. Two days later, she got arrested for shoplifting. When Courtney got home to share her good news about how well the interview went, she found out that Deneisha had been arrested. Since it was her first offense, Deneisha was charged with a misdemeanor. She was sentenced to serve twelve months in jail at the Cobb County Adult Detention Center.

Jail changed Deneisha; it made her tougher to survive inside. She ran with a crowd of rough girls. They laughed at the cutie shoplifter, but Deneisha was cool, and when it came down to it, she fought and beat the shit out of an inmate who was fuckin' with her. She beat her bloody with a tray in the cafeteria and got two weeks in the hole, but it gave her the cred she needed to be accepted and not fucked with.

"Your ass swings a mean tray," one woman joked. "You are not to be fucked with."

On the day she was to be released, Brianna, who was released early because of good behavior, picked her up in the car that she had jacked that morning, and she drove her to the apartment that they shared with Courtney. They parked the car a block away from the apartment and walked the rest of the way.

"Where's Court?" Deneisha asked.

"At work, as usual. That girl works Monday through Friday from six in the morning until six at night."

"Damn."

"She says she's making good money, so she don't mind. All she does is slice meat and flirt because you know the girl thinks she's cute."

"Who she be flirting with?"

"Customers, the guys that work at the store. They be on her like bees to honey," Brianna laughed as they got to the apartment and went inside. The place was laid out.

"You want something to drink?"

"What you drinking?" she asked, and then she laughed. "It don't matter. All I been drinking is that chain-gang liquor."

"Some of the shit be pretty good."

"It depends on who made it."

"True," Brianna said and handed her a glass of Cognac.

"Thanks," Deneisha said, watching as Brianna sat down to roll a blunt.

"They have any good weed in there?"

"Sometimes. Sometimes, it be dirt. You know how that goes."

"Well, Neisha, this here is some fire," Brianna promised and lit the blunt. She took a couple of hits and then passed the blunt to Deneisha. She hit it and immediately started coughing.

Brianna laughed. "Told your ass it was some fire."

"You wasn't lying, Breezy."

"You know I never lie. You might not like what I got to say, but I promise you it will be the truth."

"Still keeping it one hundred."

"Always. You hungry?"

"I could eat."

"What you got a taste for?"

"I been dreaming about a nice, juicy steak."

"I know that's right. I had shrimp and salmon for a week when I got free."

"Where you wanna get it from?"

Brianna got out her phone and opened the Grubhub app. She typed in steak and scrolled through the list of choices it returned.

"How about Outback Steakhouse?"

"Sounds good. What you getting?"

"I don't know. Give me a minute." She continued looking at the menu. "I'm gonna get the slow-roasted prime rib," Brianna said and handed Deneisha the phone. "Choose what you want, Neisha."

"I think I'm gonna get the bone-in rib eye."

"Anything else?"

"I was thinking about the coconut shrimp, but I didn't wanna get greedy."

"Bitch, your ass just got out of jail. You can get whatever you want."

"Then that's what I want."

"Them shits are good. I'm gonna order me some too," she said and placed the order.

When the food came, they ate and drank some more Cognac and smoked another blunt. By that time, Courtney got home from work.

"Neisha!" Courtney shouted when she came through the door.

"What's up, Court?"

She rushed up and hugged Deneisha. "It is so good to see you *not* behind that glass."

"Sure is."

"What y'all doing?"

"We ate, and now we getting fucked up waiting for you," Brianna said, holding up the blunt in one hand and the glass in the other.

"Let me get a hit, and then we're getting out of here. It's my girl's first night home. We have got to celebrate."

"I'm for that," Deneisha said.

"Cool. Let me jump in the shower first, come out of this uniform, and get sexy."

"I need something to wear," Deneisha said.

"All your stuff is in your room, right where you left it," Brianna said. "Court wanted to throw that shit out, but I stopped her."

"Why you lie so fuckin' much is beyond me," Courtney said on her way to her room.

"What you talkin' about, Court. I never lie," Brianna shouted back and laughed.

Once the three had showered, changed clothes, and gotten sexy, they walked to where Brianna had left the car and headed for the clubs. They didn't stay out late because Courtney had to go to work at the grocery store in the morning. But in the time they were out, they went to three clubs and had a ball at each stop. When they got back to the apartment, their feet were hurting from dancing all night, so Brianna parked the car in a space three buildings away, and they made the short walk back to the apartment.

After not getting nearly enough sleep, Courtney dragged herself out of bed, showered, and got ready for work. It was early, but Deneisha was already up. Mainly because she was used to getting up to be counted every morning for shift change, and she walked Courtney to the door.

"I hate you gotta go to work. I just got out," she said and hugged her.

"Gotta make this money. We can do something when I get off. I'm off on weekends, so we can party all night."

"Closing the clubs like we used to do," she said with her hands in the air.

"I'm out. See you tonight."

"See you. Don't work too hard."

"Bitch, please. I *never* work hard."

"Breezy said all you do is slice meat and flirt with the men."

"Fine-ass men. Don't get it twisted now. I leave the bums alone, and believe me, there be a bunch of them coming through there, wanting to holla at me. I pay them no mind and keep it moving. See you tonight," Courtney said and was out the door. Deneisha went back to bed.

It was after ten when she finally woke up. Brianna was in the living room getting high, watching television, when she came out of the room.

"What's up, Breezy?" she asked, sitting down on the couch next to her.

She passed her the blunt. "Waiting for you to drag your ass out from under them sheets."

"They were so soft, and the bed . . ." She shook her head. "I forgot how comfortable that bad boy is."

"Much better than that rock you've been sleeping on for the last year."

"Seriously."

"What you wanna do today, Neisha?"

# Chapter Two

"I need to make some money."

"Now you talkin'." Brianna hit the blunt and stood up. "Get dressed. We'll get something to eat, and then we'll see about putting some paper in your purse."

Once they were dressed and ready, they walked back to the car that Breezy had jacked and went to Denny's.

"What we come all the way out here for?" Deneisha asked once they were seated.

"The lick is out this way," Brianna said, looking at the menu. "You know what you want?"

Deneisha picked up the menu. "I'll probably get a steak."

"You been fiendin' for steak, for real."

"For real."

"I think I'm gonna get the braised beef skillet."

Deneisha looked at the item on the menu. "Slow-roasted pot roast and mushrooms." She nodded. "That does sound good."

"It does, doesn't it?"

Deneisha put down her menu as the server arrived.

"Morning, ladies." She held up the coffeepot. "Coffee?"

"Please," Brianna said.

"I'll have some too."

"You ladies know what you want?" she asked as she poured the coffee.

"I'll have the braised beef skillet," Brianna said.

"Make it two," Deneisha spoke up, and once the server promised to get those out as soon as possible, she left the table.

Deneisha picked up the sugar. "So, you wanna go ahead and tell me now?"

"Tell you what?"

"Why you got ghost on me for a while when I was locked up."

Brianna looked across the table at Deneisha and said nothing.

"I mean, one minute, you and Court were coming out every week to visit me, and all of a sudden, no Breezy."

Brianna rolled her eyes and looked away.

"I said, 'Court, what's up with Breezy?' She said, 'Oh, Breezy got something going on.' That's it, 'something going on.' Court got no answer. So I know something is up." She sipped her coffee. "I thought you were mad at me about some shit, so I was surprised when you came to pick me up, acting like we ain't missed a beat."

"Honestly, Neisha, I was embarrassed, and I made Court promise not to tell you."

"Tell me what?"

"While you was locked up . . ." Brianna paused. "You know I was boosting cars for Scoop, right?" One of her old boyfriends taught her how to break into and hot-wire a car.

"Right."

"Well, you know I never had no problem with stickin' a gun in a bitch face and taking his ride, right?"

"Right."

"So, he got me looking for a Lexus RZ. It's an all-electric SUV. I spot one." She leaned forward and spoke softly. "This white woman pulls up to an ATM drivin' one."

Deneisha laughed because she knew where the story was going next.

"I wait until she hit the ATM and gets back to the car, and then I step up quick. She gives up the keys, no problem, and I'm off to see Scoop to get paid." She leaned back and shook her head. "I tell Scoop how I got it, and he says he can't take it. Said he didn't need that kind of heat. I'm like, there won't be no heat; I got away clean. But he still won't take it."

"That's fucked up."

"I'm sayin'."

"So, what you do?"

"I go away empty-handed, thinking of how I'm gonna get rid of this and get paid. So, I'm drivin' around, thinkin', and then it hit me. Who would take a stolen car, no questions asked?"

"Dope boyz."

"So, I call Nate Bounce and tell him I got a proposition for him."

"A *proposition?* You actually said that?"

"It's called a vocabulary, bitch," she laughed. "Anyway, he says come through. I roll over there, and I lay it out for him, and he's in. Says he'll give me five stacks for it."

"Five?"

"So you know, I'm excited." She shook her head. "This nigga gives me five in product. All cooked up, packaged, ready to sell. I take it, I get somebody to sell it for me, and this could be a regular thing."

"Get to the part where the shit went to shit, Breezy."

"Long story short, I hooked up with the wrong nigga, and he got me to smoke some with him."

Deneisha dropped her head in disappointment and shook it. "Oh no, you didn't."

Brianna nodded. "Yeah, I did. It didn't take long before we had smoked all I had left," she said as the server returned with their food. Both ladies sat quietly, looking at each other until the server left the table. Brianna picked up her silverware and started to eat.

"I'm like, no problem. I just jack another car, and I'm back at Nate Bounce's spot. That time, he only gives me two for it. I'm mad, but I take it. I was hooked. Next time, he only gave me a G."

"Damn, Breezy. I'm sorry you went through that."

"It was my own fault. Let them dicks make me weak." She saw the look on Deneisha's face. "One big, hard dick got me suckin' on that glass dick."

Deneisha let out an embarrassed giggle. "I get it, Breezy."

"Good for you, Neisha. Anyway, I did some real, let's call it, 'questionable' shit, and I knew I had to pull up."

"What you do?"

"I told Court." She laughed. "She already knew what was up."

"She always does."

"My girl took off three weeks from work to babysit my ass because I was out of control."

"I'm glad you got that shit behind you," Deneisha said, and, figuring the sad tale was over and her friend had gotten through it. She thought nothing of it when Brianna changed the subject and moved on rather than tell her about the "questionable" things she had done.

Brianna and her boy were smoking the last package she'd gotten from Nate Bounce when his girlfriend showed up at his apartment. The three of them smoked the remaining product, and the three ended up having sex.

Sex with a woman.

Something she swore she'd never do.

That same night, she returned to Nate Bounce's spot, begging for a piece and promising she was good for it. He turned her on to a man who was at the house. She never knew his name; all she knew was that he had plenty of dope, and he was willing to let her smoke. Over the course of the next three days, Brianna had sex with him. She had sex with two of his friends who dropped by with a package at the same time.

Sex with two men at the same time.

Something else she once swore she'd never do. Since it wasn't a party without more women, they invited a couple of other women over, and she had sex with them.

An orgy.

Yet again, another thing Brianna swore she'd never do.

Once they had finished eating, Brianna drove them to a convenience store and pulled into the parking lot.

"You gotta get gas?"

"Nope. This is the lick." She reached over and opened the glove compartment. "Everything you need is in there."

Deneisha reached into the glove compartment and pulled out a 9-mm pistol wrapped in a red bandanna. She laughed.

"You a blood now?"

"Nope. But if the cops think that, it ain't my fault."

Deneisha put the bandanna around her neck.

"You ever use a gun before?"

"Nope."

"Give it here." Deneisha handed her the gun. "Always make sure you got one in the chamber," she said and showed her. "This is the safety. It's on."

"Leave it on. I don't wanna shoot nobody."

"Unless you have to," Brianna said and turned the safety off. She handed the gun back to Deneisha. "You ready?"

"Yeah," she said, holding a gun in her hand for the first time.

"How does it feel?"

"Good, I guess. I don't know," she said, but she liked the way the weapon felt in her hand.

"Okay. You're in and out. Get the money and go."

"You not coming?"

"No. This is your lick." She laughed. "You gotta bust that cherry," she said, reaching into the backseat and handing Deneisha an empty purse. "Put the money in here."

"Right," Deneisha said and reached for the door handle.

She got out of the car and walked slowly toward the store. Deneisha had made a note of the cameras and made a point not to look directly at them. Once she got to the door, she pulled up her mask, raised her weapon, and grabbed the handle. With her gun pointed at the frightened clerk, Deneisha rushed up to the counter.

"Put the money in the bag," she ordered, and then passed the bag to the clerk.

With his hands shaking, the clerk quickly emptied the register and handed her the bag again. Deneisha snatched the bag from his hand and rushed out of the store. Without looking toward the cameras, she ran to the car where Brianna was waiting and jumped in.

"How'd it go?" Brianna asked calmly as if Deneisha hadn't just robbed the store.

"Just drive, Breezy!" Deneisha shouted frantically.

Brianna laughed, put the car in drive, and slowly drove away from the store.

"I go speeding away from here like we just robbed the store, it attracts attention from witnesses."

Deneisha nodded and tried to calm down.

"Next thing you know, they're giving a description to the cops. They may even get a license plate number." She shook her head. "Slow and steady."

"I understand." Deneisha nodded. "What now?"

"Now, we ditch this car and get a new one. Tell me why," Brianna said as she pulled into a parking lot.

"In case somebody *did* see the car, and they gave a description to the cops."

"You might be all right," Brianna said, and they waited. Soon, a black BMW driven by a young white man pulled over and went to the ATM.

"There's our ride," Brianna said, holding out her hand.

"You like these two for ones, don't you?" Deneisha said, handing her the gun and the bandanna.

"Why don't you wait for me down there?" she said, pointing. "But first," Brianna said, handing her a towel, "wipe down everything. Door handles, dashboard, steering wheel, everything we might have touched. I ain't trying to get caught by no fingerprints."

Brianna got out of the car while Deneisha wiped it down thoroughly before she got out. She was looking over her shoulder as she walked away from the vehicle. She watched as the man returned to his car, counting his money.

Brianna pulled up her mask, met him at the car, and shoved the gun in his face.

"Give up the keys and stay alive," she said calmly.

"Don't kill me," the man said and handed over his keys.

Resisting the temptation to make the man open the door for her to get in, Brianna jumped into the car and drove away, laughing, as she went to pick up Deneisha.

"How you feeling?" Brianna asked as they drove away from the scene.

"I'm good."

"How much you get?"

Deneisha reached into the purse and began counting her money. "It ain't even a G," she said, disappointed in the take from her first time out.

"Fuck was you expecting?"

"More than this."

"That wasn't a bad first lick," she laughed. "But if you ain't satisfied, there are plenty more stores we can hit."

"You serious?"

"If you are."

"I'm serious."

"That's right. Fuck else we got to do until it's time for Court to get off work?"

"Might as well make some money," Deneisha said, and Brianna pulled into the parking lot of the first convenience store she got to. She parked the car, then handed Deneisha the gun and the bandanna.

"All yours. I'll be here when you get back."

"You better," Deneisha laughed and got out of the vehicle.

As she had the first time, Deneisha made sure not to look at the cameras as she approached the store. She pulled up her mask and went inside. When it was over, she rushed back to the car, thinking how easy it was. Even if it wasn't what she thought it would be, it was still a much better lick than shoplifting every day of the week.

As Brianna drove away from the store, Deneisha fixed in her mind that this was how she was going to get paid. Fuck that get-a-job shit the Courtney was talking about. Since the vehicle had just been involved in a robbery, Brianna ditched it and caught an Uber back to the apartment. When Courtney got off from work, the three got ready to hang out for the night.

# Chapter Three

It had been a week since she robbed the two convenience stores, and Deneisha's money was now getting low. She liked to look cute in whatever she wore, and the clothes she had were from before she went to jail and didn't really fit her now. And they were definitely out of style. So, she spent her money shopping. But now, she was about broke, and Brianna hadn't said anything about them hitting another lick.

"And why should she?" Deneisha asked herself.

It wasn't her responsibility to turn her on to her next hit. Deneisha had to admit that sticking up those stores was a lot easier, quicker, and more profitable than shoplifting. She had just done a year for shoplifting, and it wasn't worth it. If the stickup girl life was what she was gonna do, she needed to make it happen. And that meant she needed to get a gun of her own. But here again, she was damn near broke. It wasn't that she didn't think Brianna would let her use the weapon again, but she knew she needed her own.

Later that night, Deneisha, Brianna, and Courtney were at the apartment smoking weed and drinking when three men, Antony Hughes, Marcel Reyes, and Devonte Calderon, came by. All three were hustlers who were down for whatever made them money. Brianna had been messing with Reyes for about a month. She liked him and thought he was fine, but what she liked best about him was that he ate her pussy better than her last boyfriend.

"He didn't know what he was doing down there," she told Courtney.

Hughes had been on Courtney, trying to get with her for weeks. She had decided that his wait would end that night.

She just hadn't told him that.

When the three of them showed up, Deneisha knew Calderon had come there to meet her. He was a good-looking man, dark-skinned, which she liked, with long dreads and the cutest dimples she'd ever seen. Throughout the night, she noticed that no matter what she said, whether or not she was talking to him, he was commenting on everything she said.

*He is kinda cute,* she thought as she looked at his full lips.

And it had been a long time since she had given up any.

*You never know, this might be the night,* she thought, and finished her drink.

"Roll another blunt," Deneisha said, and she'd see where things went from there.

Calderon drained the bottle of beer he was drinking when he got there and pulled out a bag of weed. "Is there anything else to drink?"

Courtney stood up. "I got you," she said and took the bottle from him.

"What y'all drinkin'?" Reyes asked.

"We drinkin' Courvoisier and Champagne," Courtney said on her way to the kitchen.

"I want some," Reyes said.

"I do, too," Calderon said, but he was looking at Deneisha.

Brianna laughed. "I bet you do."

"I got you too," Courtney said and went into the kitchen.

Hughes got up and followed her in. When he entered the kitchen, Courtney looked up. She smiled and shook her head. She got two glasses from the cabinet, then folded her arms and leaned against the counter.

"What do you want?"

"A drink," he chuckled.

"I know that. But what do you want?"

When Hughes looked confused, Courtney broke it down for him.

"I mean, you been coming around here for weeks. We sit and talk, we watch TV, and have a good time. You take me to dinner and the movies, and I had the best time walkin' around Piedmont Park at the festival."

"That *was* nice, wasn't it?"

"It really was. So, I wanna know what you want from me?"

Once again, Hughes gave her a confused look. He knew what she was asking; he just wasn't sure how to answer.

Courtney got a bottle of Courvoisier and a bottle of Moët & Chandon Champagne from the refrigerator and began to pour the drinks.

"Are you trying to fuck me and ghost me once you hit it? Are you tryin'a have a relationship? Are you tryin'a fuck me and a bunch of other bitches? I just wanna know what's up."

Hughes was caught off guard by the bluntness of her question, but since he wasn't sure of what exactly he wanted with Courtney, he told her what he did know.

"Look, Court, it's like this. I like you. You're smart, you're funny, you're cool to hang out with, and shit. I enjoy coming around here, sitting around, and watching TV with you. And yeah, I've had the best time chillin' with you. I like taking you out to dinner and the movies and shit, and we did have fun at the park." He paused and stood up a little straighter. "And you are fine as hell. So, yeah, I do wanna make love to you and see where it goes from there."

Courtney handed him both glasses. "Give them to your boys," she said and walked out of the kitchen. Hughes followed her out.

"What happened with you and Scoop, Breezy?" Deneisha asked as Courtney and Hughes came back into the living room. Hughes handed the drinks to Reyes and Calderon.

"We cool."

"What you say?"

"I said, 'Look, I know I fucked up the last time, and I'm sorry. I ain't tryin'a bring no heat on you.' So, as a peace offering, I tossed him the keys to the car. He asked, 'What's this?' I told him it was a low-mileage Audi A6 e-tron." She giggled. "I know he's hot for electric vehicles. He looked at me for a while and said, 'What you looking for?' I said nothing. That's my way of saying I'm sorry, and the shit will never happen again."

"What he say to that?" Deneisha asked.

"The nigga looked at me for a while, and then he went and looked out the window at the car and nodded. 'You want back in? That's what this about?' I said, 'Hell yeah, I want back in.'"

"And?" Deneisha asked.

"He told me to look out for an electrified Genesis G80."

"*That's* what I'm talking about," Courtney said, fist-bumping Brianna.

"Maybe we should boost some cars," Calderon said. Reyes and Hughes nodded, but he was looking at Courtney. She laughed.

"Nigga, you know that ain't y'all thing."

"Nope," Hughes laughed. "I'm the type of muthafucka that shoves a gun in your face and take your shit."

"You right," Calderon laughed and drained his glass. "This shit was good," he said, holding up his empty glass.

"You want me to fix you another?" Deneisha asked.

"If you don't mind."

Deneisha leaned close to him. "You twist up another fatty, and I'll make you a drink."

"On it."

She took the glass from his hand and stood.

"I want one too," Hughes said and drained his glass. He held it out for Deneisha as she passed on her way to the kitchen. She stopped.

"What you gonna do for it?" She paused. "Your boy over there earning his. What you gonna do to earn yours?"

"I didn't know it was like all that."

"Don't worry, Neisha. I'll make sure he earns his drink," Courtney said, and Deneisha took his and Reyes's glasses.

"Thanks, Court."

"Don't thank me yet. You don't know what I'ma make you do to earn that drink."

"I'll shut up then," Hughes said.

Courtney patted him on the thigh. "Good idea."

When Deneisha returned to the living room, she brought the bottles of Courvoisier and Champagne and poured everyone a drink. Calderon fired up the blunt, and the party continued until they had smoked out and the bottles were empty.

"I'ma go pick up another piece," Reyes said.

"Stop at the liquor store and grab another bottle of Courvoisier and Champagne," Brianna said, even though she knew that they had more of the liquor in the refrigerator.

"No worries," Reyes said and stood up. He looked at Calderon. "Come on, nigga, let's go."

He was all up in Deneisha's ear. "What you need me for?"

"Nigga, get your ass up and let's go. I promise, she'll be here when you get back."

"Maybe," Deneisha laughed.

"I'll be here," Hughes laughed as Calderon stood up and gave him the finger before the men left the apartment to pick up some weed to smoke from a nearby trap house and stop at the liquor store.

When they came back to the apartment, an excited Reyes and Calderon rushed in.

"That didn't take long," Brianna said.

"Where's the liquor?" Courtney asked, noticing that they came in empty-handed.

"We didn't make it to the store—" Calderon began.

"Seriously?" Deneisha said, smiling and shaking her head. "You had one job. Bring back some Courvoisier and Champagne. And you couldn't even do that."

"That's because the plan changed," Calderon replied.

"To what?" Courtney wanted to know.

"We gonna rob the trap," Reyes said.

Courtney shook her head. "What?"

"We gonna hit the trap," he repeated.

"It's an easy lick," Calderon said.

"Bad idea," Courtney expressed.

"Shiiit, it's a fuckin' *good* idea," Reyes told her. "Ain't but three niggas up in there and plenty of cash. Fuck that shit you talkin', Court. We gettin' that paper."

Courtney shook her head and went into the kitchen to get some ice for her drink.

"Count me out," Hughes said. He stood up and followed Courtney.

Calderon looked at Reyes. He was disappointed that Hughes said he was out, but he sorta understood.

*The nigga tryin'a fuck Court's sexy little ass,* he thought. But that didn't change things for him.

"I think we need another man inside and someone to drive," Calderon told Reyes.

"Shit, I'll drive," Brianna said as Courtney and Hughes came back into the living room and sat down on the couch.

"What about you, Court?" Reyes asked and sat down next to her. "You in?"

"Oh, hell to the fuckin' no. I don't want nothing to do with it."

Deneisha laughed. "You scared?"

"Of going to jail on some bullshit? Yes."

"Fuck it. I'll do it," Deneisha announced.

Everybody looked at her. "That's a bad idea, Neisha," Courtney said to her, but Deneisha neither answered nor did she look in Courtney's direction.

Reyes handed her a gun. "You ever use a gun before?" Calderon asked.

"Nope," she said. Even though she'd used Brianna's gun for the convenience store robberies, she'd never actually fired one. Deneisha put one in the chamber the way she had seen it done on TV and in the movies. "How hard can it be?"

"Just point and shoot," Reyes told her, and they left the apartment.

On the way to the trap house, nobody said anything. The music was pumping, and Deneisha was thinking about what she was about to do and how much she'd get. When they arrived at the house, Brianna parked the car.

"Keep it running," Reyes said as he reached for the handle to get out.

"No, nigga. I'ma run to the store while y'all inside. I should be back in time to pick y'all up."

"Ha-ha, Breezy got jokes," Calderon said and exited the car.

"You be careful, Neisha," Brianna said as she got out and followed the men to the house.

"Y'all ready?" Reyes asked quietly when they walked through the gate to the yard.

Deneisha and Calderon nodded. Reyes kicked in the door to the house, and the three rushed inside. As expected, three men were in the house. Two were sitting on the couch playing *Madden,* while the other sat in a chair. They were caught off guard as Reyes, Calderon, and Deneisha rushed in with guns drawn.

"Don't fuckin' move!" Calderon shouted and fired several shots that hit the wall over the heads of the two on the couch. Reyes rushed to one of the men on the couch and put a gun to his head.

"You know what time it is," he shouted and pulled him up from the couch.

Reyes pushed him toward the rear of the house, where he had seen the money earlier that night.

Calderon noticed a gun on the end table, near the one in the chair.

"Don't even think about it," he warned and pointed his gun at the man's head. He put his hands up.

"Smart move." He looked at the man on the couch. "You put your hands up too, muthafucka." He raised his hands, and Reyes came back into the room with a bag filled with money. He pushed the other man down on the couch.

"Now, sit your ass down," Reyes ordered, and once he was seated, Reyes and Calderon started for the door.

With her gun raised, Deneisha was backing out of the house slowly when the man who was sitting on the chair reached for the gun. She pulled the trigger, and her shot hit him in the chest. Calderon turned quickly and fired a couple of shots wildly, and Deneisha ran out of the house.

As the two men came rushing out of the house blasting, Reyes fired several more shots as they reached the car and got in.

"Go! Go! Go!" Calderon yelled, and Brianna floored it.

"Damn, girl. You a beast," Calderon said as the four drove away from the house.

"What happened?" Brianna asked as she sped away.

"Yo," Reyes began, "your girl shot one of them when he grabbed a gun."

"Damn, Neisha," Brianna said and kept driving.

Even though she was getting mad props for what she had done, Deneisha was shaken . . . but it didn't last long.

*It was easier than I thought it would be,* she thought.

# Chapter Four

When they returned to the apartment, the four piled out. Reyes walked around to the back of the car.

"We need to ditch this car," he said when he saw the bullet holes on the bumper and trunk. Calderon came and joined him.

"I'll take care of it. Gimme the keys, Breezy." She handed them to him. "Gimme that gun, Neisha. I need to get rid of that too. Don't count until I get back," he said and got into the car. When he drove off, Deneisha, Brianna, and Reyes started walking toward the apartment.

"Don't say nothing about me shooting somebody in front of Court," Deneisha stated.

"You right. Court don't need to know nothing about that," Brianna said.

"I'm telling," Reyes said, laughing.

"Don't do that," Brianna warned and punched him lightly.

He put his arm around her and kissed her on the cheek as they walked. "Your secret is safe with me." He kissed her on the cheek again. "Happy now?"

"Very," Brianna said.

"Thank you," Deneisha said as they went inside.

"How'd it go?" Hughes asked when they entered the apartment.

"Fuck you care?" Reyes said and sat down on the couch.

"I care," Courtney said.

"Everything went fine, Court," Brianna replied. "It was an easy lick, just like he said."

"Where's Devonte?" Courtney wanted to know.

"Relax, Court. He went to ditch the car, and then he'll be back," Brianna answered.

"Y'all want a drink?" Courtney asked.

"Shit, yeah," Reyes all but shouted.

"I thought we was dry," Brianna said.

"I sent him to the store while y'all was gone," Courtney said, pointing at Hughes and looking at Deneisha as she went into the kitchen.

"I'll help you," Brianna said, and she followed Courtney.

They returned to the living room with the bottles of Courvoisier and Champagne. Then Brianna sat down next to Reyes. He put his arm around her.

"I'ma tear that fat pussy up once we split this money," he whispered in her ear.

"We'll see," Brianna said as Hughes lit the blunt.

For the next hour, they smoked and drank until there was a knock at the door. Courtney noticed the way Deneisha and Brianna looked at each other. They knew that one of them needed to tell Calderon not to say anything about Deneisha shooting somebody at the trap house.

"I'll get it," Deneisha said and got up. She went to the door and opened it. She immediately stepped to Calderon's chest. Even though the move caught him off guard, her body against his excited him.

"Don't say nothing about me shooting somebody in front of Court," Deneisha said.

"I got you," Calderon said, and Deneisha took a small step back.

"What took you so long?" Reyes asked when Calderon came into the living room with Deneisha. Calderon held up the brown paper bags that he had in each hand.

"I stopped at the liquor store."

Courtney got up, took the liquor bottles from him, and then took them to the kitchen.

"Y'all ain't let this nigga fuck wit' the money, did you?" Calderon asked as he, Reyes, Deneisha, and Brianna gathered around the dining room table and sat down.

"Naw. He ain't touch it," Brianna said as Reyes emptied the bag of money on the table and began to count.

Deneisha sat quietly, looking at the pile of cash and watching Reyes count it. What stood out to her was the abundance of one-dollar bills in the pile.

"Four thousand, two hundred, and thirteen dollars," Reyes said when he finished counting the money and splitting it four ways.

"That's it?" Deneisha questioned.

"What? That ain't enough for you?" Reyes asked as he handed the stack of bills to Deneisha.

"It's all good," she said, but she was thinking that she had killed a man, and that was all she got.

Now that the money was divided, they returned to the living room where Courtney and Hughes were watching a movie. From there, it was Champagne, Courvoisier, weed, and music. Calderon sat down next to Deneisha.

"What you do with the gun?" were the first words out of her mouth.

"I got rid of it."

"How?"

"How what?"

"How did you get rid of the gun?" she asked. She had killed a man for a little more than a thousand dollars, so how Calderon disposed of the gun was important.

"I took the gun apart, and I tossed the pieces out the window one at a time," he began.

"You know how to do that?" Deneisha asked and took a sip of her drink.

"Do what?"

"Take a gun apart."

"Hell yeah."

"You need to show me how to do that." She leaned closer to him. "And I need you to get me one."

"One what?"

"What we talkin' about? I need you to get me a gun."

Calderon leaned close to her. "You know I got whatever you need."

Deneisha patted him on the leg. "We'll see if that's true."

She stood up quickly and had to steady herself to keep from falling.

"You all right?" Calderon asked.

"No, nigga. I'm fucked up," she laughed. "I'll be back."

"I wanna go," he said as Deneisha staggered away.

"To the bathroom?" she said and kept walking, her shoulder hitting the wall as she left the room.

Deneisha went into the bathroom and looked at herself in the mirror. After a while, she turned on the cold water and cupped her hands. She allowed the water to fill her palms and leaned in. The cold water on her face felt good.

Deneisha dried her hands, and then she unbuttoned her jeans and pulled down the zipper. She turned around and was about to pull them down when there was a single tap on the door, and then it opened. Calderon boldly stepped in and closed the door.

"What the fuck," Deneisha said, but did not attempt to cover herself. "You need to get the fuck outta here, Devonte."

"Why?" he smiled and took a step closer. "I told you I wanted to go."

"What? So you can watch me piss?" Deneisha asked and leaned against the sink.

"That wasn't what I had in mind," he said and ran his hand up and down the dick print that was visible through his jeans. "You are so damn fine, Neisha."

Deneisha smiled at the sight of it. "Oh, you musta came in here to show me something," she laughed and sat down on the edge of the bathtub. "Well, come on, nigga. Stop fuckin' around and show me what you got," she commanded, and Calderon quickly complied with her request.

Even though there were no dicks available while she was locked up, at least none that she wanted, Deneisha still loved to suck dick. His dick was magnificent . . . dark chocolate, long, smooth, and thick. She slid her tongue up and down the skin, enjoying the taste of him before pulling him into the back of her throat and holding him there to adjust to his size and thickness.

His hands gripped her head, making Deneisha take him deeper into her mouth while her hands began to stroke his dick up and down. Calderon's breaths were muffled grunts as Deneisha sucked.

"That shit is so fuckin' good, Neisha," he said on his toes, and he tried to pull back, but Deneisha wouldn't let him.

She gripped his dick in her hand, stroking it as she sucked and enjoying the hard fullness in her mouth. Calderon grabbed her shoulders and pulled her up. "Stand up and turn around," he ordered.

Deneisha stood and leaned over the sink. Calderon stroked his erection and got behind her. He grabbed her hips and entered her. Her pussy was so wet, and his dick was so hard that he began to pump it in her as hard as he could.

"Give it to me harder. I wanna feel all that dick in me."

It had been so long since she felt some dick inside her, and it felt so good. He reached for her shoulders and pounded his dick into her. The feeling of her spasming pussy around his dick felt so amazing to him that he felt himself about to come and tried to force himself to pull away, but it was too late.

"Shit," he said softly as his limp dick slid out of her.

"That's it?" she said angrily.

"That shit was good."

"Whatever, nigga," Deneisha said, pulling up her jeans. She left Calderon standing in the bathroom with his limp dick in his hand. Deneisha went into the other bathroom in the apartment and locked the door in case he had ideas of following her in.

*You know what he's gonna say. I'm not always like that and beg for another chance,* Deneisha thought.

She turned on the shower.

"Not!" she said aloud.

As she undressed, she heard the front door open and close, so she figured that Calderon had gone home.

"Premie," she said scornfully and got into the shower.

# Chapter Five

The following afternoon, Courtney got off work early, and Brianna told her and Deneisha about a spot she'd heard about that had a happy hour.

"You been there, Breezy?" Courtney asked.

"Naw. Marcel told me about this spot. He said the food is good, and the drinks are strong," she replied.

"That's why she wanna go, Court. I bet you all the money I got in my pocket that Marcel gonna be there when we get there." Deneisha laughed. "Him and his premie friend."

"Whoa, slow down. Premie?" Courtney questioned. "Who we talkin' about?"

"Marcel's boy, Devonte."

"Calderon?" Courtney asked.

"Yup."

"All that swagger and shit talkin' that nigga be doin', and he's a premature ejaculator." Courtney laughed. "Say it ain't so."

"Nigga got a big dick. Big, pretty dick, but I rocked this house a few times, and the next thing you know, he's screaming, 'Oh shit!'" Deneisha shared with her laughing girls.

"I was wondering why he ran up outta here with his head down," Courtney laughed to the point of being in tears.

"Now you know," Brianna said impatiently. "So we gonna hit the spot or what?"

"Told you, Court. She's going there to meet Marcel."

"So, what if I am? At least he lasts more than five minutes."

"True," Deneisha said.

"You go get that dick, Breezy. I ain't mad at you at all," Courtney said.

"Thank you, Court. So we goin' or not?"

"Yeah, Breezy, we goin'. Just let me jump in the shower and get cute." She paused. "If that's okay with you."

"Yeah, Court. It's all right with me."

"Thank you, Breezy," Courtney said and stood up and headed toward the bathroom.

"I'm gonna change," Deneisha said, and she got up from the couch. "I don't like the way I look in this dress," she said of the red, yellow, green, and black-colored, block-striped print dress that she was wearing.

"I think you look nice."

"You think so?"

"Yeah, girl."

"I'm still gonna change," Deneisha said and headed toward her room.

"Hurry up," Brianna shouted from the living room.

An hour and a half later, Courtney and Deneisha were ready to leave, and the ladies arrived at "42" around seven that evening. 42 was a sophisticated, upscale lounge and a vibrant sports bar. The spot was a tribute to Jackie Robinson, the first Black player in major league baseball, who wore the number 42.

"This is nice, Breezy," Courtney said as they walked through the establishment and found a table.

"Told y'all," Brianna said, looking around to see if Marcel Reyes was in the house that night. She didn't know if he would be there. He told her about the place and that he liked to hang out there. Brianna also heard something about Mr. Marcel Reyes and that spot. Therefore, she was there to check it out because if there was one thing that was for certain: Brianna Commer was nobody's fool.

Once they were seated, a server brought them the food and drink menus. All three ordered Moët Spritzers, and their server promised to return with their drinks and take their food orders.

"I ain't never heard of no oxtail pizza before," Brianna said.

"That what you gettin', Breezy?" Courtney asked.

"Naw, I ain't feeling that adventurous today," she said. "What about you, Court? You know what you want?"

"I was thinking about that firecracker salmon."

"I was thinking about them crab cakes, but I'm probably gonna have some wings," Deneisha said.

"I'ma get the crab cakes then, and we can share," Brianna said as their server returned to take their order.

"Y'all are welcome to have some of my salmon bites if y'all want," Courtney offered.

It was almost ten, and after pitching Moët Spritzers for hours, all three were pretty fucked up. But they had a great time, and that was all that was important. At least, that was the case for Deneisha and Courtney. Brianna, on the other hand, was a different story. Although she had a good time hanging out with her girls, the purpose of coming there was Marcel Reyes, and he hadn't shown up.

It wasn't like they made plans to meet there or anything like that, but she wanted to catch him there and see what was up.

"I'm ready to go," Courtney announced.

"Why, Court? It's early," Brianna said.

"I gotta work in the morning. Something neither of you knows anything about."

"Sure don't," Brianna said. "If I got a job, I'd break out in hives," she giggled.

"See, Neisha, she's a bad influence on you," Courtney said.

"Maybe, but I ain't trying to get no job either," Deneisha said.

"We trying to make this paper while we can. I know you got to see that," Brianna said. At that moment, Marcel Reyes rolled up in the place.

"I do. Believe me, I do. I just ain't interested in that little nickel-and-dime shit y'all be doin'. I'm looking at something for us that's gonna make us some serious money."

"What's that?" Deneisha asked.

"I'll tell you all about it once I get it all planned," Courtney said.

"Whatever it is, if it's gonna make me some serious money, I'm all in for that," Deneisha said. "What about you, Breezy?"

"Huh?"

"She asked, 'What about you?' You down to make some of that serious money?"

"Yeah."

Courtney looked in the direction that Brianna was looking. "Oh," she laughed. "Reyes is here."

"That's why she ain't paying you no mind, Court. Her dick's in the house, and nothing else matters."

"Whatever, Neisha," Brianna said, and she gave Deneisha the finger, but she hadn't taken her eyes off Reyes as he moved around the club. She had heard from more than one person that Reyes was at 42 with another woman, and Brianna Commer was not to be made a fool of.

*Not in this lifetime,* Brianna thought as she watched him.

"Is his boy with him?" Deneisha asked.

"I don't see him," Brianna said.

"Good. I don't feel like hearin' him beg for more of this pussy," Deneisha said, definitely.

When he finally looked in her direction, he raised his hands as if he were excited to see her there and came to the table where they were seated.

"I guess you ain't ready to go now, Breezy?" Courtney asked.

"I might stay a little longer."

"No worries. I can call an Uber," she said and took out her phone to make arrangements.

"You sure, Court?" Brianna asked.

"Yeah, Breezy. It's cool."

"You want me to go with you?" Deneisha asked because she was ready to go.

"No, Neisha," Brianna said quickly. "Stay and hang out with me."

"That's right, Neisha," Courtney said. "Stay and have a good time."

"You sure?"

"Yeah, I'm sure."

Brianna stood up when Reyes got to the table.

"Hey, Sexy," Reyes said, and he kissed her on the cheek and said hello to Courtney and Deneisha. "I didn't know you was gonna be here," he said and joined them at the table.

"You was pumpin' this spot up like it was the greatest spot in the city, so I figured we'd check it out," Brianna said.

"Well, what you think?"

"It's nice. We had a good time."

"Cool, cool," Reyes said and signaled for a server. "What y'all drinkin'?"

"Moët Spritzers," Brianna said as the server approached the table.

"Another round, ladies?" the server asked.

"Nothing for me," Courtney said quickly.

"What's up wit' that?" Reyes asked.

"She gotta work in the morning," Brianna explained, and she looked at Deneisha. "You stayin', right, Neisha?"

"Yeah, I'm stayin'."

"Two Moët Spritzers. What can I get for you, sir?"

Reyes picked up the drink menu. "I'm trying to try something different every time I come here. Last time I tried the Sweet Heat."

"What's that?" Brianna asked.

"Fuck if I know." He paused as he studied the menu. "This time, I'm gonna try the Dragon Fruit Tini."

"What's that?" Brianna asked.

"Fuck if I know."

"It's made with Tito's, dragon fruit liqueur, Cointreau, and fresh lemon juice," the server said. "Excellent choice, sir."

"My Uber is outside," Courtney said and stood up.

"I'll walk out with you," Deneisha said and got up from the table.

"You coming back, right, Neisha?"

"Yeah, Breezy, I'm coming back. Order me some more of them crab cakes," she requested because she needed something on her stomach.

"See you tomorrow," Courtney said, and she walked to the exit with Deneisha.

"I know you wanna get in this Uber with me," Courtney said as they got to the car.

"Damn, sure do. But I don't wanna leave Breezy alone."

"She ain't alone. She got that nigga with her."

"You know what I mean."

"I do. So, I guess I'll see you when I get off tomorrow," Courtney said and opened the car door. "Unless you want me to wake you up before I leave," she laughed.

"Bye, Court," Deneisha said, and Courtney got in.

When Deneisha got back to the table, her drink and crab cakes were waiting for her. And for the next hour, she played the third wheel to Brianna and Reyes. She was just about to tell Brianna that she was ready to go when a woman walked up on Reyes and grabbed his shoulder.

"I knew I'd find you here," she shouted, and Reyes turned around to face her. "Who the fuck is this bitch?"

Brianna bounced to her feet and got in the woman's face. "Who the fuck you callin' a bitch, bitch?"

"You, bitch," she shouted, and Reyes took a step back.

"Only bitch in here is your bitch ass." Brianna looked at Reyes. "You need to check your bitch," she said, and the woman slapped the fuck outta her.

"Bitch!" Brianna said, and she punched the woman in the face.

She went down from the impact of the blow. Brianna stepped up quickly and began kicking the woman. That was when another woman came up behind Brianna and grabbed her by the hair. Deneisha grabbed a beer bottle from the nearest table and hit the woman in the back of her head.

The bottle broke, and the woman stumbled forward. Deneisha rushed up behind her and kicked her in the ass. She fell on her face, and Deneisha stomped her back and kicked her in the head. She had a lot of fights while she was locked up. Deneisha learned the hard way that you can't let up.

*Once you got a bitch down—finish her.*

It set an example for other women who wanted to try her.

"Get up!" Brianna shouted and kicked the woman again.

"Come on, Breezy. We gotta go," Deneisha said and pulled Brianna off the woman as a large man in a black security shirt came toward them. "We gotta go!" Deneisha yelled again, and they ran out of the club.

# Chapter Six

It was the afternoon of the following day when Deneisha woke up. After she and Brianna left 42, they went to another club. They danced and drank as much Champagne as men would buy for them until the lights came on. When she opened her eyes, the bright sunlight beaming through the window made her cover her head with a pillow.

"Damn."

The next thing that became clear was that she was hungover.

"You drank too much."

Once her eyes adjusted to the sun, Deneisha dragged herself out of bed and headed for the bathroom. Once the shower reached a good temperature, she stepped in. As the water beat down on her, her mind turned to money. She had spent almost all of the money that she got from hitting the trap house. She needed to make some, and if that were the case, she would need a gun of her own to move forward.

When she got out of the shower, Deneisha applied jasmine-scented shea butter to her body. Then she put on the Creamsicle Lace Bra and panties that she got at Victoria's Secret. She had just put on a pair of wide, barrel-leg pull-on jeans when the doorbell rang. Deneisha grabbed her throwback jersey and went to the door. She looked out the peephole and saw that it was Devonte Calderon.

"What this premie nigga want?" she questioned as she opened the door. "What's up, Devonte?"

"How you doin', Neisha?"

"I'm all right," she said and stepped aside to let him in. "You want something to drink?"

"Y'all got any brew?"

"Corona."

"That's what's up," he said and sat down on the couch. She went into the kitchen and came back with a bottle of beer. She handed it to him. "Thanks."

Deneisha sat in the chair across from him. "You talk to Marcel today?" she asked, wanting to know if Reyes had told him about what happened at 42.

"Naw, I ain't heard from him today. Why?"

"Breezy was askin' about him," she lied.

"Oh, okay." Calderon took a swallow of beer. "So, what you into today?"

"Why you wanna know?"

"If you wasn't doin' nothin', I wanted to see if you wanted to do somethin'."

Deneisha's face twisted into a frown. "Like what? Fuck?" she shook her head. "That ain't happening."

"Damn, Neisha, it's like that?"

"You didn't exactly represent the last time. So ask yourself, why would I wanna do that shit again?"

"I'm not like that. I don't know what happened." He chuckled. "Yes, I do. It's that mad head game you got goin'."

"Really? That's what you gonna sit there and tell me?" she pointed to herself. "Like the shit was *my* fault." Deneisha knew she had a mad head game, but that was no excuse, and it definitely wasn't a reason to let him back between her thighs.

"Yeah."

"I don't think so."

He smiled. “Is there anything I can do to change your mind?”

“Nope. You can’t do nothing for me.”

“Nothing?” he asked because he had a mad head game too, and all Calderon needed was a chance to show her what he could do with his tongue.

Deneisha paused for a second or two. “There is something you can do for me.”

“What’s that? Just tell me, and it’s done.”

“You said you could get me a gun.”

“You got money?”

“How much we talkin’?”

“Two, maybe three hundred.”

“I can do that. When can you make it happen?”

“We can go now if you ain’t doin’ nothin’.”

Deneisha stood up. “Let’s go then.”

When Calderon stood up, Deneisha started for the door. “You in a hurry?”

“No. But what I am is about that business.”

“I heard that,” Calderon said, and he followed the object of his desire out of her apartment. She locked the door and got in Calderon’s 1973 Chevrolet Monte Carlo. “I just got it,” he said proudly. “I’m about to trick this bitch out. New upholstery, rims, all that,” he said, but Deneisha wasn’t impressed, so she didn’t bother to comment.

“So where we goin’?”

“West End. I know a guy.”

“Cool,” she said and got comfortable.

While they drove to the West End, Calderon continued trying to talk up on some pussy, but Deneisha wasn’t trying to hear that, so she ignored him.

“How much farther?” she asked when he got off Interstate 20 at Lee Street.

“You in a hurry?”

"I told you. I'm 'bout that business," Deneisha said as he parked the car near a park.

"Well, we here."

"This it?"

"Yeah, this is it. Fuck was you expectin'? A gun store?" Calderon shook his head. "Naw, Neisha, this it right here." He pointed to a man leaning against a car. "And that nigga there is who we came to see. Come on," he said and got out of the vehicle.

Deneisha unfastened her seat belt and got out. She walked quickly behind Calderon.

"'Sup, Brick," Calderon said, and the two men shook hands.

"Makin' it." He looked at Deneisha. "Who's she?"

"I'm nobody," Deneisha said.

Brick laughed. "I like that."

"You don't need to know my name," she said.

"Naw," Calderon chuckled. "She all about that business."

"So, what can I do for you, sexy?"

"She wants—" Calderon began, but Brick cut him off.

"She can speak for herself," Brick said and turned to Deneisha. "You got plenty of mouth, so, sexy, what can I do for you?"

"First off, my name ain't sexy."

"You wouldn't tell me your name," Brick said playfully. "I gotta call you something."

"Whatever. I need a gun."

"See there, that wasn't hard at all," Brick said, and he opened the trunk of his car to reveal weapons. Handguns, long guns, semiautomatics, and revolvers for her to choose from. "You know anything about guns?"

"I know how to shoot one," she answered. Even though she knew nothing about guns, she was still insulted by the question.

"My girl is deadly with a nine," Calderon said, and got a *"You talk too much"* look from Deneisha.

Brick handed her a nine. She held it in her hand. It seemed heavier than the last time she held a gun.

"It weighs in at around twenty-eight to thirty-two ounces and has four to eight pounds of recoil. That's a good gun."

"You got anything lighter?"

Brick took the nine from her and handed Deneisha a .380. "That right there is a .380. The pistol weighs about ten ounces. It has a lot less recoil than the nine. So the .380's gonna feel a lot less forceful when fired."

"I'll take this one. How much?"

"Gimme three hundred."

Deneisha quickly dug into her pocket and pulled out her money. She counted off $300 and handed it to him.

After a quick count, Brick said, "Pleasure doin' business with you, my name is not sexy."

"Whatever, nigga," Deneisha said and followed Calderon to the car.

On the way back to Deneisha's apartment, Calderon's conversation was all about flirtation and sexual innuendos. She ignored the flirtation and laughed at the innuendos because it was kinda pitiful.

Knowing he knew he wasn't getting any, after a while, Calderon talked about the lick he was planning and asked her if she wanted in.

"Fuck that. If it's more paper than the last time, you can count me in. If it's not about more paper, I ain't trying to hear it," she said. Although she hadn't said anything about it, the fact that she killed a man for what she considered a little bit of money bothered her.

"I know what you sayin'. But Reyes wanted to hit that spot because he say he saw a table full of paper when he was in there."

"You didn't see it?"

"Naw."

"Next time, maybe you need to check shit out for yourself."

"Facts. Those is facts, for real," Calderon said because he felt the same way as Deneisha. "That's why I been scoutin' out this spot for a minute."

"Let me know what's up. If the money's right, I'm down," Deneisha said as they arrived at her apartment. Calderon walked her to the door.

"Thanks for the hookup," Deneisha said when she got to the door.

"It was my pleasure," he said and bowed slightly.

"Holla at me when you ready to hit that lick you was talkin' about," Deneisha said and took out her keys to unlock the door.

"You wanna burn one?"

"Yeah," she said and unlocked the door.

"Make yourself comfortable," she said, and went to her room to put away her gun.

She went into the closet and retrieved a shoe box containing a pair of shoes she no longer wore from the shelf. She removed the shoes, put the gun in the box, then put it back on the shelf. When Deneisha came out of the closet, Calderon was in her room.

"What are you doin' in here?"

"You said to make myself comfortable."

"That don't mean you can wander around like you own the joint." She shook her head. "It ain't like that," Deneisha said, and that was when she noticed the dick print pressing against his jeans.

"You want me to go?"

Deneisha didn't answer his question. She was getting to like him, *and he does have a big, pretty dick,* she thought.

And it was good while it lasted. Truth be told, since he teased her with that big dick, she needed to get fucked right.

"I said you can't just be wandering around like that."

"Good. Cause I wanna stay."

"You do?" she questioned and took a step forward.

"Yeah. I wanna know if we can get together. You know, do a little something."

Deneisha may have laughed, but she took a step closer. "Why should I even consider letting you back between these thighs? I mean, you didn't exactly represent."

"I told you what was up with that. That has never happened to me before," he said with his right hand raised. "I'm serious." He took a step toward her. She stepped back.

"You know, when you rolled up in the bathroom—uninvited, I was thinking we would get things started with some hot sex in the bathroom and then take it to the room." Deneisha shook her head. "But we both know that ain't what happened."

"Give me a chance to show I am *not* that guy."

She looked down at the dick print. "Your dick is hard right now, ain't it?"

"My dick been hard since you opened the door."

"I noticed."

Calderon laughed. "So, you been looking, huh?"

"It's hard to miss."

He took a step closer. "So, if I try to kiss you, would you slap me?"

"Try to kiss me and see," Deneisha said as Calderon leaned in to kiss her lips tenderly.

When their lips touched, the flame that had been simmering since that night raged inside of her. She felt her nipples brush against his chest. It made her legs feel weak, it made her wet, and it made her want him inside her.

They tore off their clothes, and then she led him by the dick to the bed. She sat on the edge of the bed, stroked his erection, and was about to take it to the back of her throat when Calderon gently touched her shoulders and pushed her down on her back. He crawled between her thighs.

Calderon eased her thighs apart and used his tongue to make circles around her clit. He licked a finger and slid it in and out of Deneisha, parting her lips with his tongue and then using his tongue to flicker back and forth across her clit.

"Shit . . ."

With her legs in the air, she held his head in place with one hand and squeezed her nipple with the other as Calderon eased his fingers in and out of her. She squeezed her nipples harder as he sucked her clit and penetrated her with his finger. Deneisha felt a wave rush over her entire body.

"Oh shit," she screamed, grabbing him by the shoulders and pulling him up. "Lie down," she demanded, still shaking from the mind-numbing orgasm he had given her. "I wanna feel you inside me."

Calderon smiled and did as she requested. Deneisha got on her knees and stroked his dick up and down, and was about to lower herself on his throbbing dick when he grabbed her cheeks and pulled her quickly to his lips.

He ran his tongue along her lips and then licked and sucked her clit. He slid his hand along her round ass. She felt herself getting wetter, and she moaned her approval for what he was making her feel. He gripped her cheeks with both of his hands, then slid his tongue inside her and sucked her moist lips gently. Her clit grew harder as he licked her with the tip of his tongue. Her body began to quiver, and then she came again.

When she tried to roll away from him to compose herself, he grabbed her hips, moved her body to his erection, and slammed her down on his dick.

"Yes . . ."

Deneisha put her hands on his shoulders and rode him hard and fast. His dick filled her up so completely.

"You're gonna make me come again," Deneisha yelled, slamming her body down on him. He was twisting her nipples, and she was screaming, "Fuck this pussy."

Deneisha started jerking her hips back and forth, sliding on his lap, and her walls began grabbing and releasing around him. She saw his eyes open wide.

"Oh shit," Calderon shouted and held her hips tightly.

"No!" Deneisha screamed, but it was too late.

His mouth and eyes opened wide, and his head drifted back . . . And he came hard.

"Not again."

*But at least he lasted longer this time. And he got a mad head game,* Deneisha thought, so it wasn't a total loss.

"That's some bomb-ass pussy you got there," Calderon mumbled.

"Whatever, nigga."

# Chapter Seven

Calderon was just coming out of Deneisha's room, tucking in his shirt, when Brianna got home. After what she had told her about him being a premature ejaculator, she was surprised to see him there.

"What's up, Breezy?"

"'Sup, Devonte?"

"Ain't nothing," he said as he headed toward the door.

When the door closed, Brianna headed to her room, but she heard the shower running.

"Oh no, she didn't," she laughed and went into the kitchen.

Brianna opened the refrigerator door, expecting to see a bottle of Courvoisier and Champagne. That was when she remembered that they crushed them the night before. She was about to head out to the liquor store, but she decided to wait until Deneisha got out of the shower because she wanted to ask her what was up with her and Calderon.

When Deneisha came into the living room, Brianna was sitting there waiting for her.

"'Sup, Breezy?"

"What's up wit' you and Devonte?"

"What you mean?"

"I mean, he just came out of your room," Brianna began as her phone rang. She looked at the display. "I need to take this," she said, and swiped the talk button. "What up, Scoop?"

Glad that she was saved by the bell, Deneisha left the living room and went into the kitchen. She opened the refrigerator door. "There were bottles of Courvoisier and Champagne in here." Then she thought about it. *Oh yeah, we crushed them last night.*

She was about to go to the liquor store to pick up some bottles of liquor, but then she decided that if she was going to go there, she might as well make it worth her while. Deneisha went into her room and walked to the closet.

"Let me see the keys to the car, Breezy," she said when she came back into the living room.

"Where you goin', Neisha?" she asked, reaching in her pocket for the keys.

"To the liquor store."

She tossed her the keys. "Don't think you avoidin' the question. I'll be right here when you get back."

Instead of going to the liquor store near the apartment, Deneisha drove past two stores before parking down the street from the one she had scoped out. There was a New York Yankees baseball cap in the backseat. She put it on and walked in.

Deneisha knew where the cameras were, so she was careful not to look directly at them. She took out her phone and made it seem like she was talking to somebody on her way to the cooler. She grabbed the most expensive bottle of Champagne in the cooler and went to the counter.

"What else can I get for you?" the clerk asked.

"A bottle of Courvoisier," she said, and held up two twenty-dollar bills as if she intended to pay once he rang it up.

When the clerk turned to get the bottle, Deneisha took out her gun and put her purse on the counter.

"And put the money in the bag. And don't do nothing stupid."

Once she had the money, Deneisha put the bottles in the bag and headed for the door. Immediately, the clerk grabbed the shotgun from under the counter and fired at her. The shot missed her, hitting the liquor display behind her. As the bottles came crashing to the floor, Deneisha raised her weapon and fired a wild shot in return. The bullet hit the clerk in the chest. He grabbed his wound and slumped to the floor.

With her heart pounding, Deneisha ran out of the store. She dropped her head and walked quickly down the street to avoid attracting attention. Once she rounded the corner, she hurried to the car, got in, and drove away.

The farther she got away from the store, the more Deneisha calmed down. It wasn't her intention, but she had killed another man. Like the man at the trap house, she just reacted. The shots were lucky. Deneisha didn't aim her weapon; she just pulled the trigger. Now, she had two bodies on her. But this one was different. In both cases, Deneisha was defending herself. The man at the trap house was reaching for his gun, and the clerk took a shot at her. But what made this one different was how Deneisha felt about taking another life.

While she was doing time, she met an inmate, Evangeline Blake, who was serving a life sentence for seven murders. She was at the county jail because she was back in court to stand trial for an eighth murder. At the time, Deneisha had never killed anybody. She'd never even held a gun in her hand. She innocently asked what it was like to take a life. The inmate told her that the first one was hard.

*"It's that whole 'thou shalt not kill' Bible shit we was all brought up on. But then you think, it was me or them." She laughed. "And it damn sure wasn't gonna be me, you know what I'm sayin'? But it still fucks with you. The second one gets easier. It's when you gotta smoke*

*a muthafucka, and it ain't a matter of you or them that it gets hard. Then when you gotta stand in front of a muthafucka and kill them, that shit is hard." She laughed. "But you get used to that too."*

Deneisha arrived at the apartment thinking that Evangeline was right. Although she didn't show it or talk to Brianna or Courtney about it, Deneisha was shaken by what she had done. Before that night, she'd never even held a gun. She was a hustler, a thief. Agreeing to join a robbing crew was a significant step up from her previous situation. Despite that, she never thought that she would have to kill somebody. Or even if she *could,* if it came to that. As far as she was concerned, she was just along for the ride and a cut of the money, of course.

She wondered what would have happened if she had hesitated when he reached for the gun. Would she be dead? Would he have shot Calderon and Reyes? She was able to rationalize that she had no choice, and that made it easier for her to deal with.

This one was easier. Deneisha felt bad after the trap house. As she got out of the car this time, she had no regret about what she had done.

*Muthafucka tried to kill me,* Deneisha said and put the key in the lock.

"Took you long enough," Courtney said. She got up from the couch and approached Deneisha with her hand out.

"You must want a drink bad, Court," she said and reached into the bag and handed Courtney the bottles.

"I really do. I had a long, hard day fuckin' with them customers," she said on her way to the kitchen. "And I come home and find that you two done drunk up all the liquor," she shouted from the kitchen.

"Sorry, Court," Deneisha said as she passed the kitchen on the way to her room.

"No worries. I'm all right now. You want me to fix you one?"

"Go ahead. I'll be out in a minute."

Deneisha went into her room, then closed and locked the door. She took the money from the purse and counted it.

"Twelve hundred and sixty," she said aloud. "Not bad."

Deneisha stood up and lifted the edge of the mattress. She counted off a few hundred dollars and put the rest under the mattress. She knew it wasn't a very secure hiding place. She would invest in a safe the next day.

When she went back into the living room, she sat down on the couch beside Courtney, who handed Deneisha the drink.

"Thanks." Deneisha took a sip. "What y'all watchin'?"

"*The Family Business,*" Brianna said.

"I never seen that before," Deneisha replied and got comfortable.

"That's cause your ass was locked up," Brianna said with her eyes glued to the screen.

"It was on before Neisha went to jail," Courtney corrected.

"I know. I just never watched it." Deneisha giggled. "Too busy in them streets."

"Shhhh," Brianna said with her finger over her lips.

"You know she don't like nobody talkin' when she watchin' TV," Courtney said.

"But let it be something you wanna watch, she'll talk the whole time," Deneisha added.

"Shhhh," Brianna said with an angry look on her face.

Neither Courtney nor Deneisha said anything else until the show was over and the credits rolled.

"So, what we gonna do tonight?" Courtney asked before the next episode came on.

"Breezy gonna sit right there and watch TV," Courtney said, getting up to get another drink.

"No, I'm not." She paused. "Well, I *am* gonna be into this for more than a minute," she giggled. "But I know about a house party we can go to later tonight."

"House party?" Courtney questioned. "I don't know if I wanna go to a house party, Breezy. Shit be hot and crowded. And then the fight breaks out."

"We ain't gotta go there."

"What about that spot you was telling me about, Breezy?" Deneisha asked.

"You talking about That Joint in Decatur? Yeah, we can go there. Now, y'all be quiet or go somewhere so I can watch my show, please."

"Okay, Breezy. We'll shut up," Deneisha said.

"That's right, Breezy. You ain't gotta tell us to shut up no more. I hate it when I'm watching something, and people be talkin' all loud and shit," Courtney said, laughing.

"Shhhh," Brianna said with her finger over her lips again.

Later that night, after Brianna had had her fill of *The Family Business,* they got ready to go out for the night. When they were dressed, they walked to the plaza near the apartment and waited near the ATM. They hadn't been there long when a woman rolled up in a midnight blue BMW and rushed to the ATM.

"Be ready," Brianna told Courtney and Deneisha. She took out her gun and walked quickly toward the BMW. The woman completed her transaction and returned to the car. The woman and Brianna got to the car at the same time. Then Brianna shoved the gun in the woman's face.

"Gimme them fuckin' keys and the money and stay alive."

"Don't kill me," the woman pleaded, handing Brianna her purse and the keys.

Brianna got into the BMW and drove away. She stopped, picked up Deneisha and Courtney, and headed for That Joint.

When they got there, they found a table near the dance floor and ordered a round of drinks. While they were sitting there, enjoying the music, Brianna spotted Chloe Mitchell. For a couple of months, before she got locked up, Deneisha was involved in a love triangle with Chloe and Antonio Freeman.

Deneisha and Chloe had known each other since she moved to Atlanta from New York. They ran in different circles, so they didn't interact much, but it was clear that neither liked the other. Deneisha met Antonio at a club and got together a few days later. It was nothing serious for either of them; it was just good sex without the burden of commitment.

She had no idea that Antonio was involved with Chloe. She hadn't seen her since high school, and that was fine with both of them. Deneisha was out one night, and she saw them together. When Antonio saw Deneisha, he excused himself and came to talk to her. After a while, the conversation was abruptly interrupted by Chloe. She grabbed Antonio by the arm.

"You fuckin' this bitch now?" she shouted.

"Who you callin' bitch?" Deneisha shouted back and came at Chloe. However, Antonio quickly grabbed Chloe and led her away. After that, Chloe found Deneisha's cell number, email, and social media. "Stay away from my man" was the focus of those interactions. Come to find out that not only was Antonio fuckin' Chloe and Deneisha, but he was also fuckin' another woman named Demi Burgess. He got her pregnant, moved to Texas, and got married.

"You know she don't like you," Brianna said, laughing at how Chloe was mean-mugging Deneisha.

"That reminds me, she gave me a message to give to you," Courtney said.

"When was this?"

"When you got locked up."

"And you just now telling me?"

"The shit wasn't relevant until now."

"Whatever, Court. What was the message?"

Courtney smiled. "She said to tell you that you're lucky you got locked up. Otherwise, she was gonna kick your ass."

Deneisha stood up and started walking toward Chloe.

"Neisha!" Courtney shouted.

"Wait, Neisha!" Brianna yelled and rushed to catch up with her. Courtney caught up with them just as Deneisha reached Chloe.

"Hey, bitch. I heard you was gonna kick my ass over that worthless nigga that got another bitch pregnant and dumped you." Deneisha took a step closer. "Well, here I am. Make a move."

Chloe got in her face. "You shouldn't have been fuckin' wit' him."

"Instead of being mad at me, you oughta be mad at that nigga and the bitch he got pregnant and married."

"No. You're the one who came between me and him. If it wasn't for you, he would never have run to her skank ass."

"You know how ignorant you sound right now?"

Chloe pushed Deneisha, and she was about to reach for her gun, but Courtney stopped her before she could get it out.

"She ain't worth it, Neisha," Courtney said.

"You're lucky. But this ain't over, and you'll never see it coming," Deneisha said to Chloe as Courtney led her away.

"That's right. Walk away," Chloe shouted, not realizing how close she had come to getting shot.

"You know where to find her?" Deneisha asked Brianna quietly when they got outside.

"I know she's a runner at Nikko's trap house," Brianna whispered.

"Where we goin' now?" Courtney asked on the way to the BMW.

"We can check out the house party I was telling y'all about."

"I don't know, Breezy," Courtney said and got into the backseat.

"If it ain't shit, we can go somewhere else," Brianna said, and she started the car.

"Right. We can just bar hop and get fucked up," Deneisha said, and the three headed for the house party.

As Courtney expected, it was hot and crowded, and the DJ was weak, so they left after an hour. After leaving the party, the three went to a couple of bars and were riding to the spot when Brianna made a turn.

"Where you goin', Breezy?" Courtney asked.

"I'm showing Neisha something," she said as she went through a neighborhood.

As they drove down the street, they saw Chloe sitting outside a house on the porch with two men.

"There she go." Brianna pointed her out to Deneisha as they drove past the house.

"Drive around the block and pull over, Breezy," Deneisha ordered.

"What you bitches fiddin' to do?" Courtney asked.

"We just gonna have a little fun, Court," Deneisha said and took out her gun.

"No, Neisha. She ain't worth it," Courtney pleaded as Brianna stopped the car.

"She's not. I ain't even gonna shoot at her," Deneisha promised.

"We can aim for the car in the driveway," Brianna said.

"Drive, Court," Deneisha said, and Brianna switched places with Courtney.

"Drive around the block, and pull over in front of the house," Deneisha said.

When they reached the house, Courtney pulled over, and Deneisha and Brianna got out and just stood there.

"Fuck y'all want?" one of the men shouted from the porch.

Deneisha and Brianna raised their guns and started firing. When the shooting started, not knowing that they weren't shooting at them, Chloe and the two men ducked and ran into the house. Deneisha and Brianna got back into the car, and Courtney drove away fast. They ditched the stolen vehicle and went home.

# Chapter Eight

It was a few days later when Reyes and Calderon arrived at the apartment. Deneisha let them in and showed them into the living room, where Brianna and Courtney were waiting.

"You and me need to talk," Brianna said with her arms folded across her chest.

"What about?"

"Let's start with your other woman."

Reyes sat down on the couch next to Brianna. "What other woman?"

Brianna gave him a look that showed her disbelief. "That's how you wanna play this, fine. I'm talking about that bitch who got her ass kicked at 42. You remember? You stepped back and watched like you ain't have shit to do with it."

"I didn't."

Once again, Brianna gave him a look. "You didn't *what?*"

"I stepped aside because I ain't have shit to do with it."

"Now you gonna tell me that you don't know who she is."

"Oh, I know exactly who she is. Her name is Jessica George."

"And?"

"And when I found out how loony tune, cuckoo for cocoa puffs she was, I stopped fuckin' wit' her crazy ass."

"She been stalking his ass ever since," Calderon said.

"I ain't heard from her since that night, so I guess that ass whipping y'all dealt gave her a different perspective on things."

"Whatever, nigga," Brianna said, waving her hand and turning away.

"Now that we got that out of the way."

"Oh, we ain't done with this. I'm just tired of talking about it now."

"Okay, Breezy. Now that we got that out of the way, let's talk about some important shit," Reyes said, anxious to change the subject.

Since nobody was satisfied with the take from the last trap house hit, Reyes had been talking up another hit and had been scouting out the spot he planned to rob.

Over Courvoisier, Champagne, and weed, Reyes laid out for Deneisha, Brianna, and Courtney how they were gonna hit another trap house. All three sat and listened.

Calderon had been talking up the lick to Deneisha, trying to get her interested. After she stepped up the last time, they were sure that they wanted her as part of their crew.

"Fuck that!" was what Deneisha would say each time he brought it up. "Call me when it's about stacking some serious *dinero*." She was tired of him bringing it up. "I don't need to hear no more about it."

"I get it, Neisha, damn," Calderon said. He didn't need or want to make Deneisha mad. He really liked her and had no intention of fuckin' it up over Reyes and the lick.

As for Deneisha, she was starting to like Calderon. Aside from being one fine-ass man, he was confident without being overconfident. She had always gravitated to intelligent men who could hold a conversation.

*I'm tired of stupid thug niggas you can't take nowhere without being embarrassed.*

Calderon didn't seem to have a problem communicating his feelings like some men do. He actually listened to what she had to say without feeling the need to mansplain everything to her.

*That is so fuckin' annoying.*

Calderon made Deneisha laugh. And, of course, he had that big, pretty dick working in his favor. She was teaching him how she liked it, and he was lasting longer each time. And, on top of that, his head game rivaled her own.

But none of that changed the fact that Deneisha wanted no parts of whatever Reyes was planning. However, that night, while he was laying it out for them, she was impressed with his preparation. The last time was spur-of-the-moment, without any planning at all. This time was different, and Deneisha believed what he was saying. This would be a lot more money for her than the last time.

"I'm in," Brianna said. She was all in from the start. Like Calderon, she had been talking about the next hit.

"Neisha?" Calderon asked.

"I'm in."

Everybody looked at Courtney. Once again, she wanted nothing to do with it.

"Fuck y'all looking at me for? I ain't about no small-time shit like that. I got something big I'm working on. But y'all go ahead and have fun. I'll be here when you get back."

"You keep talkin' up this big lick," Reyes said. "When we gonna hear about it?"

Courtney stood up and walked over to where Reyes was sitting. "I'll talk about it when I'm fuckin' ready, and you'll hear about it only if I think you need to," she said and smiled. "But like I said, y'all go ahead and have fun." She went and sat down. "I'll be right here when y'all get back."

"Whatever, Court," Reyes said, and they got ready to leave to rob the trap house.

When they arrived at the house, Reyes, Calderon, and Deneisha got out and walked around to the trunk. Reyes got a 9 mm, and Calderon grabbed the shotgun, and then they started for the house. Deneisha walked behind them, putting on gloves and pulling up her mask. She took out her gun just as they got to the door.

"Y'all ready?"

When both Deneisha and Calderon nodded, Reyes kicked in the door. They rushed in and caught the two men in the house totally off guard.

"Don't fuckin' move!" Calderon shouted.

"Y'all know what time it is," Reyes yelled.

Learning from the mistake they made last time, Deneisha immediately took their guns and their phones. Reyes pulled one up and led him at gunpoint to where he knew the money was stashed.

"That's all you got, nigga?" Reyes shouted with his gun pointed at the man's head.

"That's it. Bump came through and got the money."

"Bump, that your plug?"

When the man nodded, Reyes shouted. "Take me to him."

When they came out of the room, Deneisha had the other man on his knees with his hands on his head. Calderon saw how Reyes was looking.

"What's wrong?"

"They ain't got much of shit."

Deneisha raised her gun and pointed it at Reyes.

"Fuck is you sayin'?"

"Some nigga named Bump came and got the money."

"Who the fuck is Bump?" she wanted to know.

"That's his plug." Reyes hit the man in the head with the barrel of his gun. "He's gonna take us to him."

Deneisha shook her head. "I knew I shouldn't have fucked with you."

"Fuck that. Find something to tie him up with," Reyes said.

Calderon looked around the room and spotted the cable wire. He jerked it out of the wall and used it to tie up the man. Deneisha went into the kitchen, grabbed a dish towel, and used it to gag him.

"What about him?" Deneisha asked, pointing to the man they were taking with them.

"What about him?" Reyes asked.

"Don't you think he needs to be tied up too?" she suggested.

Calderon found an extension cord and used it to tie the man's hands behind his back, and then led him out of the house. They made him climb into the trunk.

"If this ain't the right place, I'ma put one in your head," Reyes promised and closed the trunk.

On the way to the house, Deneisha wished she had followed her first thought and had nothing to do with this lick or anything Reyes was involved in. She had a bad feeling about this move. Deneisha thought about telling Brianna to stop the car so she could get out. But Deneisha knew that Brianna was all in it for her man, so, bad feeling or not, she was staying to have her girl's back.

When they got to the house, Deneisha, along with Reyes and Calderon, got out of the car and approached the house. Reyes was about to kick in the door when someone fired several shots through the door. The rounds hit him in the chest, and the impact of the shots took him off his feet. The force of the blast blew him off the porch, and he landed in the grass.

When Deneisha and Calderon turned and ran, another man stepped out onto the porch and opened fire with an AK-47. Calderon was hit with several shots in the back as he ran. When he fell on his face, his body slid on the damp grass. The men kept firing at Deneisha as she ran. She barely made it back to the car and jumped in.

"Go!"

"I heard shooting. What happened?" Brianna asked as she put the car in gear and sped away from the house.

"Just drive!"

The two men ran out into the street and fired at the car, but it was too far away.

"What happened to Marcel and Devonte?" Brianna asked when they had gotten far enough away from the gunfire.

"They're dead," she said and told Brianna what happened. "Drive out on Cleveland Avenue. I'll let you know where to stop when we get there."

When they reached Cleveland Avenue, Deneisha told Brianna to drive to an abandoned warehouse and park where the parking lot lights were dark.

"Over by them trees."

"What we doing here?"

"We got work to do before we go. Stay in the car," she said as she got out of the vehicle and went around to the trunk. She pulled up her mask, readied her weapon, and opened the trunk.

"Get out," she ordered. The man struggled to get out of the trunk. "Walk."

"You don't have to do this," the man pleaded with tears running down his cheeks.

"Shut up."

"I swear to God, I won't say anything to nobody. I ain't seen your face. I don't know what you look like," he whimpered. "Please, don't kill me."

When he had walked away from the car into the woods at the edge of the parking lot, Deneisha said, "That's far enough."

She stepped up behind him and shot him once in the back of the head. The sound of the gunfire made Brianna flinch as Deneisha returned to the car and got in.

"Damn, Neisha. You got cold-blooded in jail."

"Just drive, Breezy," Deneisha said, slumping in her seat as she tried to come to terms with another murder.

When they got back to Courtney's apartment, they told her what happened.

"Told y'all don't fuck with no small-time shit."

"Shut up, Court," Brianna said.

"Why I gotta shut up when I'm right? Y'all shouldn't have been fuckin' wit' that bullshit. Now you got a body on you, Neisha."

"Let it go, Court," Deneisha said.

"I'll let it go," Courtney said, smiling a very satisfied smile because, once again, she was proven right. She got up and made drinks for her girls. She came back into the living room with a tray with three glasses and two bottles.

"Now, y'all ready to hear about a lick wit' some *real* money?"

# Chapter Nine

Over Courvoisier, Champagne, weed, and the honey-lemon-pepper wings she fried while they were gone, Courtney told Deneisha and Brianna about her plan.

"We're gonna rob an armored truck," Courtney said, and her girls laughed at her until they saw that she wasn't laughing.

"You serious, Court?" Brianna asked.

"I'm serious as cancer, Breezy."

Deneisha nodded. "*That's* gonna be some real money."

"But an armored truck, Court?"

"Yeah, Breezy. An armored truck. I ain't about no small-time, nickel-and-dime shit like them niggas." Courtney took a big swallow of her drink and hit the blunt. "Never steal anything small." She looked at Deneisha. "You got a body on you, Neisha, and for what?"

"You right. I ain't got shit to show for it." She looked at Brianna. "We should at least hear her out." Deneisha laughed. "We sat right here and listened to Marcel tell us his plan."

"That went all to shit," Courtney quipped.

"The least we can do is listen to what Court got to say," Deneisha said.

"Go ahead, Court. I'm listening, but I'ma go ahead and tell you right now, us hitting an armored truck sounds like more than the three of us can handle."

"What? You wanna get the fellas in on it with us?" She paused for a quick second. "Oh yeah, his stupid-ass plan got them killed and damn near the two of you along with it."

“Too soon, Court.” Deneisha giggled. “But she do got a point, Breezy.”

Brianna cracked a little smile. “You right. Going to try to rob Bump or Hump or whoever the fuck was a bad idea.”

“I started to tell you to pull over and let me out.”

“Why didn’t you?”

“I thought you’d be all about what your man wanted, Breezy.”

“That’s just how you are. You be all in for your man,” Courtney said and refreshed everyone’s drinks.

“True. But I think that I would have got out too,” she laughed. “That was a dumb move.”

“For sure,” Deneisha cosigned.

“You know, if you had said, ‘Stop the car’ and said you wasn’t going, and I threw in with you, I bet Marcel would have called it off,” Brianna said.

“Maybe,” Deneisha said. “But that mess is over and behind us. Let’s hear what Court got to say.”

“Okay,” Brianna said and took a couple of wings. “These wings is swingin’, Court.”

“Thank you.” She took a little bow. “Now, every week on Tuesday morning between ten and ten thirty, an armored truck comes to make a pickup at the grocery store where I work.”

“Just Tuesdays, Court?” Brianna asked. “I would think they’d come to get that paper more often.”

“You’re right, they do. But there’s a reason why we’re looking at Tuesday. Here’s how it goes.”

“What? You ain’t got no diagram with the layout of the store?” Brianna asked playfully.

“*Really,* Breezy?”

“Stop interrupting, Breezy. She talkin’ some real money. I wanna hear what she got to say and how she plans on pulling it off,” Deneisha said.

“Sorry, Court. You know I get silly sometimes,” Brianna said, but she was hurt because Courtney and Deneisha were talking shit about her man's planning skills, not to mention the fact that he was dead.

It was different for Deneisha; she was starting to like Calderon, but they were little more than fuck buddies.

"On Tuesday, the two-man team gets to the store. One stays in the truck, and the other goes into the store. Once he has the money, he goes back to the truck, puts the money in, and then they're gone. That's the process. Get the money, walk back to the truck, lock up the money, and go. So, you're asking, what makes Tuesday our target day?"

"I did kinda wanna know," Brianna said.

"The guard who comes into the store is messing with one of the cashiers. So, once he gets the money, she walks out with him."

"He's distracted," Deneisha said, smiling and nodding her head confidently.

"Exactly. I mean, she ain't all up on him, and he ain't all in her face, but he's distracted enough that we can step to him, and he not see it coming." Courtney paused to gauge her girls' reaction. "Questions so far? Neisha?"

"Not yet," Deneisha said. She lit the blunt.

"Breezy?"

"I'm good. Go on. Shit, this might turn out to be something," Brianna said, leaning forward because now, Courtney had her attention. Deneisha passed her the blunt.

"Here's how it's gonna go." Courtney looked at Deneisha. "When he comes out of the store, we roll up and meet him at the truck. Neisha, you get the money while I cover you. When we get the money, Breezy, you pull up, and we make our escape."

"Sounds simple," Brianna said and let out a nervous laugh.

"Too simple," Deneisha said.

"Good. I thought it was just me," Brianna said and passed the blunt.

"But you see, that's the beauty of it, its simplicity." Courtney hit the blunt. "When you get right down to it, this is a stickup. A mugging. Nothing complicated. We ain't trying to take the truck. We get the bags, and we're gone."

"When you thinking about doing this?" Deneisha asked, and Courtney passed her the blunt. She hit the blunt and chased it with Courvoisier and Champagne.

"When we're ready."

The next day, Courtney made Deneisha and Brianna get up early, and they went to the grocery store to check it out before she went to work. The purpose of this trip was for Deneisha and Brianna to get the feel of the area. Not the store since they weren't going inside. They were there to familiarize themselves with the outside of the store. Courtney had Brianna park in front of the store while she parked her car in the employee area. Then she joined them in the car in front of the store.

From where they were parked, they could see inside the store: the office, the registers, and the walkway leading to the exit. Deneisha took pictures of the grocery store with her phone, and then she got photos of the surrounding stores.

"The armored truck is gonna park there," Courtney began. "The driver is gonna stay in the truck while the bagman goes inside to get the money." Deneisha took a picture. "The amount of time he's in there depends on whether they're ready for him."

"About how long?" Brianna asked. "We gonna be sitting out there in the car, waiting."

"Like I said, it's hard to say definitely, but ten to fifteen minutes."

"Okay."

"Of course, y'all are gonna need to come back at different times to see what the place is like when it's open. And then on Tuesday, so y'all can see it going down."

"I would think we'd need to take our time and come back a few times to get down their patterns and shit,"

Deneisha said. She would be the one to approach the bagman while Courtney covered.

"Right. And you can watch how this bitch walks out with him," Courtney said.

"I think I should come inside and check that out," Deneisha remarked.

"Absolutely," Courtney agreed. "And you should check it out a few times before we make our move."

"You're right," Deneisha said and paused. "Is there any security inside the store?"

"Yeah, but he stays near the office once the bagman leaves. You'll see."

"You clock police response times, Court?" Deneisha asked.

"No."

"I'll take care of that when we get closer to the lick," Deneisha said.

"I gotta get inside. I'm running late. I'll see y'all tonight," Courtney said and reached for the handle to get out.

"See you," Deneisha said.

"Don't work too hard, Court," Brianna added.

"Never do," Courtney said and got out of the vehicle.

After Courtney went to work, Brianna and Deneisha left the parking lot and drove around the area so Brianna could get a feeling for the surrounding streets around the store.

She was the driver, so it was her responsibility to get the cars and plan their escape. They drove around the area for an hour, checking out routes that led to the main streets.

"You need to check out those police response times, for real, Neisha," Brianna said as she hit the main street and drove away.

"Tell you what. Let's go get something to eat. By then, the store will be open, and we can get started," Deneisha said.

Brianna laughed. "Surveillance, I love it. Where you wanna eat?"

"Ain't there an IHOP around here somewhere?"

"We'll find it," Brianna said and entered their destination in the navigation system. "There's one not far from here."

"Let's go. I'm hungry," Deneisha said as Brianna drove in that direction.

Brianna had the bacon temptation omelet and a Coke, while Deneisha had the big steak omelet and black coffee. Once they finished eating, they hung around for a while before returning to the grocery store.

For the rest of the week, they conducted their surveillance operation at the grocery store. Since she didn't work, Courtney joined the operation on Saturday. But they did more people-watching, laughing, smoking weed, and drinking, so not much surveillance was done, and they left early that day. After not accomplishing anything the day before, they decided that Sunday would be more of the same, so they stayed home, got fucked up, and reviewed the images they had taken previously, while discussing the importance of taking this seriously.

"Me and Breezy was taking it seriously. Shit got all out of control when you got into the car," Deneisha pointed out.

"We'll be back to serious business tomorrow, Court," Brianna promised and sipped her drink.

"The important day is Tuesday," Courtney pointed out. Deneisha passed her the blunt, and she hit it.

"Don't worry, Court, we'll be ready and sober," Brianna said as Courtney passed her the blunt, and she took a long drag. When she blew out the smoke, she hit it again before passing it to Deneisha, who, in turn, hit it and passed it to Courtney, and then she got up.

"Where you goin', Neisha?" Courtney asked.

"I got something for Tuesday," Deneisha said, and she went to her room.

When she returned to the living room, she was carrying a black Panasonic Full HD Video Camera Camcorder with an optical zoom lens and a BSI sensor.

"When the bagman is in the store, I'll be able to watch the entire exchange and see how he interacts with your girl before they come out of the store."

"Good idea," Courtney said.

"Yeah, I know," Deneisha said, brushing off her shoulders. "I try to do smart shit," she laughed. "Especially when we're planning a robbery."

"That's right, Court. You were just telling us how important it was for us to take shit seriously. Well, I think Neisha showing initiative shows how seriously she's taking it," Brianna said and chuckled.

"She is. What about you, Breezy?" Courtney asked.

"Oh, I'm taking this shit serious as cancer, Court," Brianna said, and she got up and went to her room.

"Where she going?" Courtney asked Deneisha.

"Breezy fiddin' to show you how serious she's taking this shit."

When she returned to the living room, Brianna had a box of thumbtacks and maps of the area around the grocery store. While Courtney and Deneisha looked on, she hung the maps up on the wall.

"Come here, Court, so you can see," Brianna said, and both Courtney and Deneisha joined her at the wall. "All of these are our potential escape routes away from the store. And right here," she pointed to a particular map, "this is where I'll park the second car."

"A second car, Breezy. That's smart," Courtney said, and Deneisha nodded.

"What Neisha say? I try to do smart shit, especially when we're planning a robbery."

Courtney laughed. "See, this is what we should always be doing. Finding big-money targets and planning how and when we're gonna hit them. Not that nickel-and-dime shit y'all be doing."

"Excuse me, missy, but that nickel-and-dime shit we be doing helps pay the rent in this bitch," Brianna pointed out.

"But this is better than that in the long run," Courtney said passionately.

"She's right, Breezy," Deneisha laughed. "But a bitch is broke, so she gonna have to hit a nickel-and-dime lick, so I have some paper until we make this big score."

"Yeah. Scoop been callin' me with some work, but I've been playing him off."

"Do what you gotta do for money," Courtney laughed. "You see my ass keeps showing up for work every day."

With that, Brianna called Scoop, and he gave her a target vehicle. "I need you to hunt for a BMW i4. Can you do that, Breezy?"

"I got you, Scoop," Brianna said.

"I know. You're the best hunter I got. That's why I be putting your sexy, muthafuckin' ass on the hard-to-locate shit."

Brianna accepted the compliment with pride, but she overlooked the "your sexy, muthafuckin' ass" comment because, although Scoop was one fine-ass man, and she heard he could fuck, and he eats the hell out of some pussy, Brianna knew it was important to keep this relationship purely professional.

As for Deneisha, she robbed a couple of gas stations and a liquor store to keep some money in her pocket. But all the while, she was thinking that Courtney was right. She needed to get away from doing these penny-ante licks. She only wished she had the head for planning that Courtney had. So she was glad to have her as a friend.

# Chapter Ten

When they returned to the grocery store on Tuesday, they waited patiently for the arrival of the armored truck. Brianna looked at her watch.

"According to Court, they should have been here by now," Brianna said and looked at her watch again.

"Calm down, Breezy. Here they come now," Deneisha said and pointed to the entrance to the parking lot. She looked at her watch. "Right on time, just like Court said they would be."

"I stand corrected," Brianna said and began to film their arrival on her cell phone.

When the truck parked in front of the store, Deneisha began filming on the Panasonic camcorder. She recorded footage of the bagman entering the store and interacting with the store's management. While that was going on, Brianna noticed a woman walk up.

"There's old girl," Brianna said, and Deneisha turned the camera toward her. "Look at her. The way she's looking at him." Brianna laughed. "She standing there looking at that man like she wanna fuck him on the spot."

Once the bagman had the money, he started for the exit with the woman walking alongside him. Deneisha laughed as the woman's hand drifted between her thighs for a brief second.

"No, she ain't rubbin' that pussy."

"Really?"

"Really, Breezy. I got it on tape." Deneisha shook her head as she recorded the woman accompanying the bagman. "Look at how she's looking at him. The shit is an embarrassment to all women."

When she exited the store with the bagman, they became serious and watched what happened next, as this was the spot where she would approach the bagman with Courtney covering the driver and watching her back.

Now that they had footage of the bagman, Deneisha and Brianna went home. When Courtney got home from work, she found her girls deep in preparation. That night, Courtney brought sandwiches from the deli for dinner.

"What you got, Court?" Brianna wanted to know.

"I got an Italian hoagie, a Philly cheesesteak, and a French dip."

"I'll take the Philly," Deneisha said quickly, and Courtney handed it to her.

"What's on the Italian?" Brianna asked.

"It has boiled ham, imported capicola, Genoa salami, and pepperoni."

"You got that for yourself, Court," Brianna said, and Courtney handed her the French dip. She laughed. "I did do that, so I'm glad you stuck your nose up at it," she said and sat down to eat and watch the footage of the bagman.

Courtney shook her head. "It is so embarrassing the way that woman falls all over him," she remarked.

"That's the same thing I said," Deneisha replied as they watched.

"Y'all think y'all ready to do the damn thing?" Courtney asked.

Brianna and Deneisha looked at each other. "I think we need to see it going down at least one, maybe two more times," Deneisha said, and Brianna nodded in agreement. "Just to see if they do anything different."

"Okay, that's a good idea," Courtney said.

"I got a question that we need to consider," Brianna added.

"What's that, Breezy?" Courtney said.

"What if they break up?" Brianna asked and received blank stares in response. "I mean, this whole lick is based on him being distracted by her trifling ass, right?"

"Right," Deneisha said, and they both looked at Courtney.

Courtney dropped her head. "I never thought about that." She paused to think for a moment.

"It's something we need to consider," Deneisha said. "Don't you think so, Court?"

"Yeah, we do." Courtney paused, exhaled, and then she said, "If he's not distracted by her, we call it off."

"You sure, Court?" Brianna asked. "Just cause he's not distracted don't mean we shouldn't do it. It could still work. I mean, we hit him in the same spot. Y'all take him quick, I pull up in the ride, and we outta there with a bag full of paper."

"No, Breezy, Court's right. If he's not distracted by her trifling ass, we should call it off."

"Y'all sure about this?" Brianna asked again.

"Yes," Deneisha said.

"Tell you what, Breezy. We wait another week. We go back there on Tuesday and check them out with an eye toward running the lick if he's not with her trifling ass. Sound good?" Courtney asked.

"I'm good with that," Brianna said, and they were back at the grocery store the following Tuesday. Weeks earlier, Courtney had taken the week off, so the three spent the weekend and the night before reviewing a combined two weeks of footage and decided that whether or not the bagman was distracted by the woman's trifling ass, they were still gonna hit the lick as planned.

On the day that the robbery was set to take place, Courtney was in the car with her girls when they set out for the grocery store. She had called in to her boss earlier, saying she was running late because of car problems. Brianna had stolen two cars and planted the second escape vehicle in the spot that she had selected.

They sat in the car, patiently waiting for the armored truck to come into the parking lot. Deneisha glanced at her watch and then at Courtney. She nodded in response.

"They're late." Brianna said what they were all thinking.

"They'll be here," Courtney said confidently.

"I know," Brianna said. "I'm just ready to get this over with, that's all."

Deneisha looked out the back window and pointed. "Here they come now."

"About time," Brianna said and sat up in her seat.

The three watched quietly as the armored truck parked in front of the store. Then they waited for the bagman to get out.

"What they waitin' for?" Brianna asked impatiently. She banged the steering wheel.

"Calm down, Breezy," Deneisha said. "You know they like to bullshit for a minute before he gets out."

"I know, I know. I'm just ready to get this over with, that's all," she repeated.

The bagman got out of the truck and went into the store. They watched as he went to the office in the front of the store to get the money.

"There goes old girl. Let's get into position," Courtney said.

"I'm ready," Deneisha replied.

"Good luck, y'all," Brianna said as they got out of the car to get to their designated spots outside the store.

Brianna kept an eye on the bagman as he walked away from the office. The woman joined him, and they walked toward the exit together. She gave Courtney and Deneisha the signal, and they pulled up their masks as the bagman exited the store. They moved toward him quickly with their guns raised. He didn't see them coming.

"Stop right there!" Deneisha shouted, and the bagman stopped. "Drop the bag and step back."

When the bagman dropped the bag and stepped back, Courtney quickly grabbed it. Brianna pulled up in the car, and Courtney got in the front seat. She stuck her gun out the window as Deneisha moved toward the vehicle.

"You don't make enough to do anything stupid," Deneisha warned and climbed into the backseat. Brianna dropped the car in gear and sped away from the store. She got out of the parking lot and hit the street.

They had driven for less than a minute when Brianna said, "Oh shit!"

"What?" Deneisha asked as the sound of the police siren answered her question.

"Where did they come from?" Courtney asked, looking back and seeing the blue light closing in on them.

"Does it matter?" Deneisha asked, looking out the back window. "Just get us outta here, Breezy."

Brianna floored it as the police chased them. She managed to put some distance between herself and the cops, thinking they might just be able to outrun them. She had always had dreams of outrunning the police, so this was like a dream come true.

Brianna was weaving through the traffic with ease, widening the gap with the police when she ran a light . . . and a car T-boned them.

The car spun out of control and crashed into a parked vehicle on the side of the street. The airbags deployed, and Brianna hit her head on the steering wheel.

"We gotta get outta here," Deneisha said, looking out the back window as the police closed in.

Deneisha and Brianna quickly unbuckled their seat belts, but Courtney's belt was stuck, and the car they crashed into had her pinned in. Brianna tried to help her with the seat belt.

With blood trickling down her cheek and the police closing in, Brianna tried desperately to free her friend.

"I can't get it off, Court!" Brianna shouted as she yanked on the seat belt. Deneisha grabbed the bag with the money and got out of the vehicle.

"Here they come!"

The police car caught up, then came to a screeching stop. Courtney and Brianna both pulled on the seat belt.

"I can't get it off, Court!"

"Go!" Courtney shouted, trying again to get the belt off. "Get outta here, Breezy!"

"Shit!" Brianna yelled.

She took the guns, got out of the car, and ran away from the scene, leaving Courtney to face the police alone. She put up her hands as the police approached the vehicle with guns drawn.

Brianna and Deneisha ran and made it to the second getaway car. They got away clean. The police arrested Courtney and took her to jail.

# Chapter Eleven

Courtney sat alone in the interrogation room at the Fulton County Jail for more than an hour before anybody came in to speak with her. The lights were bright, and the heat was turned up in an attempt to make her uncomfortable. Suddenly, the door swung open, and two detectives, a well-built older white man in an expensive suit, and a younger Black woman, walked in.

"I'm Detective Zamora, and this is Detective Yoder," the female cop said and sat down at the table across from Courtney. The male cop sat on the table, positioning himself to hover over and intimidate her. She looked up at him and rolled her eyes. "We'd like to talk to you about the grocery store you robbed and who was with you."

"Lawyer," Courtney said and closed her eyes.

The detectives looked at each other and stood up. They quietly left the room, and Courtney was permitted to make her one phone call. She called her mother, asking her to contact a lawyer without explaining what she had done. When her lawyer arrived, Courtney refused to tell the detectives that Deneisha Lewis and Brianna Commer were her accomplices. After that, Courtney was processed into the system, issued supplies, and taken to her cell.

It was her first day on the yard, and the first person she saw was Chloe Mitchell, the woman with whom Deneisha had gotten into it at That Joint. In retaliation, later that night, Deneisha and Brianna shot up Nikko Hensley's trap house, where she was a runner. Like Courtney,

Chloe was arrested and awaiting trial for possession with the intent to sell. It was her third arrest, and Georgia was a three-strikes law. That law mandated mandatory long prison sentences for repeat offenders. Since it was her third offense, there was a possibility that she could receive a sentence of life in prison without parole. To avoid that fate, she would need to flip on Nikko Hensley and his operation. Since snitching on Nikko was a death sentence, Chloe was keeping her mouth shut and was prepared to take her chances in court.

The night of the drive-by, Chloe assumed that it was Deneisha who shot at her at the trap house and that Courtney was with her when the shooting went down. When she saw Courtney, Chloe smiled, pointed at Courtney, and then ran her finger across her throat, a gesture universally recognized as slitting one's throat with a knife. Courtney gave her the finger and kept it moving.

Courtney was in the yard the next day when she saw Chloe coming toward her. She tried to give her a wide berth, but Chloe came straight at her. Courtney prepared for the inevitable confrontation. Chloe suddenly rushed toward her and began stabbing Courtney in the stomach. Then another inmate came up behind her and stabbed her in the back. Quickly, Chloe and the other inmate walked away, leaving a bloody Courtney on the ground, stabbed ten times. As she lay there, other inmates walked by her. By the time a guard noticed her lying there and got her to the infirmary, Courtney had lost too much blood and was pronounced dead.

# Chapter Twelve

Early the next morning, Deneisha was awakened by a crying phone call from Courtney's mother. She told her that Courtney had been murdered in jail.

"Oh my God. I am so sorry, Mrs. Fields."

"The police just told me that she had been murdered, but they wouldn't give any other information. I don't even know why she was locked up, Neisha. She just called me out of the blue and said she needed a lawyer. Can you or Breezy tell me what happened?"

Deneisha paused for a minute and carefully considered what she was gonna say. After they fled the scene of the accident, she and Brianna went back to the apartment. They gathered some clothes as quickly as they could, then made a quick exit. Since then, they've been lying low at the Crowne Plaza in Peachtree City, thirty miles south of Metro Atlanta. Brianna walked up while she was on the phone.

"Who's that?"

"Court's mom," Deneisha said softly. "I'm sorry, Mrs. Fields, but I have no idea why Court got locked up. Me and Breezy only heard she was in jail last night."

"Well, if you all hear anything, please let me know."

"I will." She paused because she felt bad about lying to Mrs. Fields. She was so nice and welcoming to Deneisha when she first moved to Atlanta from New York. "And I am so sorry for your loss, Mrs. Fields," Deneisha said as tears rolled down her cheeks.

"I know you girls were close," Mrs. Fields said. "I will call and let you know when we are going to lay my baby to rest," she said and began to cry. It was as if the realization that Courtney was really dead suddenly hit her. "I'm sorry, but I gotta go, Neisha," she said and hung up the phone.

"I understand," Deneisha said to dead air. She looked at Brianna and practically fell on the couch.

"What's wrong, Neisha?" Brianna asked because she was crying. "What did Mrs. Fields say?"

"Court's dead, Breezy."

"*What?*"

"She said she was murdered."

"By who?"

"She didn't know. Cops won't tell her anything."

Brianna began to cry, and she sat on the couch beside Deneisha. The two best friends hugged and tried to comfort each other.

Two days later, Mrs. Fields called again. She commented that she was surprised that neither she nor Brianna had come to the house to offer condolences.

"But I understand. You girls were so close. I imagine this must be hard on you."

"It has been hard, Mrs. Fields. Some days, I don't even feel like getting out of bed. But that's no excuse. We could have come over and paid our respects."

"I know that you and Breezy will be at the service."

Deneisha said nothing at first. "When will the service be held?"

"The wake is going to be on Friday night at Wilson Funeral Home, and the service to lay her to rest will be at Saint Paul's AME Church."

"We'll be there, Mrs. Fields, I promise," Deneisha said, and after offering her condolences once again, she ended the call.

She dropped her head into the palms of her hands and began to cry because, once again, Deneisha had lied to Mrs. Fields about coming to Courtney's funeral service. She had thought long and hard about it, and she had decided that she wasn't going to attend. Deneisha felt bad about her decision, but she was convinced it was the right decision under the circumstances.

She couldn't be sure if Courtney told the police that she and Brianna were with her when she robbed the grocery store. In either case, she was sure that the police would be at the funeral looking for them, so she wasn't going to the wake or the funeral.

"Fuck you mean you ain't goin' to Court's funeral?" Brianna asked angrily.

"Exactly what I said, Breezy. I ain't goin', and you shouldn't either."

"Why the fuck not?"

"I got a feeling that the cops will be there looking for the two women who got away."

"How they gonna know it's us outta all the people that's gonna be at the funeral?"

"They're the cops, Breezy. Don't you think they been investigating Court? By now, the cops know everything about her. Where she worked and where she lived, and they know we're her roommates."

"So?"

"Fuck you mean, so?"

"So what? They know we roommates. That don't mean we was in on the robbery with her."

"Are you willing to take that chance?"

"Fuck yeah, Neisha. I'm going. And you should too. Court was our girl, and it would be fuckin' disrespectful for us not to go."

"I know it will be, but I am not willing to take that chance, and you shouldn't either." Deneisha and Brianna looked at each other for a minute. "I know it's disrespectful, Breezy, and I feel bad about it, but my mind is made up. I'm not going to Court's funeral, and you shouldn't either."

Brianna pointed at Deneisha's face. "That's fucked up, Neisha," she said, storming out of the room.

"I'm sorry," Deneisha shouted as she heard Brianna's door slam, and over the next few days, the two best friends sat around the hotel room, not speaking and exchanging dirty looks.

Deneisha was right. Detectives Zamora and Yoder were indeed investigating Courtney Fields. They knew where she lived, where she worked, and who her roommates were. The detectives had already obtained a search warrant for the apartment. At this point, Deneisha Lewis and Brianna Commer were persons of interest in the investigation and were being sought for questioning.

"I'm willing to bet you a month's salary that these two are involved in the robbery," Yoder said, tossing their mug shots on Zamora's desk. She picked up Deneisha's file. "They both have priors. Both Lewis and Commer did time for shoplifting."

"True. But armed robbery of a grocery store is a big step up," Zamora said.

"You sayin' they don't look good for it?"

"No. That's not what I'm sayin'. I just said it was a big step up." She paused and looked at Brianna's file. "The way I see it, Fields came up with the idea. She convinced the other two to throw in with her."

"Agreed. But we don't have enough for a judge to grant us an arrest warrant for them."

"So, what now?"

"I say we make an appearance at the funeral. These girls were tight, thick as thieves. Let's see if they show up at the funeral."

"It's worth a shot," the younger detective said.

The next day at Saint Paul's AME Church, Courtney was laid to rest. Reverend Marcellus had known Courtney since she was born, and he gave a eulogy that brought tears to the eyes of many. Several of Courtney's friends spoke, but when it came time for Brianna to eulogize her best friend, she was overwhelmed with grief after a few words and broke down in tears.

"I can't do this," she said, and had to be led away by friends.

The repast was held in the basement of the church. Members and family friends brought food for the solemn occasion. Brianna mingled with Courtney's family and old friends at the repast. She grew so tired of people asking her, "Where's Deneisha?" that she considered recording her answer to play for everyone who asked.

"Deneisha isn't feeling well. She's running a high fever and throwing up. She wanted to come, but I made her stay in bed. I told her there was no point in making herself sicker by coming, not to mention making the rest of us sick." She laughed. "I told her, 'No, girlfriend, you stay your ass right there in the bed. Courtney knows your heart, and that's all that matters.'" That answer seemed to satisfy those who asked.

Brianna had just gotten a plate and was on her way to sit down at the table with the Fields family when the two detectives arrived. So many people there were paying their respects that Brianna didn't know. She assumed the detectives were merely people Courtney worked with, paying them little attention as they moved around the repast and spoke with others.

"There she is," Zamora said, discreetly pointing Brianna out to her partner. "You wanna take her now?"

"No," Yoder said and got in line to get some food. "I don't want to make a scene. That would be disrespectful to the family." He picked up a plate. "We'll wait until she leaves and take her outside."

"You think the other one will show up?"

"No. If she's not here already, she's not coming. Smart," he said, and glanced at Zamora. "You're not eating?"

"I don't know who made that shit," she said, frowning and shaking her head. "But you have at it. I'll keep my eyes on Commer."

After she ate, Brianna chatted with old friends until the repast began to break up. She said goodbye to Mrs. Fields, apologizing once again for Deneisha's absence, and expressed her deepest and heartfelt condolences for her loss before leaving.

Zamora tapped Yoder. "She's leaving," she said, and the detectives went after her.

Brianna had called for an Uber to take her back to the hotel and was about to get into the car when the detectives approached her.

"Brianna Commer?" Zomora said.

"Yes."

"I'm Detective Zamora, and this is my partner, Detective Yoder. We want to ask you some questions about Courtney Fields. Would you mind coming with us?"

"Not like I have a choice," she said and went with the detectives.

When they arrived at the station, Brianna was taken to an interrogation room. Zamora told her that they would be with her in a minute and left the room. As they did with Courtney, they left Brianna in that room for over an hour with the lights on and the heat turned up before they returned. They came in hot and went hard at her.

"Look, we know it was you and Deneisha Lewis who robbed the grocery store with Fields," Yoder got in her face and shouted. He shoved a still image of Brianna in the car in the parking lot at the grocery store. "That's you!" he shouted, and then he got in her face. "Ain't it, Breezy?" Yoder said with a smug smile.

"We can charge you right now with armed robbery, brandishing a firearm, and conspiracy. You're facing ten years to life in prison. Do yourself a favor. Cooperate. Tell us where to find Lewis and the money."

"What happens if I tell you what you wanna know?"

Zamora and Yoder looked at each other. "You were just the driver," Zamora began. "You tell us where Deneisha Lewis is and aid in the recovery of the money. We'll drop the armed robbery and brandishing a firearm charges. You plead guilty to conspiracy and testify at her trial, and then you do five years in prison."

Yoder leaned in. "Five years is a whole lot better than doing life."

"He's right. Do the smart thing, Brianna. You're a young woman with your whole life ahead of you. You'll be out in five years," Zamora said, holding up five fingers. "Less for good behavior. You can still make something of yourself and have a life."

Brianna sat quietly and contemplated what the detective said. Five years was a whole lot better than doing life. But it meant that she would have to give up Deneisha. She did not doubt that they would charge her with armed robbery, brandishing a firearm, and conspiracy if she didn't cooperate. She'd be condemning her friend to life in prison. Brianna thought back to her time in prison. She couldn't do life.

"She's at the Crowne Plaza in Peachtree City."

"Is the money there?" Yoder wanted to know.

"Yeah, it's there."

"Is she armed?" Zamora asked.

"Yes."

The detectives stood up. "I'll get started on an arrest warrant for Lewis," Zamora said and left the interrogation room.

"Stand up, Miss Commer, and put your hands behind your back."

Brianna did as she was told, and he cuffed her.

"You're under arrest for armed robbery, brandishing a firearm, and conspiracy."

"What? But you said—"

"You have the right to remain silent. Anything you say can and will be used against you in a court of law."

# Chapter Thirteen

Meanwhile, at the Crown Plaza Hotel, Deneisha was feeling bad about her decision not to attend Courtney's funeral, but she was sure she'd done the right thing. And it wasn't long before she was proven right. She had just gotten out of the shower when she heard her phone beep with a text message from Ceyonna Bradshaw, a friend who knew them in high school.

I'm not sure, but I think Breezy got picked up by the cops.

"Damn it, Breezy. I told you not to go," she said aloud and sat down on the edge of the bed.

Although she felt that Brianna would stand tall and not give her up, there was no way to be sure if she flipped on her. Deneisha knew she needed to get outta there. She bounced up from the bed and began dressing. When she finished, she packed her clothes, got the money and the guns, and headed out. She had no idea where she was going, but anywhere was better than sitting in that room, waiting for the cops to arrest her. She tossed the stuff in the backseat of the old Honda Accord that Brianna used as the second getaway car after the robbery and drove south on local roads.

Deneisha found her way to State Route 19 and continued heading south, away from Atlanta. The next big city was Albany, Georgia, 180 miles south of Atlanta. She thought she could hide out there until she figured out what she was going to do. Deneisha had over $25,000 from the robbery, so she'd be all right for a minute as far as money was concerned. The farther she got away from Atlanta, the more she began to think that Albany wasn't far enough.

If there were a warrant for her arrest, it would go out statewide, and she'd have every law enforcement officer in the state on the lookout for her. Deneisha needed to leave the state of Georgia. She remembered that her mother had a friend when they were living in New York named Vivian Tate. She had moved to Jacksonville, Florida, around the same time that Deneisha moved to Georgia.

She was in Atlanta visiting Carlitha and told Deneisha that if she were ever in Jacksonville, to give her a call. Deneisha took out her phone and scrolled through her contacts until she found the number. She called Vivian and told her that she was relocating to Jacksonville. Vivian offered Deneisha a place to stay until she got settled.

Now that Deneisha had a plan and a destination, she dumped the phone and continued driving south. But she was driving a stolen car, and there was a chance that she could get stopped. She was passing through a small town called Leesburg when Deneisha saw a small used car dealer. She parked the car, took $10,000 of the money, and walked to the dealership. Even though it was a small dealership, all the vehicles were imported.

Deneisha fell in love with a burgundy 2004 Jaguar XJ, but thought it might be too conspicuous. But she wanted something nice, so she settled on a 2006 3-series BMW.

"I'll take this one."

"How much did you want to put down?"

"I'm going to pay cash."

"Right this way to the office, and we'll get you riding."

The car was listed at $4,995 plus tax, tag, and title. Deneisha put six in cash on the desk. When he asked to see her driver's license and proof of insurance, Deneisha put another thousand on the desk.

"Let's say we forget about the whole license and insurance requirement."

The dealer smiled. "For another thousand, we can forget about that messy paperwork altogether." Deneisha counted off another thousand. The dealer took the money and stood up with his hand out.

"Congratulations."

And Deneisha was on her way to Jacksonville.

She stayed on state routes and off the interstate, careful to obey traffic laws as she passed through small town after small town.

It was late on Sunday afternoon when Deneisha crossed the state line from Georgia into Florida. She cruised down Highway 301 and rolled into Jacksonville from there. Vivian Tate owned a house in the Murray Hill neighborhood of Jacksonville. She was sitting outside on the porch when Deneisha parked in front of her home. She stood up when Deneisha got out of the car. The first thing that hit her was the stifling humidity.

"Hey, Miss Vivian," she said and waved.

"Hey, Deneisha. How was your drive down?" she asked, coming to the vehicle.

"It was a nice, quiet ride," Deneisha answered as she opened the trunk and got her bag.

"You need help?"

"No, Miss Vivian. I got it, thank you," she said and followed Miss Vivian into the house, thankful that she had the air-conditioning on blast.

"Well, this is it," Miss Vivian said when they came into the living room. "It's not much, but you're welcome to stay as long as you need to."

"Thank you, Miss Vivian. I appreciate you letting me stay here. I promise not to be the houseguest who don't know how to leave. As soon as I get myself situated, I'll be outta your hair."

"Like I said, you are more than welcome to stay as long as you want. It'll be nice to have someone in the house. It's been kind of quiet since Serena and the kids moved out."

"How is Serena?"

"She's doing fine. Excited to see you."

"I'm excited to see her too," Deneisha lied. Although she and Serena grew up around each other, they weren't friends. Deneisha thought that Serena was fake and liked to start and keep shit going. Serena thought Deneisha was a gossipy backstabber and saw her as competition, and was jealous of her popularity with the boys.

"I heard she got married. How many kids does she have?"

"Two. A boy and a girl. She's 7, and he's 5. You'll see them tomorrow. I'm having a little barbecue and invited a few friends over for the holiday."

"That should be nice."

"Are you hungry?"

"Starving."

"Well, come on into the kitchen. I fixed pork chops, mashed potatoes with gravy, and snap beans."

"You didn't have to go to all that trouble, Miss Vivian," Deneisha said as she followed her into the kitchen.

"Trust me, child, cooking is no trouble at all." She chuckled. "It's my love language." Miss Vivian pointed to the table. "Now sit down and enjoy this meal." She stopped and looked at Deneisha. "Unless there's something that you don't eat."

"No, ma'am." She sat down at the table. "Watch me tear them pork chops up like a greedy crack fiend."

"Good. I like to see people enjoy their food," Miss Vivian said and served Deneisha her food, and, as promised, she tore those chops up like a greedy crack fiend. "You want another pork chop?"

"Yes, please."

After dinner, Miss Vivian showed Deneisha to her room. "It used to be Serena's room, and the kids sleep in here sometimes when they stay overnight, which isn't nearly as much as I'd like." Miss Vivian shook her head. "Denny, that's her husband; he can be so controlling. But she seems to like being told what to do, who to speak to, and where to go. I've learned to see and not see and mind my own business."

"Sometimes that's the best policy."

"As long as she's happy, I'm happy for her."

"I hate it for her, but if she likes it, I love it," Deneisha said as Miss Vivian handed her some towels and then showed her where the bathroom was. After she showered and freshened up, Deneisha went into the living room. She sat and talked and watched television with Miss Vivian until she got ready to call it a night. Finally, she stood up.

"I'm going to bed. You're welcome to stay up as long as you like. Don't worry about the television being loud. I can sleep through anything," she laughed.

"I might go out for a while. Get the lay of the land."

"Well, in that case, you're gonna need a key. You show up here ringing the bell, thinking you gonna get in . . ." She laughed and went into the kitchen. "You'll be sleeping in your car." She opened the drawer, picked up the key ring, and handed it to Deneisha.

"It's comfortable, but no, thanks, Miss Vivian." She pocketed the keys.

"Well, good night, Neisha. I'll see you in the morning. I'll cook breakfast for us."

"Because it's your love language, right?"

"Right."

"Good night, Miss Vivian," Deneisha said and followed her out of the kitchen.

She went into her room and lay across the bed. Deneisha looked at her suitcase and thought about unpacking. Then she thought that she wasn't planning on staying long, so why go through the trouble of unpacking? Finally, she stood up.

"Because living out of a suitcase when you don't have to is ghetto," she said, answering her own question.

Once she had put away her clothes, Deneisha looked in the mirror. She was wearing her comfortable jeans and that Michael Vick throwback jersey. It was her standard, *I ain't doing shit around the house,* look. But if she was gonna hit the streets, she needed to change.

"But what? It's so fuckin' hot here," she said aloud and went to the closet.

She chose a V-neck cotton dress that she picked up on sale at Nordstrom's with some Lisbeth slingback pointed-toe pumps, grabbed her keys, and headed out. Since she had never been to Jacksonville, Deneisha had no idea where she was going. So, she decided just to drive.

"Get the lay of the land," she giggled and started the car.

Although it was late, Deneisha drove toward the beaches. She hadn't been to the beach since she was a little girl growing up in New York. She knew she would return, but she wanted to savor the roar of the waves and the fresh, salty air. When she arrived at Jacksonville Beach, she found bars open, so she decided to pick a spot and have a drink after hitting the beach. With that decided, Deneisha got her gun from her purse and exited the car.

"Ain't no point fuckin' around," she said aloud as she walked toward the beach.

# Chapter Fourteen

The next morning, Deneisha woke up to the smell of breakfast cooking in the kitchen. After she showered and got dressed, she made her way to the kitchen.

"Good morning, Miss Vivian."

"Hey, Neisha. You want some coffee?"

"Yes, ma'am. Where are the cups?"

Miss Vivian pointed as she continued frying the bacon. "In the cabinet there."

"Thank you. How are you this morning?" she asked as she filled her cup.

"I'm fine. Unless you take it black, I got flavored creams in the refrigerator."

"I take it with cream," she said, and opened the refrigerator to find a variety of creams. There was Crème Brûlée, Peppermint Mocha, Caramel, and Pumpkin Spice. She chose the Caramel and poured it into the cup.

"That's my favorite too," Miss Vivian said as Deneisha sat down at the table. "After I saw how you ate last night, I got a little carried away with breakfast, so I hope you're hungry," she said, setting a plate of eggs, bacon, and waffles in front of her.

"You gonna make me fat," she said and picked up her fork. "Me and my girls used to eat out a lot; we ate a lotta fast food," Deneisha admitted and started to eat.

"Can you cook?" Miss Vivian asked and sat down across from Deneisha with a plate of food.

"That depends on what you mean by 'cook,'" she laughed. "I can boil water for hot dogs, and I can scramble some eggs. I'm hell with a microwave, but that's about the extent of my cooking skills."

"I could teach you some stuff, if you wanna learn."

"That would be nice, Miss Vivian. Thank you."

After Miss Vivian and Deneisha cleaned the kitchen, Miss Vivian began prepping the meats for the grill—chicken legs, wings, and hamburgers. There would also be hot dogs and brats on the menu. Once that was done, she got a couple of racks of ribs from the refrigerator. Mis Vivian got ready to make her famous dry rub for the ribs.

"Pay attention, child."

"Yes, ma'am."

"The brown sugar's gonna make it sweet and savory," she said, starting with three tablespoons of brown sugar. "Paprika's gonna give it that warm, smoky, deep flavor that I like. Now, a little salt and cayenne pepper," Miss Vivian said as she added the ingredients to the mix. "And some garlic powder."

Once the dry rub mix was finished, she turned on the stove and set it to 295 degrees. She washed her hands and began to rub the mixture she had prepared all over the ribs.

"You not putting those on the grill?" Deneisha asked.

"Why? So they can be tough and burnt up? No, Neisha, I slow cook my ribs in the oven. That way, the meat is tender and falls off the bone. But I put them on the grill once they're cooked with some sauce to give it that smoky barbecue taste and smell."

"See, I learned something," Deneisha said, proud of herself but not knowing when she'd ever use this skill.

Now that the ribs were in the oven, they went outside and fired up the grill. Miss Vivian planned to serve a variety of dishes, including baked mac and cheese, collard greens, shrimp pasta, macaroni, potato salad, corn soufflé, hush puppies, baked beans, and fruit salad. She had prepared those items the day before Deneisha arrived and had them in the refrigerator.

Her barbecues were an annual event among her friends and family, so she went all out. She used to spend hours making cakes and pies for the occasion. However, in recent years, Miss Vivian decided that store-bought pastries were good enough.

Once everything was done, Miss Vivian sat down on her chair on the porch. It was at that moment that Serena, Denny, and the kids pulled into the driveway and parked.

"She always gets here after everything is done," Miss Vivian laughed. "I think she plans it that way," she said as the car doors opened and her grandchildren came running out. She stood up to greet them. "There are my babies."

"Hey, Grandma!" they both shouted and rushed into her arms.

"And who are these beautiful children?" Deneisha asked, crouching down to their level.

"This is my granddaughter, Chrystal, and this handsome little man is my grandson, Michael. Say hello to Miss Neisha."

"Hello, Miss Neisha," they both said, and Michael offered his hand.

"It is nice to meet you both. How old are you?"

"I'm 7," Chrystal said.

"And I'm 5," Michael said.

"No, you're not. You're still 4 years old."

"I'll be 5 next month."

"That means you're still 4, silly."

"I am not silly."

"Yes, you are. Just a silly little boy," Chrystal teased.

"Chrystal," Serena said sternly when she and Denny arrived on the porch. "What I tell you about calling your brother names?"

"Not to do it."

"Apologize to your brother."

"I'm sorry, Michael."

"Now go inside and wash your hands," Serena said, and they ran inside. She turned to Deneisha and broke into a big smile. "Hey, Neisha," she said and hugged her like they were the best of friends who hadn't seen each other in years.

"Hey, Serena," Deneisha said, caught completely off guard by the reception.

"How have you been, girl? It is so good to see you," she said and hugged her again. Serena let her go and turned to her husband. "Neisha, this is my husband, Denny. Me and her grew up together in New York."

"Nice to meet you, Neisha," Denny said, looking at her as if she were a fried pork chop dripping with hot sauce. "It's always nice to meet Serena's old friends. They always have the best stories about her."

Serena looped her arm in Deneisha's. "Moving right along," she said, rolling her eyes at Denny and going into the house, "how long are you going to stay here in the 'ville?"

"The 'ville?"

"That's just what we call it." Serena giggled. "How long do you plan on staying in Jacksonville?"

"I don't know. I needed a change from the ATL, so I came here to check it out. If I like it, I'll stay."

"You are gonna love it here. The weather is amazing, the atmosphere is laid-back, not that New York or Atlanta pace, and the beaches are awesome."

"I needed to slow down and chill out."

"Living that fast life in the ATL." Serena nodded as Denny and Miss Vivian came into the house. "I hear you."

Miss Vivian went into the kitchen, and Denny sat down on the couch next to Serena. She rolled her eyes as he put his arm around her. The children came running into the room, and Chystal turned on the television, tuning it to *Nickelodeon.*

"Come on, Neisha," Serena took her hand. "Let's go into the kitchen and see if Mommy needs any help," she said, once again, rolling her eyes at Denny. Deneisha followed her, leaving Denny with his children.

# Chapter Fifteen

Later that afternoon, Miss Vivian's guests began arriving along with their appetites. Before they came, Deneisha went to get ready. She put on an African-ethnic Kente sleeveless minidress with stripes. When she went into the backyard, Miss Vivian took Deneisha around and introduced her to family and friends.

The sun was setting in the western skies, and Deneisha was thinking about getting out of there when something happened to make her want to stay.

"Who is that?" Deneisha asked the woman sitting next to her.

"His name is Dallas."

"He family?"

"No, just a friend of Miss Vivian and them."

Deneisha nodded at the sight of this fine-ass specimen of a man. He was a sexy, chocolate, six-foot-three specimen with bulging biceps that were straining the sleeves of the Bob Marley shirt he wore. And then he turned in her direction and smiled as he talked with Miss Vivian. Deneisha got a little moist and knew that she needed an introduction. She stood up, smoothed out her dress, and walked across the yard to where they were standing. Dallas noticed her as she walked, and he became a little tongue-tied in his conversation with Miss Vivian.

"Who is that?" he asked, thinking that she was the prettiest woman he had ever seen in his life.

Miss Vivian glanced at Deneisha as she strutted across the yard. She smiled.

"That's Deneisha Lewis. She's visiting from Atlanta." She looped her arm in his. "Come on. I'll introduce you. That is what you were gonna say, right?"

"You know everything, Miss Vivian," Dallas said, and they met Deneisha in the middle of the yard.

"Dallas, this is a family friend, Deneisha Lewis. Neisha, this is Dallas."

He bowed at the waist and took her hand in his. "It is truly a pleasure to meet you, Deneisha."

She looked up into his intense, dark eyes. "Nice to meet you too, Dallas."

"Miss Vivian," a woman walked up and said.

"Yes, dear?"

"Serena wants you in the kitchen."

"Would you two excuse me?" she said and walked away with the woman.

"So," Dallas took a step closer to Deneisha, "what brings you to Jacksonville?"

"I needed to get away," she began. "I was living life in the fast lane and needed to take it down a bit for a minute."

Dallas flashed that smile and chuckled. "Well," he leaned forward, "you came to the right place."

"So Serena tells me."

"A man told me once that Jacksonville was a good place to take a nap," Dallas said, and they both laughed. His laugh was intoxicating, and Deneisha felt powerless to stop herself from falling under the spell he was casting.

"Look, I'm gonna make myself a plate, but I want to talk to you some more."

"I think that could be arranged," Deneisha said. "I was thinking about getting a slice of the cherry pie. I already made a pig of myself on ribs, chicken, and mac and cheese, and didn't have room for dessert."

"Miss Vivian's food will make a pig outta anybody," Dallas said and extended his hand toward the food.

Once Dallas had fixed his plate and Deneisha had her pie and two scoops of vanilla ice cream, they sat down, and the getting-to-know-you flirtation conversation continued. His voice was a deep baritone and so fuckin' sexy, Deneisha was thinking as they chatted about this and that.

"You gonna get you some dessert?" Deneisha asked when Dallas finished eating.

"No. I was actually thinking about getting something to drink." He leaned close to her again. "Something *stronger* than iced tea."

"Not here."

"No, Miss Vivian will feed you until you're full, but this is a dry house."

"I could stand a drink myself."

"You're welcome to come with me. There's a spot on Edgewood not far from here."

"Let me tell her I'm leaving and get my purse. I won't be long," she promised and started to walk away from him. He quickly caught up with her.

"I need to say goodbye too," he said as he walked alongside her.

After they said their goodbyes to their host, Deneisha went to get her purse. As she was on her way, she noticed that Serena was looking at her, and she didn't look happy. She figured that Denny must have said something to her and kept it moving. She had noticed the tension between them when they were introduced.

"You ready?" Dallas asked when she came back into the yard.

"I am. Let's go."

They waved goodbye and left the yard, heading for the car. She took out her keys and was about to turn off the alarm.

"Why don't you ride with me?" he said, pointing to a Lexus coupe.

Deneisha paused for a moment and looked at him. She had just met him, so jumping in the car with him wasn't her first choice.

"Okay," she said, even though her better judgment told her it wasn't a good idea.

"I promise to be a perfect gentleman." Dallas unlocked the car and held the door open for Deneisha to get in.

"See that you do," she said and got into the car.

After a short drive, they found themselves at a bar called Moon River. They sat down at the bar and ordered drinks. Deneisha looked around the crowded bar.

"A lotta white folks in there," she said as the bartender returned with their drinks.

"Tell you what, we'll finish these and go to a private club I know about."

Deneisha shot her drink. "I'm ready when you are."

Dallas chuckled and shot his drink. "Let's go."

Once they were outside and headed for the car, Dallas said, "I take it you don't like white people."

"Not in groups like that. Crackers get dangerous when they get around each other."

"You can't lump all white people together," he said, unlocking the car.

"Why can't I?"

"Because they're not all bad."

"Granted. Some of them can be all right if you catch them one-on-one," Deneisha said, and Dallas smiled. "What?"

"Muhammad Ali, the greatest fighter that ever lived."

"Word."

Dallas smiled. "You like boxing?"

"I do."

"Anyway, Muhammad Ali said if 10,000 rattlesnakes were coming after me, but I had a door that I could shut, and I knew that a thousand of those rattlesnakes were good and didn't want to bite me . . ." He paused and started the car. "Should I let all these rattlesnakes come down, hoping that the thousand will get together and form a shield around me? Or should I just close the door and stay safe?"

"You better slam that door quick," Deneisha said, laughing hard.

When they got to the private club, the place was packed and jumping. The music was pounding through the speakers, and the DJ had skills. They went to the bar and ordered drinks. It wasn't long before somebody Dallas knew came up to him and invited him to join a poker game.

"I would, but I'm with somebody tonight, man."

"Go ahead and get your gamble on. I'll be over there in a few."

"You sure?"

"Yes." She pointed. "Go."

He smiled. "Okay. I'll be right over there if you need me," Dallas said and walked away with his friend, thinking that made Deneisha just that much more desirable. While Dallas was gambling, Deneisha was approached by a man who started up a conversation.

"Let me buy you a drink," he offered.

"Sure."

"What you drinkin'?"

"Courvoisier on the rocks," Deneisha said to the bartender.

"Let me have one of them too," the man said to the bartender.

While the bartender fixed the drinks, another man started talking to Deneisha, so she didn't see that the first man who was talking to her had slipped ketamine, a well-known and powerful date rape drug, into her drink. The drug makes a person less able to say no or fight back.

"I don't feel so good," Deneisha said when she began to feel the effects of the drug.

"Here, let me help you," one of the men said and pulled her up from her seat at the bar. Each man took an arm and walked her to the door.

"Where are you taking me?" she asked as they helped her walk out of the bar.

As they were leaving, Dallas saw them taking her out. He cashed out of the game and followed the men outside. They took Deneisha to their truck, which was parked in the darkened area of the parking lot. While one held her down on the flat bed and covered her mouth, the other started pulling up her dress when Dallas walked up. When he saw what was happening, he took out his gun and fired with his .44 Magnum.

The first shot hit the man standing in the chest. He was patiently awaiting his turn. The impact from the shot at close range from that cannon took the man off his feet and blew a massive hole in him. The other man jumped up and tried to run. Dallas raised the weapon again and fired, hitting him in the back. After that, he walked up to each one and put a bullet in their heads. Then Dallas went back to the truck and fixed Deneisha's clothes.

"What happened to me?"

"Niggas was about to rape you."

"What happened to them?"

"They're dead. Come on." Dallas helped her get up and out of the truck.

"You killed them?"

"Yes."

"Thank you."

"Can you walk?"

"I think so," Deneisha said. She took a step and fell into his arms.

"Guess not," he said and picked her up. He carried her to the car and put her in the front seat. Then he got in, started the engine, and drove away.

# Chapter Sixteen

The following morning, Deneisha woke up, sat up in bed, and wondered where she was. All she knew was that the king-sized, four-post bed she was lying on was so comfortable. In addition to not knowing where she was, she had no idea how she got there. She pulled back the covers. She was still wearing the dress she had on the night before. And then, it all began to come back to her.

"Dallas."

But that didn't explain where she was or how she got there. Deneisha got out of bed in search of a bathroom. She found her way to the living room and found Dallas asleep on the couch.

She tapped him lightly on the shoulder, and he opened his eyes.

"Good morning," he mumbled.

"Hey," she said and waved.

"How do you feel?"

"I'm feeling a little . . . I don't know, kinda groggy. What happened to me last night?"

"You don't remember?"

"No. I don't."

"What's the last thing you remember?" Dallas sat up to ask.

"I remember us goin' to some club, but what happened after that, I have no idea."

"Two guys slipped something in your drink and tried to rape you."

"You serious?"

"Yeah."

"You did say they just *tried,* right? They didn't actually—"

"No. They didn't."

"What happened to them?"

"You really don't remember any of this?"

"No, Dallas, I really don't remember anything."

"They're dead."

"You killed them?" a wide-eyed Deneisha asked.

"Yes, Deneisha. They were about to rape you, and I killed them instead."

"Thank you. But somehow, that doesn't seem like enough."

"No problem."

"Where's your bathroom?"

Dallas stood up. "Come on. I'll show you." On the way, he stopped in the linen closet and handed her a towel. "In case you want to freshen up."

"Thank you."

"Bathroom's this way," he said and led the way. "You hungry?"

"I could eat," she said as she reached the bathroom.

"Cool. When you're ready, we can go get some breakfast or something."

After showering and putting on the same clothes as the night before, Dallas took Deneisha to the Maple Street Biscuit Company on San Marco Boulevard.

"I eat here all the time."

"You must like the food."

"I do," he said, and they both ordered the hash brunch bowl, with onions and topped with goat cheese, bacon, and eggs.

After breakfast, Dallas took Deneisha back to Miss Vivian's house. He parked the car, turned off the engine, and turned to her.

"If you don't have any plans for the day, I'd like to spend the day with you."

"I'd like that. Give me a minute to change clothes, and I'll be right back," she said as she got out of the car.

She was also surprised when he got out of the vehicle and walked with her to the door. Deneisha was even more surprised when Dallas came into the house with her. While she changed clothes, he sat in the living room talking to Miss Vivian.

"Ready," Deneisha said when she came into the room.

"Ready," Dallas said, standing and smiling at the sight of Deneisha in the pink floral one-shoulder draped mini-dress that she was wearing.

"Where are you two off to?" Miss Vivian asked.

"I don't know. I was thinking of taking her to the beach."

"You're not planning on getting in, are you, because I don't have a bathing suit."

Dallas chuckled, and she enjoyed the sound of it. "No, I wasn't. But we can go shopping for one if you want."

"Not today. To be honest with you, I never liked shopping with men."

"Neither do I," Miss Vivian offered. "You men be in too much of a rush to get outta there."

"Just an offer," he said with his hands up. "So, I say again, you ready to go?"

"No. Since we're going to the beach, these shoes are not going to cut it," she said, pointing to the slingbacks she was wearing. Dallas sat down again.

After a quick change, Deneisha returned wearing sandals, and they left for the beach. They walked along the boardwalk, and then they took off their shoes and walked along the edge of the water. On the way back to the car, Dallas asked if she wanted to get a drink. After Deneisha accepted his offer, they headed to the nearby Margaritaville Beach Hotel, where they enjoyed drinks outside at the LandShark Bar and Grill. Cocktails and fascinating conversation followed. Deneisha found Dallas to be a very intelligent man, and she enjoyed the wide range of topics he seemed to be knowledgeable about.

To her, it was the best and most potent aphrodisiac.

One other thing that was making her want him even more was that this intelligent man had killed two men who tried to rape her.

"That is so hot," she said louder than she intended.

"What did you say?"

"Nothing. I was just thinking out loud."

Dallas nodded. He leaned closer to Deneisha. "What is so hot?"

Deneisha leaned back. "You." And then she leaned close to him. "*You* are so fuckin' hot, and the fact that you killed two muthafuckas who tried to rape me is even hotter."

"You're pretty fuckin' hot too."

"What should we do with all this hotness?"

"I think I should pay the check, and we get a room and get naked."

"Waiter," she said with her hand in the air.

"Yes, ma'am," one said as he approached the table.

"Check, please."

Dallas stood up, reached into his pocket, and pulled out a hundred-dollar bill. "Handle that. I'll go get us a room."

She picked up the money. "See you in a minute."

As soon as they got to the room, they began undressing each other. He pulled out a rubber and covered himself with it. The sight of him putting a condom on that dick had Deneisha biting her lip in anticipation of what would come next. Without a word, he spread her legs open and moved in between her thighs, entering Deneisha slowly and gently. It caused her back to arch.

"That feels so good inside me," she breathed out once his entire length was buried deep inside her.

"Not nearly as amazing as it feels to be inside *you,*" Dallas offered.

Deneisha quickly wrapped her legs around his waist, and with that long, hard dick, Dallas pounded that pussy with slow, constant strokes. He was sliding in and out of her just like Deneisha needed, and she wanted to feel every sensation, every nuance that his lovemaking had to offer.

Suddenly, Dallas began to move faster, and Deneisha quickened her pace to match his.

"You're gonna make me come all over this dick," she shouted and exploded.

Before she had a chance to compose herself from the orgasm, Dallas smiled and kissed his way down between her trembling legs. His lips were sucking and nibbling Deneisha everywhere she wanted him to. What he was doing was making her clit swell.

He let out a guttural moan, and he squeezed her titties together, taking them into his warm mouth to lick, lavish, and suck her hard nipples. He tapped one of her tits and began sucking both nipples like they were the sweetest things he had ever tasted.

Dallas kissed a trail down her stomach until he was between her thighs. Deneisha closed her eyes as his lips and tongue began circling her already swollen clit. The sensations that he was making her feel were intense as Dallas parted her lips with his tongue.

"Yes!" she shouted, holding his head. "This shit is so fucking good."

Dallas had her toes curling as he used her tongue to make circles around her clit. He spit on her pussy, licked his fingers, and slid them in and out of her slowly while his wet tongue flickered back and forth across her clit.

"Oh shitttt!" Deneisha shouted, and she came hard again.

With her legs in the air, Deneisha squeezed and then sucked her nipple as Dallas eased two fingers in and out of her. She squeezed her nipple harder and felt a wave rush over her entire body.

"I'm coming," she screamed and pulled him up from between her thighs. He rolled over on the bed beside her. His dick was hard and erect. Deneisha ripped off the condom and quickly took Dallas to the back of her throat.

She teased his head with her tongue and slowly worked her way down his shaft. Then Deneisha slid her lips and tongue up and down his length. When she felt it getting harder, she relaxed the muscles in her throat and used the roof of her mouth to apply a little pressure on his shaft.

"Damn, Deneisha, suck that dick," he moaned in a voice barely above a whisper.

"I know you like that shit," Deneisha said, lifting her head. "But I'm not ready for you to come yet."

"Okay."

"Lie down."

Dallas did as he was told, and Deneisha straddled his body and rode him hard and fast.

"Fuck me and make me come," Dallas said, and Deneisha slammed her hips back and forth, bouncing on his dick and then shaking and jiggling her ass before she dropped down on him again. Deneisha ran her fingers through her hair.

"Fuck me with that dick."

Dallas arched his back and began tossing it up to her as deep and as hard as he could. His powerful thrusts knocked Deneisha forward, and she collapsed on his chest, but she kept bringing it down on him as hard as she could.

"Yes, yes!" he shouted when his whole body locked.

Deneisha's head drifted back, her eyes and mouth opened wide, and she screamed, thinking that she had never come so much, so hard in her life.

# Chapter Seventeen

After sex, Dallas fell asleep, and Deneisha wasn't far behind. When she woke up, she got out of bed and, once she had finished in the bathroom, sat on the edge of the bed. She looked at Dallas, who was still asleep. She exhaled and thought about the love they made.

*That shit was so fuckin' good.*

She was about to get back in bed, cuddle up next to him, and go back to sleep, but that was when she saw his gun. It was sitting on the table in the room. She was so caught up in them kissing and removing their clothes that she didn't see him put it there. Deneisha stood up, walked over to the table, and picked it up. It was a .44 Magnum, the kind of gun Clint Eastwood carried in the Dirty Harry movies. It was a big gun, much heavier than her .380 or Brianna's 9 mm. She stood naked in front of the mirror and raised the weapon.

"Go ahead, make my day," Deneisha said, quoting a line from the movie *Sudden Impact*.

"You know how to use that thing?" Dallas asked.

His deep voice startled her, and she spun around. "Let me put it to you this way. I know how to use one, but I don't know what I'm doing."

Dallas laughed. "What does that even mean?"

"It means that I've used a gun before, but I don't know how to use one correctly if that makes sense."

"It does," he laughed. "I could show you."

"I'd like that."

"So you used a gun before, huh?"

"Yup."

"You ever kill anybody?"

Deneisha looked at Dallas for a moment without answering.

"I'll take that as a no."

"And you'd be wrong."

He laughed. "Who your sexy muthafuckin' ass killed?"

Once again, Deneisha said nothing.

"What's the matter?" He chuckled. "I just dropped two bodies to keep you from getting raped. Come on now, give it up."

"We robbed a couple of trap houses. I shot one of them when he went for his gun, and the other is a long story that I don't feel like getting into, but I shot another muthafucka who took a shot at me when I robbed his liquor store."

"People tend to do that when you rob them."

"I heard that too," she laughed and paused. "I'll just say that the other nigga I had to kill was covering up for somebody else's mistakes."

Dallas nodded his head. If he wasn't already deep into everything Deneisha, the fact that they had something else in common was great.

"So you a robber. A stickup girl."

"I was. Shit got hot in the ATL, so I relocated south."

He looked at Deneisha and decided to do something he'd never done before with a woman, but he had a feeling that she was special. He told her the truth.

"I'm a robber too." Dallas paused to enjoy the smile that crept across Deneisha's lips. "I don't leave the house for less than ten grand. I come through the door blasting. I don't like to leave any witnesses or muthafuckas who wanna come after me when I robbed them."

"People tend to do that when you rob them."

"Yeah, I heard that too," he laughed. "You got a gun?"

"Two. A nine and a three eighty."

"Which you prefer?"

"The three eighty."

Deneisha paused and looked at Dallas, trying to decide how open with him she was going to be. She wasn't sure of what she was feeling. It could be, and probably was, the afterglow of amazing sex, but she liked him.

"To be honest with you, two of the people I killed were lucky shots. I didn't even aim."

Dallas laughed. "How you killed two people, and you ain't aim the gun?"

"I just pulled the trigger."

"What about the third guy?"

Deneisha paused before saying, "I shot him in the back of the head."

"Point-blank?"

Deneisha nodded.

"That was to cover somebody else's fuckup?"

"Yup."

Dallas nodded, carefully considering what he was about to say.

"My old partner got himself locked up, so I'm looking for a new one. You interested?"

"In what? In being your partner?"

"Yeah."

"I'm interested."

Dallas nodded. "Come here."

Deneisha walked back to the bed. Dallas pulled back the covers. She smiled when she saw that his dick was already hard. She got in bed with him.

"I'm starting to think you like me," she said and took his dick in her hand.

"What was your first clue?"

"This rock-hard dick in my hand," she said, slowly stroking up and down.

"Yeah, Deneisha Lewis, I really like you."

"That's good because I really like you too."

Deneisha licked the tip and sucked his dick, in and out her mouth, until she felt as if she was about to gag. Dallas ran his fingers through her hair with both hands, gently guiding her head up and down. She looked up at him; his eyes were focused on her. When she felt his dick twitching, Deneisha reached for a condom from the nightstand. She put it on him, got on her knees, and quickly straddled him. She put her hands on his shoulders and took her time sliding down on his dick.

"Fuck me, Deneisha."

She began riding him harder and faster. His dick filled her up so completely, and it wasn't long before she was screaming in ecstasy.

"Yes, Dallas, yes! You're gonna make me come again," she shouted, and he brought her to a thunderous orgasm.

The following day, Dallas took Deneisha back to Miss Vivian's house, but they didn't stay long. She changed clothes and, knowing that she might be with Dallas for the night, Deneisha tossed a few things in a bag. When Dallas saw her come out of the room with a bag, he stood up and took it from her.

"You ready?"

"Let me leave a note for Miss Vivian so she doesn't worry or think I'm disrespecting her house," she said, sitting down at the dining room table to write. "Now I'm ready," she said, folding the note.

Dallas and Deneisha drove out of the city to Palatka, a town in Putnam County, about seventy miles south of Jacksonville.

"Who lives here?" she asked.

"I grew up here."

"Wait, I thought you were from Dallas."

"I was born in Dallas and lived there for the first thirteen years of my life. Then my family moved here, and this is where I grew up, where I became a man."

Deneisha giggled. "Dallas from Dallas. How your mama name you after the city you was born in?"

"She didn't name me Dallas. My name is Calvin Goodwin. When I moved here, people started calling me 'Dallas,' and it stuck."

"Yeah." Deneisha nodded. "When I first moved to the ATL, people called me 'New York' for a minute." Dallas smiled. "What?"

"Just wondered what else we have in common and thinking about how interesting it's gonna be finding out."

"I ain't like no other woman you ever met."

"I see that. And I'd like to see more."

"Maybe you will," Deneisha said. "So, how long have you known Miss Vivian?"

Dallas paused for a second before he answered. "I've known her for six years."

"How did y'all meet?"

"I met her through Serena."

"Really?" Deneisha paused, and then she asked the question that Dallas wished to avoid but was prepared to answer honestly. "How do you know Serena?"

"We used to date."

"You did?" Dallas saw the look on Deneisha's face as she did the math.

"Serena had separated from Denny when we met," he said, and he could tell that she had more questions. "Yes, there was some discussion about whether Michael was my son, but he turned out to be Denny's son, and she went back to him. I didn't even know she was married until she told me that she was pregnant, and it might be his baby."

"Did you love her?"

"No," Dallas said quickly. "You know Serena. She's got some serious issues."

"Always did. She's mean and petty." Deneisha looked away from Dallas but turned back quickly. "So, why were you with her?"

"You've seen Serena, right? I mean, she can't carry your water, but she is kinda fine."

"So you were just fuckin' her?"

"Yes. To me, it was all about the physical, nothing mental."

"What was it like for her?"

"What do you mean?"

"You said you were just fuckin' her, right?"

"Right."

"What was it like for her? Was it all about that dick?"

"To be honest with you, I don't know."

Deneisha may have laughed, but she was still mad. "Yeah, you were just fuckin' her, and you didn't care about her feelings, did you?"

Dallas scratched his beard. "Not really."

*She was just pussy to him,* she thought.

However, strangely, knowing that Dallas wasn't interested in Serena's feelings made her feel better about the situation.

"That's why Serena was looking at me all crazy when I was leaving with you."

"Probably."

They drove in silence as Deneisha reconciled her feelings, and Dallas was just glad that they weren't talking about it anymore and hoped that they were done with it.

"We're here."

Deneisha looked out the window. "Where is 'here'?" she asked as Dallas got out of the car. It appeared to be an old, abandoned farm.

"This is an old shooting range. It's been closed for years, but people still come out here and shoot."

Dallas walked around to the back of the car and opened the trunk.

"What are we doin' here?"

"I wanna see if you can hit what you aim at." He took out two 9-mm handguns and handed one to Deneisha. Then he got some shooting targets. "Come on," he said, and led her into the first building, where he set up some targets.

Dallas gave her a brief class on how to load, how to hold the gun with both hands, and how to shoot. Next, he turned her loose.

"Okay, Deneisha, let's see what you got."

Deneisha set herself the way Dallas had just shown her. She raised the weapon and started shooting.

She hit nothing.

Over the next couple of weeks, he taught Deneisha how to use the weapon properly. He explained how to clean it, load it, and store it safely before letting her shoot again. Then he taught her how to aim and fire the weapon.

"Now, let's teach you how to aim."

"Okay, let's do that."

"To shoot a gun properly, you gotta aim." He took the gun from her and pointed to the sight on the barrel of the weapon. "You need to make sure that your eyes are focused on the gun sights and not the target."

"Okay. Focus on the sight, not the target."

He handed her the gun again. "Go ahead. Line up your shot."

Deneisha raised the weapon and focused on the sight.

"See how the target looks a little blurry?"

"Yes."

"But you should still be able to see it."

"I can."

"Go ahead and fire one shot."

Deneisha fired, and this time, she hit the target. It wasn't a bull's-eye; it wasn't even close to being a bull's-eye, but she hit what she was aiming at. And they celebrated her accomplishment. As the days went by, her skills improved.

"You're almost ready," he said.

"Almost?" Deneisha raised her weapon and fired. She emptied the magazine. Each round hit the center mass. "Nigga, I'm raw with this here."

"Run."

"Run?"

"Yeah, nigga. You so muthafuckin' raw with that nine, let me see you hit your target on the run."

When Deneisha just looked at him like he had lost his mind, he explained why.

"Look, listen, and understand. In my business, ain't no time for hesitation. We come through the door blasting, so there ain't no time to stop and aim."

"Got you."

"So, make like you following me through the door. What you gonna do?"

Deneisha took a deep breath and started running and firing at the targets. Once again, she hit nothing. Dallas laughed. However, over the next few days, they ran the same drill until Deneisha was hitting her target with every shot.

"You're almost ready," he said and walked away. "You coming?"

Deneisha rushed to catch up with him, and he led her to another building on the property. As they walked through the building, Deneisha saw that it was a maze, and there were shot-up wooden targets that appeared to be cops, crooks, and civilians. Dallas stapled targets to the cops and the crooks.

"The targets aren't gonna move, but I don't want you to run. Move quickly, like you need to do what you came to do and get outta there."

"Got ya."

"Let's see what you got."

She did all right for the first time. She hit most of her intended targets, but she shot a few civilians that day. As the days rolled into weeks, her skills improved to the point where Deneisha was hitting her targets every time she raised and fired her weapon.

"*Now* you're ready."

# Chapter Eighteen

There wasn't any doubt in her mind that, for the first time in her life, Deneisha was in love. She had previously said the words and had them said to her, but it never felt like this. In the three months that she had been in Jacksonville, they'd spent every minute of every day together. And that was something that she wasn't used to. Deneisha never considered herself the type of woman who always had to be around her man, or she'd go crazy.

In fact, she was the opposite. Deneisha liked her space, enjoyed hanging out with her girls, and appreciated the freedom to date other people if she felt like it.

She thought back to Tyquan Reynolds. They dated for less than a month, but it was really over after the first week. Deneisha had gone out with Brianna and Courtney one night. Tyquan called before she left, and she told him she was going out.

*"Where you going?"*

*"Out with Court and Breezy."*

*"Yeah, but where y'all going?"*

*"I don't know. We just going out. Ain't no telling where we gonna end up," Deneisha said, and that's the moment she knew that it wouldn't last.*

*"Fuck you mean, you don't know?"*

*"It means I don't know where we're going."*

*"You going to hook up with some other niggas. I know that shit."*

*"Look, Tyquan, I'm going out with Court and Breezy. So, I'll talk to you later."*

*Deneisha ended the call, and he called her back fifty times that night. It was so annoying that she put her phone on silent and eventually turned it off. The next day, he came to her apartment, apologized, and promised that it would never happen again. But it did happen again . . . and again, and he quickly moved to stalker mode. He only stopped when some friends of Deneisha's told Tyquan at gunpoint that if he called her again, sent another text message, or showed up somewhere she was, even if it was an accident, that they would find him, then kill him and his whole family. Deneisha never heard from Tyquan again.*

Bottom line was that Deneisha liked her space, but that wasn't the case with Dallas. She paused to think about the fact that she didn't know anybody in Jacksonville other than him and Miss Vivian. Did that make a difference?

*Maybe,* she thought.

But it didn't change the fact that she wanted to be wherever he was, doing whatever he wanted to do.

It was the same for Dallas. He couldn't stand to be fenced in by a woman. *I belong to the streets. I'll see you when I see you,* was what he was known to tell the women he'd been involved with over the years. He had never committed to one woman. Dallas enjoyed the endless variety of women: Black, white, Puerto Rican, Asian; it didn't matter. Dallas loved them all . . . just not for long.

*He was entertaining a woman when another woman rang the bell. Naturally, he didn't answer the door. When the woman began banging on the doors and windows and yelling, I know you're in there with some other bitch, he called the police. She was still at the door, banging and yelling at the top of her lungs when the police arrived. With Dallas looking out the window, they tried to lead her away from the house, but she screamed, "Get your muthafuckin' hands off me!"*

*She proceeded to fight with the officers until they were able to restrain her long enough to handcuff her. Even then, she struggled and resisted until they got her into the car.*

Now, there was Deneisha, and he couldn't get enough of her. At first, it was just that she was fine as hell, and he wanted to fuck her. But then she turned out to be someone he enjoyed spending time with. Next, he discovered she was a robber who had dropped bodies, and he recognized her potential. And then there was the sex.

Dallas had always seen himself as a pleaser. Making a woman come, more than once, was what he was about. His philosophy was that if you make a woman come hard, she will fuck the shit outta you. It was a philosophy that he'd always found true, so awesome sex was the norm for Dallas.

And it was no different with Deneisha. He made her come violently, and she came at him with a crazed look in her eyes. What was different for Dallas was that Deneisha had him grabbing the sheets while *his* toes were curling. It was his body that was rigid and his mouth open, screaming, "Oh shit."

Dallas thought he had found the perfect woman for him. He paused to wonder how many people in the world were feeling the same way about their mate that he was feeling at that moment, looking at Deneisha. She was beautiful, smart, funny, and fun to be with, and she was sexy. Now, she could hit a target on the run.

"Shit, she's perfect."

"What did you say?" Deneisha asked. His deep, baritone voice was enough to wake her up.

"Nothing. Just thinking how lucky I am that . . . Whatever happened, happened, and you had to run from the ATL and ended up here in my arms."

Dallas wrapped his arms around her and kissed her shoulder. He wasn't ready to call it love, at least not yet. But it was a fact that he was into everything about Deneisha. They could talk about any and everything. And one day, she felt comfortable enough to open up to him.

"Me and my girls, Court and Breezy, stuck up a grocery store," she said and told Dallas how it went down. "What we couldn't figure out was how the cops got onto us so fast. I clocked the normal police response at five minutes and seventeen seconds, but they were on us damn near as soon as we were out of the parking lot."

"Did you use any kind of jammer?"

"What?"

"A frequency jammer?" Dallas asked, and Deneisha looked confused. "A jammer blocks signals from cell phones and radio traffic. Nothing like that?"

Deneisha shook her head. "Nope, nothing like that."

"The driver probably called into his base on the radio, or he called the police from his cell phone. In either case, that's why they were on you so fast."

"I never even thought about that," Deneisha said, and she was glad that she met Dallas for more than one reason. She felt like she could learn so much from him *and* get fucked right in the process. She considered it a win-win.

In the time that they'd been together, he taught her how to handle, shoot, clean, dismantle, and reassemble a gun. Deneisha worked hard and was so proud when Dallas said that she was ready.

Although they spent their days in the country shooting, they spent their nights in the streets of Jacksonville. When they met, Dallas told Deneisha that he didn't leave the house for less than $10,000. He didn't hit trap houses.

"Not enough money at no trap house to make it worth my time," he said.

"Tell me about it," she replied.

Dallas had heard about a deal between Mitchell Potter, one of the biggest drug dealers in the city, and Oscar Pennington, who was rumored to have connections to the Sinaloa Cartel. Over the next few weeks, they followed those individuals and their people. They talked to people who knew and paid attention when those people were talking with other people in the know, so they knew when the deal was to take place. What they needed to know was where and what time.

"We could just follow Potter or Pennington, and they lead us to the spot," Deneisha said. They were sitting in a car parked down the street from the home of Hutch, Potter's bagman. Dallas was sure that Hutch and his boys, Isaiah and Jayden, would be the ones doing the deal.

"We could, but I would much rather know where the spot is so we can check it out in advance and be there, set up, when they get there. Doing shit blind is how shit goes wrong. When that happens, the police get involved, and people die."

"What happens if we don't find out where the deal is gettin' done?"

"We walk away," Dallas said firmly, and Deneisha nodded. "I don't take chances when I'm doing work."

Deneisha pointed. "There's Hutch."

He came out of the apartment building and ran to his car. Dallas started his vehicle as Hutch got in his and drove away.

"Wonder where he's going in such a hurry," she said as Dallas followed him.

He stopped in front of a storefront and parked. When Dallas and Deneisha arrived, they noticed that all of the stores on that block were abandoned. They parked a little way down the street and waited for something to happen or someone to show up. Their wait wasn't long when a tricked-out Mercedes-Benz rolled down the street and parked behind Hutch.

"I think this might be the place," Deneisha said.

"I think so too."

Dallas and Deneisha watched as the car doors opened, and four men got out.

"That's Potter," Dallas said as Hutch got out of his car.

The men shook hands, and then they went into one of the abandoned stores. They came out ten minutes later, shook hands again, got in their cars, and drove away. Dallas waited until both vehicles were out of sight before he reached for the handle.

"Come on."

Deneisha got out of the car, followed Dallas behind the building, and watched as he picked the lock.

"You need to show me how to do that."

"What kind of robber are you that you can't pick a lock?" he asked as he worked.

"The kind that sticks a gun in a muthafucka's face and takes what the fuck she wants."

Dallas smiled at her and shook his head. "I'll teach you," he promised as the door opened, and they entered.

"I can't see a fuckin' thing," Deneisha said and reached for her phone. She turned on the flashlight. "Much better."

"Keep it pointed at the floor and not at the windows."

"Got it," Deneisha said, and they walked through the rear of the building until they reached the storefront.

"This is definitely the place," Dallas said when he saw the table set up in the middle of the room. He began looking around the room for the best place to get them in a crossfire. "Let's get outta here."

It was two days later when Dallas and Deneisha returned to the storefront and let themselves in the back door. Since they had talked about where each one would be, no words were spoken as each went to their spot and set up. Deneisha would take Potter's people, and Dallas would handle Pennington's.

It was less than an hour later when the door opened, and the first of that evening's prey arrived. Three men came in and settled around the table. One of them was Jerome, one of Oscar Pennington's men. The other two were Hakeem and Malik.

Deneisha had seen each one with Pennington while they were watching them. While she was waiting, she thought it would be easier if they just shot the three men, took their place, and killed Hutch and his crew when they got there.

Just then, the door to the store opened, and Hutch walked in with two other men that Deneisha had never seen before. She assumed that they were his boys, Isaiah and Jayden. But it didn't matter who they were, she thought as she raised her weapons and lined up her shots. When all six men had gathered around the table, Deneisha and Dallas readied their guns.

When Hutch unzipped the bag with the money, Deneisha and Dallas opened fire. His first shot hit Hakeem in the head. Deneisha's first shots hit Isaiah and Jayden before they got their guns out. As Jerome and Malik tried to grab their product, Dallas shot Malik in the chest.

Jerome dove to the ground, pulled out his gun, and returned fire. Hutch grabbed the money from the table, fired several shots in Deneisha's direction, then ran.

Deneisha returned fire, came out from her perch, and went after him, mad at herself for not shooting him first. He was closest to the money. Had she initially shot him, she wouldn't be running now.

As Dallas shot it out with Jerome, he saw Deneisha run after Hutch and the money. He knew he had to finish Jerome and then pursue her. When Jerome stopped to reload, Dallas stood up and walked toward him, firing with two .44 Magnums. When Jerome stood to return fire, Dallas shot him in the chest. The impact of the blast knocked Jerome off his feet, and Dallas fired again. That bullet hit him in the head and blew away half of his head before he hit the ground.

Next, Dallas ran in the direction he saw Deneisha go after Hutch and the money. He used a speed loader and reloaded his weapons on the run, and then he heard shooting. He ran in that direction and found Deneisha shooting it out with Hutch. He joined the firefight, giving Deneisha a chance to reload. She came up firing. Hutch fired his last shot.

"Shit!"

Hutch paused and thought that if he ran and left the money, they might not kill him. When the shooting stopped, Hutch came out from hiding and ran. Deneisha saw that he didn't have the bag with the money, and she lowered her weapon.

Dallas stepped up, aimed, and fired one shot that hit Hutch in the back as he raced away. He stumbled to the ground.

"Why didn't you shoot him?" Dallas asked.

"He didn't have the money."

"What I say about leaving witnesses alive?"

"They come after you."

"Go get the money. I'll get the dope," he spit out and walked away from Deneisha.

She went to get the money, knowing that she fucked up, and vowed that it would never happen again.

# Chapter Nineteen

Deneisha sat quietly as Dallas drove away from the storefront. She wouldn't even look in his direction because she was sure he was mad at her for not shooting the last man. Dallas hadn't said a word to her since he told her to get the money. Deneisha couldn't help but wonder if that would end their partnership and their relationship before it had a chance to really get started.

When they got off the Buckner Expressway heading toward Ponte Vedra Beach, a wealthy suburb of Jacksonville, Deneisha wanted to ask where they were going, but she kept silent. As they drove past fabulous homes, she wondered if there would come a day when she could live like this. When Dallas pulled into the driveway of a magnificent house, she was curious to know who he was visiting. But once again, Deneisha remained silent.

"Come on," he said when he turned off the car. "There's somebody I want you to meet."

Dallas got out of the car and came around to open the car door for Deneisha. Another thing she liked about him was that Dallas was a gentleman who knew how to treat a lady. He insisted on opening doors for her and helping her with her coat. It was a little thing, but she loved it. He treated her with a type of respect that no man had ever shown her.

Dallas opened the trunk and removed the duffel bag containing the stolen product. He shut the trunk and started for the house, with Deneisha following behind. He rang the bell and looked at her.

"You are so beautiful." He smiled and kissed her forehead. "Even dressed like that," Dallas said of her in the baggy black overalls she was wearing. "You are still the prettiest thing in life I've ever seen."

"You're not mad at me?"

"For what?" he asked as the door opened.

"Dallas!"

"What's up, Preach?"

"Getting money."

"*That's* what's up," Dallas said as Preach stepped aside to let them in.

"Now, you must tell me who this amazing creature is."

"Preach, this is my partner in everything, Deneisha Lewis. Baby, this is Preach."

"Nice to meet you, Deneisha."

"It's good to meet you too."

Preach pointed at the duffel bag. "That for me?"

Dallas handed it over to him. "It is."

"Well, let's see what you got," Preach said and walked into the living room.

"Go ahead. I'll be there in a minute," Dallas said, and Deneisha knew that he was getting ready to let her have it. It was the one thing he repeated over and over. *We don't leave any witnesses or muthafuckas that wanna come after us.* If Dallas had a rule, that would be it.

"What's wrong with you?" Dallas asked when Preach was out of earshot.

"I thought you were mad at me 'cause I didn't shoot Hutch 'cause he didn't have the money."

Dallas smiled. "That why you were sitting over there in the car, mean muggin' me?"

"Yes," she said shyly.

"It was your first time out." He stepped closer to her and took her hands in his. Deneisha's chin was resting on her chest.

"Look at me, Deneisha."

She lifted her head and looked into his eyes.

"It was your first time out, and you did great." Deneisha smiled. "And no, I'm not mad." Dallas laughed. "I'd be mad if he got away. But he didn't. I got him. That's all that matters."

"It won't happen again."

"And if it does, I'll have your back, just like I know you'll have mine." He paused. "It's a mind-set, a philosophy that you need to embrace. In your mind, it's all about gettin' the cash and gettin' gone. But let's play that out. One night, you and me are at a restaurant, enjoying a nice meal. Without our knowing, Hutch walks in, he sees us, walks up to the table, and kills us both because you let him live."

"I understand. And it won't happen again. I promise."

Dallas chuckled. "That's probably what he was thinkin' when he ran off without the money. It's all about gettin' the cash and gettin' gone. 'I leave this money, and they'd let me get away.'"

"You're right. Because that's exactly what I was thinkin'. Like I said, it won't happen again."

"Come on. Let's go get paid," he said, and Deneisha fell deeper in love with Dallas. His understanding and the compassion he showed blew her mind. It was the exact opposite of what she was expecting. Instead of being mad, he said that he was proud of her.

Dallas led Deneisha through the living room to a door that led to the basement. He opened the door.

"After you."

"So, Preach, what's his deal?" Deneisha asked as they went down the stairs.

"His daddy's a preacher, so he knows the entire Bible and can quote it word for word." Dallas chuckled. "And the nigga has been known to drop a verse before he killed you."

"A brother will betray his brother to death, and a father his child. Children will rebel against their parents and have them put to death. Mark, chapter thirteen, verse twelve," Preach said and went back to his task.

Preach was standing at a counter, testing the cocaine's purity. Using a simple Scott Reagent, he watched it turn blue when it came into contact with the cocaine.

Deneisha leaned close to Dallas as she watched what Preach was doing. "You gonna have to explain what he's doing." Dallas nodded.

"It's got the color I'm looking for," Preach said, scooped some up on his fingernail, and took it to his nose.

"That's pretty pure."

"I wouldn't know," Dallas said.

"And why would you?"

"No reason."

"What you looking for?"

"Thirty."

"How 'bout twenty-five and my word to make it right on the next one?" Preach said with his hand out. Dallas glanced at Deneisha.

"Deal," he said, and the two shook hands.

Preach went to the safe and entered the combination. He took out five stacks of bills and closed the safe. He placed the stacks on the counter in front of Dallas.

"Twenty-five grand."

"And your word." Dallas shook his hand. "Which, to me, is more valuable than money."

"True. But you are gonna take that money."

"Shit yeah. Me and my baby worked hard for this," Dallas said as he collected their money. "How's Yvette?"

"Mean as a rattlesnake and sexy as fuck," Preach said as he led them out of the basement. "She'll be home soon. You know she'll want to see you."

"Let her know I still love her, and I'll catch her next time."

"You makin' it hard for me," Preach said when they got to the door. "Deneisha, it was a pleasure meeting you."

"The pleasure was all mine."

Preach paused and looked at the way Dallas was looking at Deneisha. "I have a feeling that I'll see you again."

"You just might." The two men embraced. "Be easy, brother," Dallas said.

"Always, my nigga," Preach replied, and then he opened the door. He stood in the doorway and watched until they got into their car, then waved and went inside.

"Where we goin' now?" Deneisha asked.

"All work and no play makes Dallas and Deneisha sad and bored," he said and put his hand on her thigh.

She smiled and held his hand. "So, we goin' to have some fun?"

"We are gonna handle a little business, then it will be a whole lot of us having a whole lot of fun."

"I like the sound of us doin' anything."

The pair caught a flight to Las Vegas and checked into the Palms Casino Resort. Upon arrival, they checked into the hotel's one-bedroom penthouse suite with a Jacuzzi. Once they were settled in their room, they put fifty of the seventy-five thousand they had in the safe. The twenty-five they got from Preach and the fifty they had from previous jobs. Then the couple had dinner at the hotel and hit the casino.

"I don't gamble," Deneisha admitted on the way out of the restaurant. "I never even learned how to play. Never had any interest. It was giving away money, and I've always been about taking it."

"You don't mind if I do?" Dallas asked as they went to the window to get chips.

"No, but I hope we didn't fly all this way for you to gamble away all of our money."

"Exactly the opposite, my love."

Dallas got his chips and walked away with Deneisha.

"We're here to make this dirty money clean." He put his arm around her and kissed her cheek. "Do a little gambling and have a lot of fun. Take in a show or two, maybe see a fight if one's in town."

"Now you talkin'. How does it work?"

"I just gave them incorrect identifying information. We converted that dirty money into casino chips. Now we, or I should say, I'm, gonna play various games before being cashed out with clean money in the form of a check."

"That's it?"

"Yeah, that's it. We'll hit another casino tomorrow," Dallas said and sat down at a poker table.

The buy-in was five thousand. The small blind is five thousand, and the big blind is $10,000. The dealer dealt the flop with the nine of hearts, the eight of hearts, and the five of hearts.

"Check," one player said.

"Five," another said and threw in her money.

"Bet?" the dealer asked Dallas.

He racked and stacked $5,000 in chips.

"Call," he said, smiling as he pushed his money into the pot.

"Three players," the dealer said after two players folded, and then she dealt the nine of clubs.

"Fold," one said and tossed in his cards.

"Call," Dallas said and put up the cash.

"Call," the other player said and matched Dallas's bet.

The dealer dealt the river, the last of the community cards. "Two of hearts. Showdown, please."

"Fuck," Dallas said as the woman turned over the two of spades and the two of clubs.

"Full house. Duces full of nines," the dealer said as Dallas tossed his cards.

"You lost?" Deneisha whispered in his ear.

"Winning ain't the point."

"What's the point?"

"Cashing out with clean money at the end of the night. Tomorrow, we'll hit another hotel."

"Cool," Deneisha said, and she sat patiently watching Dallas play different games: poker, blackjack, roulette, and craps. He won some, lost some, and cashed out with a little over $22,000.

Deneisha had never been to Vegas, so she was excited to do as much touristy shit as she could fit in. After they left the casino, Dallas took her to *Purple Reign,* the Prince tribute show. The following day, they caught the *All Motown* show and *The Motown Brunch, Flashback: Tina Turner & Friends Tribute,* and she sat through and grudgingly enjoyed *The King of Diamonds,* a Neil Diamond tribute because Dallas was surprisingly into his music. And they went to *The Rat Pack Is Back* show.

"You never heard of The Rat Pack?"

"Nope."

"The Rat Pack was Frank Sinatra, Dean Martin, Sammy Davis Jr., Peter Lawford, and Joey Bishop."

"I heard of Frank Sinatra and Sammy Davis Jr., but I have no clue who the rest of them were."

"Not important," he said and sat down to enjoy the show.

But it wasn't just the shows they went to. During the day, they took pictures in front of the "Welcome to Fabulous Las Vegas" sign. After that, Deneisha dragged Dallas to the Bellagio Conservatory & Botanical Garden, and then it was off to the Grand Canyon's Hoover Dam and Grand Canyon Deluxe Helicopter Tour the following day. Dallas and Deneisha also took the Las Vegas Helicopter tour. They went on the Big Bus Tour, and, of course, they hit a different casino each night. Before they left Vegas, the pair had gambled at the Hilton Vacation Club Desert Retreat, The Berkley, the Four Seasons Hotel, the Flamingo, and The Palazzo. After that, they flew back to Jacksonville with checks totaling over $67,000.

"Money laundered," Deneisha said and rested her head on Dallas's shoulder for the flight home.

"Not bad for a few minutes of work."

"And weeks of preparation," she added. "But it ain't bad at all."

# Chapter Twenty

*Six Months Later . . .*

Deneisha and Dallas were in love and were no longer afraid to say it. They planned a future together and had set a goal for themselves. Once they had a million dollars, they would retire and open a business.

"Ready?" Deniesha asked.

"Let's do it," Dallas replied, and the pair emerged from their positions and began shooting.

Dallas had heard of a drug buy, and the word on the streets was that this one was gonna be big. The problem for Dallas was that nobody could tell him how much, nor could they tell him when or where the deal would take place.

"It's goin' down tomorrow night," Zaki Burgess finally told Dallas.

"Where?"

Zaki shrugged his shoulders. "That I can't tell you."

"Thanks."

In the last six months, they had robbed two more buys. As a consequence, dealers have become more security-conscious. They kept information about the buy to only a select few who needed to know.

"Nobody knows anything, and if they do, they're not talkin'," Dallas told Deneisha as they lay in bed together.

"Where does that leave us?"

"Out in the cold and out of the money."

"That's fucked up."

"No shit," he said and closed his eyes.

It wasn't like they were desperate for money. They were currently sitting on more than a quarter of a million dollars. Years before he met Deneisha, Dallas had opened an account in Curaçao, a Dutch Caribbean island located off the coast of South America. At the time, he was dealing with Maisy Humphrey, a woman involved in running financial scams. She told him that having offshore accounts was essential to her business, and she recommended that he get one.

"You might not need it now," she chuckled. "You may not even understand what their purpose is. But one day, you *will* need it and understand why, and you'll thank me for it."

She opened an account for him, and after he completed the next job, she showed him how to deposit money into that account. It wasn't long after that that she began getting more possessive and demanding of his time. Therefore, it wasn't long after that that he stopped seeing her, and he never used that account again.

One day, he and Deneisha were talking about their relationship in comparison to every other relationship they'd had in the past. She told him about Tyquan Reynolds, the guy who quickly moved to stalker mode, and he told her about Maisy Humphrey. When he was through telling his story, Deneisha had questions, not about the relationship. She wanted to know about the importance of having and using offshore bank accounts.

"Why aren't we using it?" Deneisha found the answer Dallas gave was unacceptable. "We're going through all these steps to clean this money. Putting our clean money," she said using air quotes, "into a perfectly legal offshore account is the next logical step."

Considering the goals that they set for themselves, Dallas had to agree that it made sense to use that account. Since then, they've deposited most of their laundered money into that account.

Every time he looked at her, every word she spoke, and everything she did made Dallas fall deeper in love with Deneisha. The idea of spending the rest of his life loving her made him anxious to reach the bright future they had painted. That's why he got excited about this deal, and he tried to find out all he could about it. The fact that he couldn't was frustrating him.

"Somebody knows what's up, and we'll get them to tell us what we need to know," Deneisha said and kissed Dallas on the cheek. Just then, Dallas got a text message.

"It's from Zaki. He says the spot is a vacant building on Lenox Avenue."

"That's it?" Deneisha questioned as they got out of bed and got ready to hit the streets.

"That's it."

"You know how many vacant buildings there are on Lenox?"

"We're about to find out."

As they cruised down Lenox Avenue, Deneisha spotted a 1987 Buick Grand National GNX, driven by Rehan James, one of the key players in the deal they were pursuing.

"Follow him," she said, pointing to the car. Dallas made a U-turn and followed James to his house.

"What now?"

"Drive back on Lenox. I think it's around here somewhere," Deneisha said, and, sure enough, it wasn't long before they came up on a spot. "What do you think?"

"Could be. Let's go check it out," he said and parked a block away from the spot.

They walked around to the back of the building, which faced Interstate 10, and picked the lock. Once inside, they took a look around and found that a table had been set up in the large room near the front of the space.

"This is the place," Dallas said.

"Yeah, but it's not a good spot for us."

The way they operated was to know where the deal was taking place and being set up, and then waiting for the right opportunity to kill everybody and take the money and drugs.

"There is no place for us to hide," Deneisha pointed out.

"You're right," he said and turned to leave.

"And?"

"And that means the only advantage we'd have is the element of surprise," he said as they left the building and headed back to the car.

"Seems like I'm missing something."

"Deals goin' down in the front room, right?"

"Right."

"We come in the back. Make our way through the building to the front and do what we do," he said, and opened the car door for her.

"Thank you," she said and got in.

"You know," Deneisha began the second Dallas got in the car, "I started to take some pictures of the room, but I didn't think we'd need it. But you talkin' about us catchin' them niggas off guard by coming through that narrow-ass doorway."

"I come in blasting, you come in behind me blasting, and the only advantage we'll have is the element of surprise. We need to kill as many niggas as we can on that first round. After that, it gets deep."

"You sure you don't wanna walk away from this?"

"Yeah, I'm sure. We're gonna make this money."

"Okay," Deneisha said. "Glad I invested in body armor."

She also bought earpieces so they could stay in contact during the job.

Later that night, Deneisha was sitting in a car parked where she could see the front of the building. Dallas was parked near the back of the building. She would let him know when that evening's prey arrived, and then she would join him around back to make their entrance.

From her vantage point, Deneisha watched as three men entered the space and put a bag on the table. She didn't know if drugs or money were in that bag. It wasn't until Mookie came in with three other men that Deneisha knew who was who. Mookie worked for Whale, and Deneisha knew that they were looking to expand, and that meant Mookie had the money.

"You know what I think?" Deneisha asked as six men gathered around the table.

"What do you think?"

"I think we should maintain our positions and come in shooting. Get them in a crossfire like we always do."

"I think you're right," Dallas agreed, and when the time came, they were ready. Once the players were in place, the new plan was for Dallas to come in through the back and be in position when Deneisha reached the front door.

"Ready?" she asked.

"Let's do it," Dallas replied, and the pair emerged from their positions and began shooting.

Dallas hit one, and Deneisha shot another as the rest of the men took out guns and returned fire. Mookie grabbed the bag with the money and fired at Deneisha as he moved toward the door. The man who came with the product grabbed his bag and flipped over the table for cover. He took out his gun as one of his men pointed his weapon at Dallas, who put two in his chest before he could get off a shot. Deneisha fired at Mookie while he ran. He returned her fire and kept firing until he reached the door. Deneisha set herself, aimed, and fired at him. Her shot hit him in the head. He fell to the floor and dropped the bag. One of the men made a run for the money. He picked it up, and when he turned to shoot, Deneisha shot him twice in the chest.

One man began firing at Dallas, and then he dove to the floor. He was about to fire again when Deneisha lit him up before he could shoot Dallas. Now, there was only one man left. Once he fired his last round, he put up his hands and surrendered.

"Please don't kill me," he begged as Dallas walked up to him.

"Go get the money," Dallas said to Deneisha before he shot the last man twice in the head.

Once they had the money and the product, they were out of there and on their way to see Preach. However, they were a little disappointed because the deal wasn't as large as they had been led to believe. When they left his house, they had almost $200,000. Their next stop was Jacksonville International Airport for a flight to New Jersey. After a short layover in Fort Lauderdale, they exited the plane in Atlantic City.

After checking into a spacious Social Suite at Ocean Casino Resort, Dallas and Deneisha hit the casinos. The next night, they went to Caesars Resort & Casino. Before they boarded their flight back to Jacksonville, they had laundered money checks from the Tropicana, the Hard Rock Casino, Resorts Casino, and Bally's, most of which they deposited into their account in Curaçao.

They had been back in Jacksonville for a week when Dallas dropped by Deneisha's condo in Ponte Vedra Beach. She took some of the money she earned from that first job and the money she had left from the grocery store robbery and had a fake identification created. That allowed her to make a substantial down payment on a condo. Deneisha found a one-bedroom condo for $200,000 on Sandiron Circle.

"You got anything goin' on tonight?" Dallas asked.

"Not really. Why?"

"We've been invited to a pool party. You wanna go?"

"Yeah, we can go. I just need to run over to Town Center to get a bathing suit."

"This might sound like a stupid question, but I'm gonna ask it anyway."

"No, I *don't* want you to come with me."

Dallas smiled. "Okay, if you're sure."

"Yes, I'm sure."

"Cool, I'll be here when you get back," he said and made himself comfortable on the couch.

"Whose party is it?" Deneisha asked as she got dressed.

"A friend of mine."

"This friend got a name?"

"Sherick Powers."

"Real friend or business associate?"

"Sherick's a friend. Me and him go back some years. But yes, he is up-and-coming in the game, if that answers your question."

"It does," Deneisha said as she stood in front of Dallas. "How do I look?" she asked, referring to the Donna Karan sleeveless midi dress she was wearing.

"Like I need to strip you out of it and prove to you, once again, how much I love you."

"I don't think that's necessary. I know that you love me," she said, taking off the dress she just put on. "But you can show me anyway," she said as the dress dropped to the floor.

"If you insist," Dallas said, and then he stood up. He picked her up and carried her to the bedroom.

Later that night, at the pool party, Deneisha showed off the Agua Bendita floral bikini top she had bought earlier in the day. Since she had no plans to get in the pool, she completed her look with Khaite straight-leg jeans and Stuart Weitzman sandals. Before they left her condo, Deneisha and Dallas ordered dinner from Maggiano's Little Italy and had it delivered.

They drank a bottle of Pinot Grigio with dinner and another while they watched a movie. Between that and the blunts they smoked, they were fucked up by the time they left for the pool party.

The drive to the party allowed Dallas to sober up a little by the time they arrived at Sherick's house, but not Deneisha. She was still pretty fucked up when they got there.

"I'm gonna go holla at Sherick. You gonna be all right until I get back?"

"Yeah, I'll be fine," she said, and Dallas left her sitting in a lounge chair by the pool.

Deneisha was minding her own business, smoking a blunt, when a woman stood in front of her.

"What the fuck are you lookin' at?"

"Who the fuck you think you talkin' to?" Deneisha stood and asked the woman.

"I'm talkin' to *you,* bitch," she said, and she slapped the shit outta Deneisha.

Deneisha started to reach for her gun, but then she realized that she wasn't armed. She punched the woman in the face, and she swung back. The two women began to wrestle.

While that was going on outside, Dallas was in the house talking to Sherick. He was telling his old friend what a wonderful woman Deneisha was and how happy she'd made him. Not only was she a good woman, "She's also the best partner I ever had," Dallas was saying when Sherick noticed that an argument had broken out by the pool.

"Check it out," Sherick said. "Two women are fighting by the pool."

Dallas came and looked out the window.

"Oh shit."

"What?"

"That's Deneisha," Dallas said as Deneisha's bikini top was ripped off, and the two women fell into the pool.

Sherick laughed. "Go see about your girl."

"Right," Dallas said and rushed out of the house.

By the time he got out of the house, Deneisha and the woman she was fighting were separated by two men. When he arrived at the pool, somebody had helped Deneisha out of the water. Dallas took off his shirt and handed it to her.

"Cover them pretty titties, and let's get outta here," he said and escorted her out.

# Chapter Twenty-one

When Deneisha woke up, she sat up, yawned, and got in a good stretch.

"That felt good," she said, and that was when she saw Dallas. He was fully dressed and ready to go.

"Where are you going?"

"Going to talk to Preach."

"What does he want?"

"He didn't say. He just said we need to talk about some business."

"You want me to go with you?"

"You can if you want."

"You ain't goin' to see no other woman, are you?"

Dallas laughed. "No."

"What's so funny?"

"Your question."

"Why is my question funny to you?"

"Because the idea of me seeing a woman other than you is funny, that's all." He sat on the bed beside her. "What could I possibly get from another woman that I can't get from you?" He paused. "Go ahead, I'll wait."

"Wait for what?" Deneisha asked with a smile.

"For you to tell me what I could possibly need from a woman that I'm not already getting in abundance from you." He slowly pulled back the covers. "Ain't nobody as fine as you."

"True. I am a bad bitch."

"And I don't know of any woman who can clear a room the way that you can."

"I can't think of any."

"Where else am I going to find another perfect woman?"

"You can't because she doesn't exist." Deneisha kissed Dallas on the cheek. "Do you realize that this will be the first time since we met that we won't be together?" she asked and lay down.

Dallas paused to think. "You're right."

"I know."

"You wanna come with me?"

"No. I'm gonna go get my nails and my toes done."

"You sure? I wouldn't want to break our inseparable streak."

"It's not that serious. And besides, you wouldn't invite me if you were going to see some other woman."

"I could, but you'd have to wait in the car until I got finished with her."

"Which might take hours with you, stamina man."

Dallas stood up. "I'll be back as soon as I can. Then we can do something."

"What do you have in mind?"

"I don't know. You choose."

Deneisha got out of bed and walked him to the door. "Call me when you're on your way so I can be ready when you get here."

He took her in his arms and kissed her once they reached the door. "I'll call you," he said as he left the condo. Deneisha locked the door and headed to the bathroom to shower and get ready to go to the salon.

When Dallas arrived at Preach's house, he parked in the driveway and paused to think about what he could want that he would say, 'I need to talk to you alone.' Knowing he would find out in a minute, Dallas got out of the car and approached the house.

"Thank you for coming," Preach said and looked around outside. "Come on in."

"So, what you wanna see me about that Deneisha couldn't hear?"

"Straight to business." Preach chuckled. "Can I at least offer you a drink?"

"Sure."

"What are you drinkin'?" Preach asked as they entered the living room.

"Whatever you're pouring."

"I'm drinkin' that Tanqueray No. Ten Gin."

Dallas sat down. "Pour 'em up, my nigga."

While Preach poured the drinks, Dallas took out his phone and texted Deneisha.

I'm here.

Preach handed Dallas his drink. "Thanks." He took a sip. "So, let's talk," he said as he got a reply from Deneisha. It was a picture of her standing naked in front of a mirror. The caption was, You don't know what you're missing.

And he replied, Yes, I do. That's why I'm in such a hurry to get back to you.

"Always straight to business." Preach chuckled. "Okay, here's the deal," he said and laid it all out for him. When he finished, Dallas stood up.

"I'll let you know whether I'm in."

"When?"

"Tonight."

"Cool," Preach said and got up to show Dallas to the door. "I wouldn't ask if it wasn't totally necessary."

"I know. We'll talk tonight."

Dallas walked away from the house, knowing that he was all in for whatever Preach needed. What concerned him was Deneisha and how she might feel about it. Then there was the question of how much he would tell her. Would it be enough to simply say, "This is what we're doing," without explaining? That wasn't how things had been between them. He told Deneisha everything. If there were something, anything, they would talk about it and come to a joint decision. He picked up his phone and called her.

"Hey, baby," she answered.

"Where are you?"

"At Muse, gettin' my nails and toes done. You on your way home?"

"Yes."

"Pick up something for us to eat. I'll be there in about an hour."

"What do you have a taste for?" he asked, but he knew the answer.

"I don't know. You pick something. You know I ain't picky," Deneisha replied as she always did.

He chuckled. *One day, she's gonna tell me exactly what she wants to eat,* he thought and laughed aloud. "Just not today."

"What's not today?"

"Nothing, baby. I'll see you when you get home," Dallas said, and he ended the call before she could ask any more questions.

Since he had a taste for ribs and Deneisha loved them, Dallas drove to The Bearded Pig BBQ on Kings Avenue. He ordered jalapeño poppers and Deneisha's favorite, pimento cheese with saltine crackers as an appetizer, along with macaroni and cheese, potato salad, collard greens, and a full rack of spareribs.

When he got to the condo, Deneisha hadn't made it home yet, so Dallas took the opportunity to set the dining room table. All he would have to do was serve the food when she got home. Once that was done, he poured himself a drink, twisted up a blunt, and went out on the balcony. He leaned over the rail and lit up. Then he took a sip of his drink and thought about Deneisha. She was his world. He drained the glass.

"I don't know how I survived all those years without her," he said aloud as the door opened and in walked Deneisha. He came back in and went into the kitchen.

"Hey, babe," she said, and saw that the table was set. "What did you get us to eat?"

"I went to The Bearded Pig and got jalapeño poppers and pimento cheese crackers."

"My favorite," she said and kissed him on the cheek.

"I also got mac-n-cheese, potato salad, collard greens, and a rack of ribs."

"You sit down, I got this," she said and brought out the plates. "What you want to drink with that?"

"Just some water."

"You want me to squeeze a lime for you?"

"Naw, I don't want you to go to any trouble," he said and sat down at the table.

"No trouble at all," she said as she sliced the ribs and put them in the microwave with the mac-n-cheese, poppers, and the greens. While that was heating up, Deneisha cut a lime in half and squeezed it into the glass of water she had poured for Dallas, because that's how he liked it, and she would do anything to make him happy.

"So, what did Preach wanna talk about?" she asked when she brought out the food and sat down.

"He's got a job he needs done."

"What's the job?"

"It pays $50,000."

"Not a whole lot of money. What's the job?" she asked again.

"It's a high-stakes poker game, so in addition to the fifty, there should be a lot of cash. He couldn't tell me how much."

"Okay, that sweetens the pot. What's the job?" she asked as she took a bite of rib.

Dallas hesitated.

Deneisha put the bone down and looked at him. "What's the job?"

"The buy-in is two hundred thousand. The small blind is ten thousand, the big blind is twenty, so you know there's gonna be some real money in the house."

Deneisha let out a little laugh. "Do I need to get my gun to get you to tell me what the job is?"

"It's an assassination. The four people at the game and the houseman."

"Now I *know* why you were fuckin' around. An assassination? *Really,* Dallas?"

"Yes, Deneisha. An assassination."

"I don't know, Dallas. What did these people do that Preach wants them dead?"

"I don't know. I didn't ask."

Deneisha nodded. "Of course you didn't. That would be unprofessional." She ate some greens. "How'd you leave it?"

"I told him I'd let him know," he said and started eating. "I love their mac-n-cheese."

"I do too. But don't change the subject. An assassination?"

"Yes, Deneisha. It's an assassination."

"Okay." She picked up her rib and took a bite. "I know you told him that you would let him know, but I know you, Dallas. I know you're gonna do it."

"You don't have to come. I can handle this by myself."

"No. That is *not* how we work. If you're in, then I'm in."

"Like I said, you don't have to come. I can handle this by myself."

"Okay." Deneisha nodded. "You go by yourself. Let's play that out. You go in by yourself." Deneisha stood up and demonstrated. "You shoot the houseman first because you know he's armed."

"Right."

"Then you systematically shoot the rest of them, starting with whoever is closest to the houseman."

"Right."

"You cap two of them, but when you turn to shoot the third man, he's had time to get his gun out, and he kills you because you went in by yourself. No, Dallas, if you're in, then *I'm* in."

Dallas chuckled. "I can't argue with your logic."

"No, you can't because I'm right."

"You usually are."

"And the smart play is for us to go in *together*. You shoot the houseman first because you know he's armed, and I shoot the one farthest from him. Then we systematically shoot the rest of them, with you shooting whoever's closest to the houseman first."

"Here again, I can't argue with your logic."

"No, Dallas. You can't argue with my logic because you know I'm right." Deneisha ate some more greens. "When is this assassination gonna happen?"

"Tomorrow," he said, and he waited for Deneisha's fiery response. But there was none. She just continued eating.

All she said was, "You're right. This mac-n-cheese is swingin'."

The following evening, Deneisha and Dallas arrived on Starling Avenue in the Greenfield Manor area of Jacksonville. Since she didn't like the dynamics in the room, Deneisha picked up a little something extra to ensure that they didn't get shot. Dallas parked in front of the house where Preach told them the game was taking place. They checked their silencer-clad weapons.

"You ready?" Dallas asked.

"Yeah, I'm ready."

Deneisha wasn't with the assassination, and it showed in her attitude.

"You can wait here. I told you, I can handle it," he said.

Deneisha rolled her eyes, grabbed the door handle, and got out.

"And I told you that is *not* how we work."

"Okay. Let's go do this," Dallas said, and he started for the house.

"Right here with you," Deneisha replied as she walked alongside him.

The game was being played at the dining room table of the house, but it was a straight shot from the door. When they got to the door, Dallas looked at Deneisha. When she nodded, he kicked in the door.

Deneisha tossed in a flashbang grenade. The loud noise and bright light disoriented the men. Dallas fired and hit the houseman with a shot to the chest, and Deneisha shot the man farthest away from him. Next, Dallas shot the two men who were closest to the houseman on the right. Deneisha shot the last man. And just like that . . . It was over.

Deneisha and Dallas looked at the pile of cash in the center of the table and the neatly stacked bills in front of the players. She took the bag from around her neck and began filling it with money. He began searching the house for the rest of the money. She looked at Dallas and saw an angry look on his face.

"What's wrong with you?"

It was evident that he was disappointed by the take. "That look like eight hundred thousand to you?"

"No, it doesn't," she said and put the last of the money in the bag. "You can take that up with Preach." Deneisha zipped up the bag and started for the door. "But right now, we gotta go."

"Right," Dallas said and followed her out of the house.

He tossed her the keys. “You drive.” Deneisha knew he was mad because he never wanted her to drive.

“I don’t like this,” Dallas said once they were in the car. “How much you think that is?”

“Two hundred max. Yeah, if Preach told you there’d be at least eight hundred grand—”

“He lied to me.”

Dallas sat quietly, fuming, looking out the window. Deneisha knew how mad he was, so she said nothing. But she had been with him long enough to know what he was going to do next.

“Take me to Preach’s house,” he said after a while, and then he noticed where they were. “You’re already on your way to his house, aren’t you?”

“I knew you couldn’t let that stand without talkin’ to him about it.”

“I love you.”

“I know.”

# Chapter Twenty-two

After his conversation with Preach, Dallas seemed to be much calmer when he got back into the car. He reported that all five men were dead, as he requested. Preach nodded, and he went to get their money. Once Dallas had the fifty thousand he promised, he counted it, and then he took out his gun and pointed it at Preach's head.

"Whoa. What's all this?"

"You lied to me."

"Wait a minute, wait a minute, man. Slow down."

"Fuck that, Preach. You *lied* to me," he said and pressed the gun harder into Preach's head.

"Okay, okay!" Preach shouted, leaning back with his hands up. "I lied to you, and I'm sorry. But I needed them gone."

"Why?" Dallas shouted and hit Preach's head with the butt of the gun. "Tell me why you needed them dead so badly that you figured you had to lie to me?"

"Okay, Dallas. I'll tell you the whole story. Okay? Just take the gun away from my head 'cause you know if you fuck around and kill me, the shit is gonna eat you alive, regardless of whether I deserved it."

Dallas took a breath and moved the gun. "You're right, it would." He put the gun down. "Tell me why you thought you had to lie to me."

"You remember Yvette's niece, Shekita?"

"Yeah, what about her?"

"She was working as an escort, and she worked one of their parties. They drugged her and raped her. All of them."

"A lot of that goin' around," Dallas commented since the same thing almost happened to Deneisha.

A tear drifted down Preach's cheek. He wiped it away quickly. "She reported it to the cops. They told the cops that the sex was consensual, and besides, she was well paid for her work that night."

"I told him something had to be done," a female voice spoke up.

When Dallas turned, he saw Preach's wife, Yvette, standing in the doorway.

"I'm sorry to interrupt men while they're talking, but if you came to kill somebody, you came to kill me."

"Hello, Yvette. How are you?"

"I'm fine, Dallas."

Yvette came into the living room and kissed Dallas on the cheek before she sat down next to Preach.

"I'm the one who urged Preach to do something to make this right." Preach took her hand in his. "If they did that to Shekita and got away with it, imagine how many other women they've done that to."

"I get all that, Yvette. I really do." Dallas looked at Preach. "But you didn't have to lie to me to get me to do it. We go back years. All you had to say was. 'I need this,' and I was all in."

"Something had to be done, and I know you don't do that type of work. So, I sweetened the pot to get you interested."

"You lied, Preach. After all you and me been through together, you decided that you needed to lie to me."

"I'm sorry."

"I am too." Dallas looked Preach in the eyes. "Now, how can I trust what you tell me?"

"Hopefully, in time, I can earn back your trust."

"Maybe," Dallas said, but he knew things would never be the same between them going forward. He had known Preach since he moved to Palatka from Texas, which made him sad.

"I'm sorry too, Dallas," Yvette said. "I'm the one you need to blame. Preach was just doing what I asked him to do."

"I hope we can put this behind us and move forward," Preach said.

"I hope so too." Dallas stood up. "Always good to see you, Yvette."

"It's good to see you too, Dallas, and I am so sorry. I hope you can find it in your heart to forgive us."

"I hope so too, Yvette."

When he got back into the car, Dallas was much calmer, but he was hurt. When he moved to Palatka, Preach was the first person he met. He lived around the corner, and Dallas's family went to his father's church. That's how they met. The church's youth ministry had a program designed to keep boys off the streets. Dallas's parents all but forced him to attend, and he sat next to Preach at the first meeting he went to. Preach, being the son of the preacher, made him acceptable to Dallas's family. That left them free to hang out and get into all kinds of trouble. That's why Dallas was so disappointed that he felt he had to lie.

"All he had to do was tell me what was up, and I would have been all in," he told Deneisha when he got back into the car. "Especially after what happened to you."

"I know," Deneisha said as she drove him away from there. "But he had no way of knowing what happened to me. I'm sure you didn't tell him."

"Of course not. That's personal."

"Right. That probably is the reason that they felt they had to lie to you."

"Like I told Preach and Yvette, I get all that, but they didn't have to lie to me. I just can't get past that."

"I understand. A muthafucka ain't got but one time to lie to me. But you and Preach go back years. All I'm sayin' is that you should cut him some slack."

"On the strength?" Dallas chuckled.

"Yeah." Deneisha smiled and nodded. "On the strength of y'all's friendship."

"Okay." They drove in silence for a while. "No more poker games. We rob drug dealers when they're doing business."

"Good. I was feeling some kind of way about killing civilians."

And that was that. Deneisha and Dallas went back to doing what they did best, and three months later, they were back at work. Dallas liked the additions that Deneisha brought to their last job. He thought that the ability to stay in contact was a great idea, and wearing body armor just made sense.

"You know, just in case a muthafucka wanna shoot back before we kill everybody," Deneisha said.

However, the addition that Dallas liked best was the inclusion of flashbang grenades, which were produced for military and law enforcement use. The ATF classified flashbangs as a destructive device. Therefore, they weren't available for commercial sale. But Deneisha had a contact who was able to get them for her.

Soon, after weeks of surveillance and planning, Deneisha and Dallas hit another drug buy. Dallas kicked in the door, and Deneisha tossed in the flashbang grenade. It produced a blinding flash of light and a deafening bang that made the victims easy prey. Dallas and Deneisha shot the four men in the house. They quickly got the money and the drugs, and they were out of there.

"What now?" Deneisha asked as they drove away from the scene.

"What you mean?"

"I mean, are we going to see Preach?"

"Yes." Dallas stopped at a red light and looked at her. "Unless you know somebody else that we can sell these ten keys to."

"No, I don't."

"Preach it is."

"So, you two are cool?"

"No. Not by a long shot, but this is business. I trust him enough to do business." There was silence in the car. "And I do understand why they felt the need to lie to me."

"Thank you."

"I just don't appreciate it because it wasn't necessary."

"I'm just glad you can move past it."

"Why are *you* glad?"

"Because you feeling whatever it was you're feeling about Preach betraying y'all's trust affects everything you do, including your relationship with me. So, yeah, I'm glad you've reached this point. I like my Dallas unbothered by bullshit."

When they arrived at Preach's house, it didn't matter that it was almost three in the morning. Since Dallas had called them earlier in the day, Preach and Yvette were up waiting for them. Deneisha went inside with Dallas, and he proudly introduced Yvette to her. Yvette and Deneisha soon became fast friends, and Yvette insisted that they stay and eat breakfast before they boarded their 8:30 a.m. flight to Las Vegas. She served bacon, eggs, hash browns, and waffles, accompanied by delicious Tequila Sunrise Mimosas.

Since they had been there to launder their money recently, they stayed at the Desert Rose Resort, this time, and Dallas did his gambling at the Ellis Island Hotel, the

South Point Hotel Casino, the Platinum Hotel, and the Desert Paradise Resort. While he was gambling, Deneisha busied herself with other activities. She attended a burlesque show and then went bar hopping at some unique establishments. She tried zero gravity, visited a ghost town, took a horseback tour around the Nevada desert, and went to every pool party she heard about.

When Deneisha and Dallas visited the Graceland Chapel, they passed on a marriage officiated by an Elvis impersonator. But they had the most fun at Minus5°, a unique, one-of-a-kind ice bar where they were given gloves and a faux fur coat and drank cocktails from glasses made entirely of ice while enjoying an LED light show and upbeat music before returning to Jacksonville with laundered money.

# Chapter Twenty-three

When Deneisha and Dallas returned to Jacksonville, nothing was going on. No jobs were available to get them paid. So, for the first time since they'd been together, they had time to relax and simply enjoy life.

"It's been so long, I don't know if I still remember how to do that," Dallas said.

"I'm not too far behind you. When I was in the ATL, me and my girls was always on the lookout for the next lick."

"You talk a lot about your girls." Dallas paused to think about how he was gonna ask her the question. He figured it had to be a touchy subject, so he decided to tread carefully. "Y'all were pretty tight, huh?"

"Yeah, we were," Deneisha said, and Dallas could hear a hint of sadness in her voice. "When I moved to Atlanta from New York, Breezy was the first person to befriend the 'new girl with the bad attitude.'"

"You, bad attitude?"

"Yeah, that was me. When I made the move, I was all excited about it. I had heard so much about the ATL, New York South, you know what I'm sayin'?"

"I hear you."

"I get down there, and compared to the city, it was country as hell to me." Deneisha laughed. "I mean, one day, I'm Fort Apache, The Bronx, and the next day I'm in Mayberry. But Breezy and Court were cool." She giggled. "Kinda country cool, but they were my girls."

"What happened with y'all?"

Deneisha got quiet for a while. "Court is dead, and I don't know what's up with Breezy."

"I'm sorry about Court. How did she die?"

"All I know is that she died in jail. I never knew what happened."

"What about Breezy? You said you don't know what's up with her."

"I heard she got arrested."

"You heard?"

Deneisha hadn't confronted her feelings about what went down, and she wasn't sure that she wanted to. She just tried to move on and not dwell on it. Her meeting Dallas and them hitting it off on her first day had a lot to do with that. Deneisha looked at Dallas and saw the compassionate look in his eyes. He had always been there for whatever she needed. Perhaps he could offer the emotional support she needed to confront her feelings.

"Our last job didn't go well."

"The grocery store robbery?"

"Yeah. I told you about the cops getting on to us right away."

"I remember."

Deneisha took a deep breath. "We got into an accident, and we couldn't get Court's seat belt off, so she told us to leave her. Cops arrested her, and then Court's mother told us that she was murdered in jail. Breezy wanted to go to the funeral, but I didn't think it was a good idea. I felt bad about it, and Breezy stopped speaking to me over my decision." Deneisha paused. "Turns out, I was right because the cops arrested her at the funeral. I didn't wait around to see if she flipped on me. I got the hell outta Dodge and came here."

"You did the right thing. If you had hung around, you would have gotten arrested too. Y'all was roommates, right?"

"Yeah."

"Cops would have come for you sooner or later, regardless of whether Breezy snitched on you. Three women rob a grocery store. They catch one, they gotta be thinking her two roommates were in on it with her."

"That's what I tried to get Breezy to see. But she wasn't trying to hear what I was sayin'. To her, it was all about my not paying my respects to Court's family by not attending the funeral. And I agree with her. It was disrespectful for me not to go to the funeral, and yeah, I feel awful about it, but I was right. Problem with that is being right don't make me feel any better about it," Deneisha said, and Dallas hugged her.

He didn't know what he could say or do to make her feel better, so he said nothing. All he could do was hold her tight and be there for her when she needed him to be.

"But we're supposed to be relaxing and having fun," Deneisha said. "Enjoying the fruits of our labor."

"I'm for all that. What do you wanna do?"

"I don't know."

"We could—" Dallas started, but Deneisha interrupted him before he could continue.

"Let's have a picnic on the beach."

"That sounds like fun."

"We could get some picnic food, set out a blanket, and relax. I recall the first night I arrived. I went to the beach, listened to the waves, and breathed in the salty air. It was great."

"Did you get in the water?"

"No," she said emphatically. "It was dark, and I was alone and had no desire to become the morning headline."

"Cutie moves from Atlanta and gets murdered at the beach on her first night in the city."

"No, thank you. But this time, I'm gonna get in the water . . . something I haven't done in all the time I've been here."

"You haven't?"

"No. I've gotten dressed up in a cute bikini and hung out at the beach. And I've been there, walking and holding hands with you. But me goin' in the water . . ." She shook her head. "Hasn't happened."

"Well, it will today. Come on," Dallas said and got out of bed.

"Okay, okay," Deneisha said, and she followed him into the bathroom.

He turned on the shower, and when the water reached the right temperature, he got in, and Deneisha followed him. They made love in the shower, then took it to the bed, and afterward, they had to take another shower separately when they were done.

Once they were dressed, they drove to the Publix grocery store. Since neither she nor Dallas liked flats, Deneisha got all drumette wings and macaroni and potato salads so they would have choices. She also ordered a small deli sub selection and a mini deli fresh fruit platter, accompanied by chips and dip.

"You know this is more food than we can eat, right?" Dallas pointed out as they drove away from the store.

"Maybe."

"On second thought, I've seen you put away some food."

"That's true, and I'm hungry, so it might be just enough."

Then they went to the liquor store and picked up bottles of Courvoisier and Champagne. Because they preferred a more private beach experience, they headed for Ponte Vedra Beach, which was less crowded than the rest of Jacksonville's beaches. While they were at the beach, Dallas received a call from another childhood friend from Palatka. His name was Peter Falkner, but since he was younger than Dallas and Preach, they called him The Kid.

"What up, Pete?"

"Oh, we being formal today. Bet. What's up, Calvin?"

Dallas laughed. "I'm good, man. How about you?"

"I'm awesome, as always. But listen. I'm having a party next weekend, and I want you and that amazing woman I've been hearing so much about to come."

"Her name is Deneisha, and yeah, she is amazing. She's sitting right here next to me. You wanna go to a party in Miami?"

"I would love to go to a party in Miami."

"She's in, so we're coming."

The Kid laughed. "Now, I know she must be special."

"What makes you think so?"

"Because you asked her if she wanted to go. The Dallas I knew would have just told her we're goin' to a party in Miami, and that would have been that."

"What can I say? I'm evolving."

"Right. See you next weekend, Mr. I'm Evolving."

"See you next weekend, Kid."

The following weekend, Dallas, Deneisha, Preach, and Yvette boarded a flight to Miami. They booked a room at the Four Seasons Hotel and rented a car to go to the party. Since Deneisha had never been to Miami, Dallas showed her the city.

The event was to be held in the Grand Ballroom at the Miami Marriott, their largest capacity event room, located at Biscayne Bay. The Kid had invited over 500 people to celebrate his big announcement. Since the affair was semiformal, Deneisha bought Dallas a navy Pal Zileri silk-blend dinner jacket and slacks, and she wore a Johanna Ortiz Ocean Of Secrets maxi dress with an open back and a sweetheart neckline.

The event was catered and featured an open bar, so by the time The Kid made his announcement, many people were already drunk or on their way to becoming intoxicated. The Kid got up and went to the podium that was set up for the event. He quieted the crowd.

"First off, I want to thank all of you for coming. I'm glad I got the grand ballroom. Niggas and free food and drinks. Yeah . . . Wasn't nobody missing this party."

The guests laughed.

"So, I hope everybody is full from that delicious meal they prepared for us. Give it up for the hotel staff," The Kid said to a round of applause. "Now, I guess some of you are wondering why is The Kid springing for free food and drinks. And some of you don't give a fuck. Free food and drinks, right? Who cares why?"

The guests laughed again.

"To answer that question, for those who give a fuck, I need Tomesia Chambers to join me at the podium. Tomesia, come on up here," he said to a round of applause that continued until she was standing beside him, and he quieted the crowd. "For those of you who don't know this astonishing woman, her name is Tomesia Chambers, and she has been by my side every step of the way as I built the empire that's feedin' you niggas and getting y'all drunk," he said to laughter. "I invited y'all here tonight to bear witness to me making a fool of myself or me becoming the happiest man in the world."

Tomesia's eyes got big when The Kid got down on one knee and pulled a box from his pocket.

"Tomesia Chambers, will you marry me?"

"Yes, yes!" she all but shouted.

Larry Graham's "When We Get Married" began playing in the background. The crowd of guests erupted in applause as The Kid slipped an 18K yellow gold diamond radiant-cut solitaire engagement ring on her finger.

"I need Preach and Dallas to come on up here. Preach, Dallas, where y'all at?"

The crowd clapped as The Kid's two best friends joined him on stage.

"Baby, I want you to meet Preach and Dallas. These my niggas from way back."

While Dallas went on stage, Deneisha was alone. They had been standing at the bar when the call went out for Dallas to join The Kid on stage. Deneisha was one of those people that The Kid was talking about.

Deneisha was fucked up.

She and Dallas were talking about getting out of there after The Kid made his big announcement. They had no idea that Dallas would be called up on stage. Deneisha was clapping for her man as he went up on stage, and she accidentally bumped into the woman standing next to her, and her drink spilled on the woman's dress.

"Oh, I am so sorry," Deneisha said.

"You stupid bitch. Look what you did to my dress."

"I said I'm sorry, but I ain't gonna be your bitch."

"When you do stupid bitch shit, you get called a stupid bitch," the woman yelled.

"Y'all need to take that shit outside," a man said because they were disturbing The Kid's big announcement.

"Come on," Deneisha said and walked away from the woman.

"Don't walk away from me, bitch. You need to pay for this fuckin' dress you ruined," she shouted as she followed Deneisha out of the Grand Ballroom.

Once they were outside the ballroom, the argument turned into a fight when the woman pushed Deneisha, who pushed her back, and then she came at Deneisha with her arms swinging, in a windmill-like motion. When she punched the woman in the face, she lost her balance and fell down the stairs.

"Get up, bitch! You was talkin' all that shit. Now, get up!" Deneisha shouted as she came down the stairs.

When Dallas arrived on the scene, he saw what was happening. He rushed past Deneisha and went to check on the woman. He saw how she was lying, so he quickly checked for a pulse and found none.

"I think her neck is broken," he whispered to Deneisha when she came down the stairs. He grabbed her hand. "Come on, we gotta go," he said softly, and they walked quickly out of the hotel and to their car. As people came out of the party, Dallas drove them away from there with the lights off, so nobody could report the license plate number.

"What happened back there?"

"I bumped into the woman standing next to me, and her drink spilled on her dress. I said, 'I am so sorry,' but she called me a stupid bitch. I said, 'I'm sorry *again,* but I ain't gonna be your bitch.' Then a man said that we needed to take that shit outside. When we got outside, she pushed me, and I punched her in the face. She lost her balance and fell down the stairs."

"Damn, Deneisha, your ass can't stay outta trouble."

# Chapter Twenty-four

It wasn't long after they collected their belongings from the hotel where they were staying and drove away. Deneisha fell asleep. Dallas shook his head and turned up the music. He got on Interstate 95 North and headed back to Jacksonville.

"Where are we?" Deneisha asked when she woke up from her nod.

"We're on I-95 goin' north." Deneisha saw a sign for Riviera Beach.

"Riviera Beach?" she questioned.

"It's about an hour and a half north of Miami. It's a small town, so there isn't much to do there."

"Well, I need to use the bathroom. You think we'll find a bathroom open at this hour?"

"I'm sure we will."

Dallas got off at the exit and found a Wawa gas station with a restroom. While Deneisha was using the bathroom, Dallas paid for the gas and a couple of bottles of water.

"What's to do here?" he asked the clerk.

"Not much doing here. But, hey, are you a Mets or an Astors fan?"

"Big-time Astros fan," Dallas replied.

"You should go to Port St. Lucie. The Mets hold their spring training at Clover Park, and they're playing the Astros today."

"How far is Port St. Lucie?"

"It's about an hour north of here."

"What's about an hour north of here?" Deneisha asked when she came to the counter with some chips and a bottle of Mountain Dew.

"Port St. Lucie."

"What's in Port St. Lucie?"

"Baseball. The New York Mets play their spring training games there, and they're playing the Houston Astros today," Dallas said as they walked back to the car.

"Oh joy," she said as Dallas pumped the gas.

"I take it you're not into baseball?"

"No, I'm not."

"Why not?"

"Because it's as interesting as watching paint dry."

"Baseball?"

"Yes, Dallas, baseball is boring." She got into the car.

Dallas finished pumping the gas, and then he got in the car. "Baseball, boring?" he questioned as they got back on the interstate.

"Yes, it is boring as hell. All that standing around waiting for somebody—anybody—to do something—anything. And when the batter finally hits the ball, everybody goes crazy, and then it goes right back to being boring again until something else happens."

"Yeah, but there is nothing like the excitement when they hit the ball."

"Whatever, Dallas. Boring," she all but shouted.

"Okay. Let me suck up a day of spring training, and I promise to make it up to you."

"How?"

"We'll do something you wanna do."

"Problem with that is, you wanna do what I wanna do."

"True. But I'm sure you'll find something."

"Maybe. In the meantime, it can be something I hold over your head for years to come," she laughed and settled into her seat.

"Deal."

It was early in the morning when Dallas and Deneisha arrived in Port St. Lucie.

"It is way too early for any baseball to be playing," she pointed out as they drove through the near-empty streets. Undeterred by her comment, Dallas found his way to a Bob Evans restaurant.

"I see what you're doing. You always think you can feed me, and I'll do whatever you want me to do."

"I only do it because it works. How am I doing?"

"I like Bob Evans, so we'll see," Deneisha said as Dallas got out of the car and came around to her side of the vehicle.

He opened the door for Deneisha and extended his hand to help her out of the car as he always did. She appreciated the fact that he treated her with such love and respect, and it went a long way toward convincing her to do what he wanted. That was mostly because she wanted to do what he wanted to do too.

*No point in letting him know that,* Deneisha thought as she walked to the restaurant.

Dallas held the door open for Deneisha, and she entered.

*The food does help, though,* she thought as the hostess seated them.

The New York Mets were playing a spring training game against the Houston Astros that afternoon at 1:10 p.m. at Clover Park. That still left them with plenty of time before the game started. Therefore, after breakfast, Dallas got them a room so they could relax and freshen up before heading to Clover Park to watch the game.

After watching baseball in the hot sun all day, they decided to stay the night in Port St. Lucie. When they got back to the room, Deneisha immediately began shedding her clothes.

"I stink, and so do you. I'm gonna take a shower."

"Go ahead. I got a call I need to make," Dallas said. He needed to call The Kid to see if the woman was actually dead and if anybody could identify him or Deneisha.

"I'll try to save you some hot water, but no promises," she said and disappeared into the bathroom. As soon as the door closed, Dallas reached for his phone.

"What's up, Dallas?"

"I'm good. Everything all right down there?"

"Yeah, everything is lovely. Just wondering why you ran up outta there like you did. I asked Preach if you had said anything to him, and he didn't know where you ran off to. So, what's up?"

"Deneisha had too much to drink, and she wasn't feeling good, so we left, and I took her to a hotel."

"She all right?"

"Oh yeah, she's fine. She just needed to sleep it off. We're on our way back to Jacksonville. We stopped in Port St. Lucie and saw an Astros game. So, that was cool."

"That's right. The Mets play their spring training games there. It's one of those things that you mean to do but never get around to."

"I know what you mean. I wouldn't have known anything about it if not for a guy at the gas station who told me about it."

"I'll get up there one of these days."

"Sorry if my leaving like that ruined anything you had planned."

The Kid laughed. "Wasn't you that ruined the night."

"What you mean?"

"A woman got drunk and fell down the stairs and broke her neck. Cops came, so you know, with the crowd of niggas that I had up in there, the party was over."

"Cops sure do know how to fuck up a good party." They both laughed. "But what was up with the woman falling down the stairs?"

"That shit was crazy. I didn't see it, but people say that she must have fallen."

"Yeah, that shit is crazy. Didn't none of that blow back on you, right?"

"No. What does some bitch getting drunk and falling down the steps got to do with me?"

"When did the cops ever need a reason to fuck with a nigga over some bullshit?"

"True that, true that. But they bagged and tagged her and got the fuck on."

"That's good," Dallas laughed. "Especially with the crowd you had up in there."

"That's why niggas got the fuck on at the first sign of blue lights." The Kid paused. "But look, I need to handle something important right about now, but Jacksonville ain't that far from Miami."

"The door swings both ways. You could bring your ass to Jacksonville."

"You know, Preach said the same thing. And I'm gonna make it up there."

"Right. I remember you said that after the last time the three of us got together."

"And I will."

"Maybe now that you're settling down, you might have time to make the trip."

"I'm getting married. Ain't nobody said nothing about me settling down. Gotta go."

"I'll holla," Dallas said and ended the call.

Now that he knew that the police weren't looking for Deneisha, he got undressed and went into the bathroom. Deneisha was drying herself.

"I guess I'm too late," he said, walking toward her.

Deneisha dropped the towel. "I saved you some hot water," she said, walking around him and leaving the bathroom.

"I guess I really am too late."

When Dallas came out of the shower, Deneisha was dressed and looking at a travel magazine.

"Get dressed."

"Where are we going?"

"We're going to do something *I* wanna do."

"What's that?" he asked as he began to get dressed.

"We're going to play video games at Dave & Buster's."

"Oh joy."

"I know you think playing games is a tragic waste of time."

"Because it is."

"But it's fun, and I like to play games and have fun. You know, just like you like watching boring-ass baseball in the hot-ass sun."

"Right. So, let's go play games."

Once Dallas was dressed, they went to Dave & Buster's, and much to his surprise, he had a good time. When they got back to the hotel, the pair relaxed and watched television in bed, but they ran out of liquor.

"And I'm hungry," Deneisha said.

"You're always hungry."

"But I don't feel like getting up."

Dallas got out of bed. "What do you have a taste for?" he asked, knowing that he wouldn't get an answer.

"I don't know. Whatever is on the way."

He kissed Deneisha. "I'll be back," he said and left the room.

Dallas went to the liquor store and then to Babalu's Cuban Café for a palomilla steak and their Cubano especial sandwich, before heading back to the hotel. On the way, the police pulled him over.

"Shit," Dallas said when he saw the blue lights come on behind him. "This is the last thing I need." He took the gun from his waist, put it in the glove compartment, and got the car rental paperwork before he pulled over. He got out his driver's license and rolled down the window as he waited for the officer.

"Evening, Officer," Dallas said when the cop got to the window.

"Do you know why I stopped you, sir?"

"I have no idea."

"You were doing forty-five in a thirty-five-mile-per-hour zone and failed to signal when you made that last turn. License, registration, and proof of insurance, please."

Dallas handed the officer his documents. "It's a rental."

The officer took the documents. "Remain in your vehicle, and I'll be back."

As Dallas sat waiting for the officer to return with a ticket, he noticed that another police car had arrived on the scene.

"This is not good," Dallas said, and knew that he was going to jail. He thought about Deneisha as the officer got out of his cruiser. The two officers talked briefly before one of them approached.

"Have you been drinking tonight, Mr. Goodwin?"

"I had a drink earlier this evening."

"Would you mind stepping out of the car and submitting to a breathalyzer test?"

"Sure."

After Dallas failed the test, he was arrested for driving under the influence and put in handcuffs. That was when the second officer on the scene searched the car and found his gun in the glove compartment. Since Dallas was on probation, he knew they would violate him and take him to jail.

Deneisha fell asleep while she was waiting for Dallas to return to the room. She was startled when the phone rang at three o'clock in the morning. Although she was startled by the call, she was happy . . . until she looked at the display.

"Andre?" she questioned. "Why is Andre calling me at this hour?"

He was Dallas's lawyer. Like Preach and The Kid, Dallas had known Andre for years.

"Hello," she said tentatively.

"Hello, Deneisha. I'm sorry to be calling you at this hour."

"It's okay, Andre, just tell me what's wrong?"

"The police in Port St. Lucie stopped Dallas."

"Oh no."

"They found the gun. So in addition to violating his parole, he's going to be charged with DUI, improper lane change, and carrying a gun without a permit."

"That is not good."

Andre chuckled. "You sound like Dallas. He said the same thing."

"Do you know when and where he's going to court?"

"No, I'm sorry, but I don't. To my knowledge, they haven't contacted the parole officer yet. Once they do, and he sets the process in motion, I'll get back to you with all the information."

"Thank you, Andre. What's the worst-case scenario?"

"Worst case, he's got six months left on the aggravated assault charge, and the gun charge is a misdemeanor that might result in up to one year in jail and or a fine."

"Thank you for letting me know, Andre."

"No problem, Deneisha. I'm just sorry to be the bearer of bad news. But I'll be in touch when I have more information for you."

"Thank you, Andre."

# Chapter Twenty-five

The following morning, Deneisha woke up and waited to hear from Andre. Then there was the minor issue of how she was going to get back to Jacksonville. She didn't have a credit card, so renting a car was out of the question. So it was going to be her catching a bus back to Jacksonville. She thought about calling and asking Miss Vivian to come to pick her up, but it was 250 miles to Jacksonville, and although she was sure she wouldn't mind, Deneisha didn't want to impose. So, the bus was it.

Once she packed the few things that she and Dallas had unpacked, Deneisha called an Uber, and they took her to the bus station. It was Monday afternoon when she heard from Andre. He told her that Dallas would be in court in Tallahassee the following morning.

"Why Tallahassee?"

"That's where he picked up the aggravated assault charge."

"I see," Deneisha said, and she was in Tallahassee when Dallas was arraigned on the gun charge and the parole violation. He received an additional year on his sentence and would be out in eighteen months. She wasn't able to talk to him; all she could do was wave to him with tears in her eyes as they led him away.

The bus ride back to Jacksonville was long, but it gave her a chance to think about her future. Dallas would be gone for the next eighteen months. The question of whether she was going to wait for him wasn't even a question. To her, there was no doubt in her mind that she would be waiting for him when he got out. Dallas had treated her better and shown her more respect, kindness, and understanding than anybody else she'd ever met, man or woman.

The question was what she was going to do for the next eighteen months until he got out. They had almost $600,000 in the account in Curaçao. With that money, she could relax for the next eighteen months and live comfortably and still have plenty of money left over when he got out. Or maybe she would take the next step in the plan. She would find a country that didn't have an extradition treaty with the US, buy a house, and open a small business there.

However, that list included Russia, Zimbabwe, Venezuela, Switzerland, Iceland, Nicaragua, Bolivia, Cuba, Ecuador, and China. Deneisha wasn't the slightest bit interested in living in any of those places.

She briefly entertained the idea of going back to Georgia and seeing what was up with Breezy, maybe even going to see Mrs. Fields to pay her respects for the loss of her daughter, but she quickly ruled that out. As badly as she wanted to do both of those things, there was too much risk in returning to Georgia. Therefore, she resolved herself to remain in Jacksonville until Dallas got out in eighteen months.

One afternoon, Deneisha was at Chili's Restaurant at the River City Marketplace, enjoying a Surf & Turf rib eye at the bar when a man came and sat down next to her. He told the bartender that he was there to pick up a takeout order.

"I'll get that right out to you, sir," the bartender said once the man had paid for his order. While he was waiting, he looked closely at her.

"Deneisha?"

She put her hand on her gun and turned to him slowly. "Yes?"

"You used to run with Dallas. That's you, ain't it?"

"Who's asking?"

"My name is Sherick, Sherick Powers. You came to a pool party at my house."

Deneisha chuckled. "Not my finest hour," she said, recalling that it was the night that she got into a fight with a woman, and they fell into the pool.

"I heard about Dallas getting locked up."

"Off some bullshit."

"Yeah, I heard that too. But anyway, Dallas said you were the best partner he ever had."

Deneisha smiled proudly. "He said that about me?"

"He did. And trust me, that was high praise coming from Dallas."

"I know," she laughed. "Like I said, Dallas never told me that. He wasn't big on passing out compliments."

Sherick moved closer to her and spoke softly. "So, if you don't mind me asking, what you doin' these days?"

Deneisha leaned back and hesitated before asking. "What's it to you?"

"If you're not into anything right now, I may have some work for you. You interested?"

"I'm listening."

"Here's the deal. Dallas sayin' that you were the best partner he ever had meant you don't mind killing a muthafucka, and you're good at it." Sherick paused to wait for her response.

"I'm still listening."

"I got some issues I need to deal with. You would be sort of a bodyguard."

Deneisha looked at and pointed to the man standing by the door who came in with Sherick.

"What about that big gorilla-looking muthafucka right there? Ain't he your bodyguard?"

"He is. But he's more of a blunt force object, and there are times when I need something a little more 'delicate.'" He looked at the man and leaned close to Deneisha. "And besides, in case you haven't noticed, you are much easier on the eyes than he is."

Sherick paused as they handed him his food, and he gave the bartender a big tip.

"Thank you very much, sir. Have a good night," the bartender said and walked away to serve another customer. Sherick turned to Deneisha.

"You don't have to give me an answer right now. Think about it." He signaled to his man.

"Morris, this is Deneisha. Give me a pen."

When Morris gave him a pen, he wrote a number down and handed it to her. She looked at the number and put it in her purse.

"Thank you, but you can have my answer now," Deneisha paused. "If you want it."

"And what would that be?"

"I'm in." She looked at the bartender. "Check, please."

When the bartender got her check, Sherick paid for her meal, and they left Chili's together. As Morris took the food to the car, Sherick walked Deneisha to hers.

"Give me a call tomorrow anytime. We'll get together then and talk about compensation and who and what needs to be done."

"Sounds good." Deneisha shook his hand. "I'll call you tomorrow."

"I will look forward to hearing from you, Deneisha," Sherick said and walked back to his car. Morris opened the door for him, and he got into the Ferrari Purosangue.

"Who was that, Boss?"

"That, my friend, is Deneisha Lewis."

"What's her deal? Other than being fine than a muthafucka, I mean," Morris asked as he started the car and drove away.

"She definitely is that, but Deneisha Lewis is the answer to our Martin, Coleman, and Young problems."

"So I can't fuck her?"

Sherick laughed. "That's Dallas's woman."

"The chick from the pool party?"

"The same."

"Nice titties."

"Yeah, she's definitely rockin' some twins," Sherick said and paused. "But do you wanna fuck with Dallas's woman?"

"Shit, no. Fine as that muthafucka is, that nigga will bust out of jail to kick my ass over her fine ass," Morris laughed. "No, thank you."

"Wise decision, my friend; a wise decision," Sherick said.

# Chapter Twenty-six

The following day, Deneisha tried to call Sherick to discuss what he had in mind for her to do. However, each time she called, Morris answered and told her that Sherick was indisposed and that he would call her back as soon as he was available. That had been going on for the last week, and she hadn't gotten a callback from him. But each time Deneisha called, Morris assured her that, despite appearances, Sherick did want to talk to her, and he definitely had work for her.

"Just be patient with him; he's got a lot goin' right now."

"Okay, Morris. I'll call him back tomorrow." She paused. "How are you doing today, Morris?"

"I'm doing fine. How are you?"

"I'm awesome." She spent more time talking to Morris than she did talking to Sherick, so she thought she might as well try to get to know him.

*Since we're gonna be coworkers,* she thought.

"Hoping I get to see you guys again."

"I know. And I promise you, he wants to see you, and he needs your help. And I personally want to see you again because you are so beautiful. And I mean that in the most respectful way." He laughed. "I certainly don't want you to tell Dallas that Morris is nice, but he be trying to hit on me."

"You don't have to worry about that. He asked, and I told him you've been nothing but sweet to me."

"Thank you. The last thing I need is for Dallas to be mad at me."

"Talk to you tomorrow," Deneisha said, and then she paused. "On second thought, I'll just be patient and wait for him to return my calls. How about that?"

"I'll miss these little conversations, but that'll be fine."

"I'll miss you too, Morris. So maybe you can bug him into calling me."

"I'll see what I can do. Enjoy your evening, Deneisha."

"You too, Morris," she said and ended the call.

Deneisha knew that she needed to be patient with Sherick. Dallas had told her that he was a stand-up guy, and if he said he needed her help and was going to call, then that is what he would do.

"Sherick just has a lot going on," Dallas told her on one of their nightly calls.

Every night at eight, he would call Deneisha, and they would talk until the guard ran him off the phone. It was what kept her going. Those calls were all she had to look forward to. However, Deneisha wondered if she could do this for the next 540 days.

"It's just time."

And time was the one thing that she had plenty of. She didn't go anywhere; she didn't do anything. The only people she knew were Miss Vivian, Preach, and Yvette. Dallas had been her entire world for the last year. She had to laugh at herself because she had become the kind of woman that she constantly criticized.

*A woman who had to be around her man twenty-four-seven, or she'd go crazy.*

So, Deneisha tried to find things to keep herself busy. The only thing that she really enjoyed doing was shopping, but with no money coming in, that wasn't a good idea. She actually gave some thought to planning and executing another job. She could ask Preach to put her on somebody to rob. Deneisha had long suspected that the dealers they robbed were people he put them on to. But she quickly talked herself out of that one. She never thought that she had the head for that planning. And besides, she would need a partner to pull it off. It was times like this that made her realize how alone she was, and that made her miss her girls even more.

She reached out to Ceyonna Bradshaw, the friend from high school who had sent her the text message about Brianna's arrest. She went to the nearest convenience store, bought a burner phone, and made the call. Ceyonna didn't answer the first two times Deneisha called, but she kept calling, and she finally answered.

"Hello."

"Hey, Ceyonna, it's Deneisha."

"Girl."

"That bad?"

"Yeah, Neisha. Breezy flipped on you. She told the cops that it was you and Court with her when she robbed the grocery store. But I heard the cops reneged on the deal they offered her to give you up. They charged her with armed robbery, brandishing a firearm, and conspiracy, and she got ten years. Cops is for sure looking for you, Neisha."

"Thanks, Ceyonna," Deneisha said, and she quickly ended the call.

She removed the SIM card from the phone and retrieved the hammer from the drawer. She spread out a paper towel on the counter and mashed the card. Then she used it on the phone and hit it until it was in pieces. Deneisha took a moment to think that if, by some outside chance, the police were monitoring Ceyonna's phone, they could use the cell phone data and see that the call pinged off a cell tower in Florida.

"Stop it, girl, because now you trippin' for real," she said, shaking her head. "You be watching too many crime shows," a habit she picked up because she was bored. "The cops aren't monitoring Ceyonna's phone."

The following morning at eight o'clock, Deneisha was startled out of her sleep by her phone ringing. She looked at the display and didn't recognize the number. She had made a practice of not answering calls from numbers that she did not recognize. Then she thought about Sherick and decided to take a chance.

"Hello."

"Good morning, Deneisha. I'm sorry if I'm catching you at a bad time."

"No, I was just sitting by the telephone waiting for you to call."

"My bad." Sherick chuckled. "I know I've had you on hold for a minute, and I apologize. I know this may not be any consolation, but I had a lot going on in my little corner of the world. But I *am* sorry about that. It was unavoidable."

"No problem."

"Yes, it is. I know you have better and more important things to do than sit around waiting for me to call."

*If you only knew,* she thought.

"As I said, not a problem," she repeated instead of admitting that she had nothing else to do. "When can we get together?" she asked.

*Please say today,* she thought and crossed her fingers.

"Do you like Indian food?"

"I've never tried Indian food, but I am a foodie, so I am always willing to try new food."

"Great," Sherick said excitedly. "I'm a foodie too. We will get along just fine. Do you know where Masala Mantra is? It's an Indian bistro on North Main Street."

"I can find it."

"Are you free for lunch today?"

"I think I can move some things around to fit you in," Deneisha said, knowing that she had nothing to do and no place to go.

"Great. I'll text you the address and a time. And again, Deneisha, I apologize for having you on hold while I straightened out some things."

"I tell you what. You show up and be on time, and it will go a long way toward you making this right."

"I will see you for lunch."

"And please, remember what I said about being on time," Deneisha said, ending the call. It was something that Sherick didn't appreciate. However, he understood and respected it.

Later that afternoon, Deneisha arrived at Masala Mantra, the Indian bistro on North Main Street, for her lunch meeting with Sherick. When she walked into the place, she was pleasantly surprised to see him sitting at a table, waving, and Morris seated at the bar.

"Thank you for coming, Deneisha," Sherick said when she was escorted to the table and sat down. "You see, I took your request seriously that I be on time."

"And I appreciate it," she said and picked up the menu. "So, what's good here?"

"I recommend we start with the flatbread. It's freshly baked in a clay oven. You said this was your first time having Indian food, right?"

"Right."

"Then I suggest we keep it simple for your virgin palette," Sherick said as the server arrived at the table.

"You folks know what you want?"

"Yes. We're going to start with some of your flatbread."

"Plain? Garlic, onion, or chili?"

"Deneisha?"

"I'll try the garlic."

"And I'm gonna do the chili. She's going to have the Bombay lamb chops, I'll have the Masala Mantra special, and the gentleman at the bar will have the biriyani with shrimp," Sherick ordered, and once their server promised to get that in for them, she disappeared. "Now, let's get down to the business at hand."

"Let's."

"I have some people that I need eliminated."

"Who and how many?"

"Three. Kameron Martin, Javon Coleman, and Tyrell Young."

"Your competition, I take it?"

"Correct."

"Any particular way you want it done?"

"Not really. But I don't want them all to go at once, if you know what I mean."

"I get it. You plan to consolidate power by killing off your competition, but not make it look like you're consolidating power by killing off your competition."

"Exactly," he nodded.

Not only did he find Deneisha to be extremely attractive, but he was also impressed with the way she carried herself. He thought about the advice that he had given Morris about messing around with Dallas's woman.

*Even from jail, Dallas is a dangerous man,* Sherick thought, and thought about Yvette and her repeated threats to cut him down to the white meat when he got to messing around with her too much.

*One word from Dallas, and I'll never see it coming.*

"Here's how I see it going. I'm gonna introduce you to them. You get to know them and how best to go about it."

"I can work with that," Deneisha said as their food arrived. "Any time frame you need this done by?"

"No. Take as much time as you like. The point here is not speed. It needs to be done and done right."

"How much is this job worth to you?" she asked once the server was gone.

"Ten thousand a man."

Deneisha put down her fork and extended her hand. "Consider it done."

With their business concluded, Sherick and Deneisha enjoyed their meal, and he had a chance to get to know her. He found her to be smart, funny, and engaging. She was different from most of the women that he came across. Most of them were only there to see what they could get from him. Deneisha was confident, self-assured, and independent. By the time they said goodbye and agreed to meet the following day to put the plan in motion, Sherick had decided that Deneisha Lewis was worth the risk.

*I can take her from him, and he'll never see it coming,* he thought and laughed aloud. *That nigga's in jail.*

# Chapter Twenty-seven

Deneisha drove away from Masala Mantra feeling good about what she was about to do for Sherick. She had to laugh because now, she was a paid assassin. She had gone from shoplifter to stickup girl, and now, she was an assassin. She paused as she drove to think about what she had signed up for. She wasn't, by any stretch of the imagination, an assassin.

"I'm a stickup girl, not a hit girl," Deneisha said aloud and giggled as she thought about the kick-ass movies and the character "Hit Girl."

But it was true. Deneisha was a stickup girl. She was the kind that sticks the gun in her mark's face and takes their shit. She remembered what Evangeline Blake told her.

"It's when you gotta smoke a muthafucka, and it ain't a matter of you or them, that it gets hard. When you gotta stand in front of a muthafucka and kill them. *That* shit is hard."

*It was good advice,* Deneisha thought.

Well, now that she had taken the job, she was about to find out just how hard it is to stand in front of a muthafucka and kill them.

The following day, Deneisha called Sherick, as promised, to meet one of her targets. He asked if she'd ever been to Venue 841 Riverfront.

"No, I haven't," she said, thinking about the fact that she never went anywhere.

"It's primarily a wedding event venue, but they take anybody's money. On Saturday night, Javon Coleman is having a party for his daughter's twenty-first birthday. I'm gonna introduce you to him socially, of course, as somebody I'm interested in," he said, because he was *very* interested in Deneisha. "From there, I'll leave it to you as to how you go about . . ." he paused and smiled, "completing the assignment before we move on to the next one."

"I know I asked you this once before, but since you have an order that you want this done, do you have a time frame in mind?"

"Not at all," Sherick paused to think about it. "As a matter of fact, it would be better if you take your time. Your plan needs to be tight so none of it blows back on me."

"Naturally," she laughed. "Otherwise, you'd do the shit yourself."

"See, you understand everything, and that is something that everybody can't do. Can't see the forest for the trees. Most of my people, unfortunately, are so focused on the minutia of the situation that they can't even imagine, much less understand, the bigger picture."

Deneisha laughed. "I'm sure some of them don't even know what 'minutia' means, much less understand what you're trying to accomplish."

"And that is why I believe wholeheartedly that I am desperately in need of your skills and your services, Deneisha."

"I'll try not to disappoint you."

"I know you won't. So, listen, I'm gonna pick you up in a limo, and we'll go together to the party."

"I'll text you my address."

"No need. I already know where you live."

"You do?" she questioned angrily. "I don't know how I feel about that."

"Don't you think it makes sense that I know everything about the people I work with?"

"It does, but I still don't know how I feel about that."

"Understandable. But, believe me, it is absolutely necessary for me and the way I like to conduct my business."

"No worries," she said because it wasn't worth making an issue of. She had expressed her displeasure, and now it was time to move on. "So, since you know where I live, what time are you planning on picking me up?"

"About tenish."

"I'll be ready."

"I know I don't have to tell you this, but," Sherick paused. "Wear something nice—no, wear something that will stop the show and turn some heads."

"No, Sherick, you didn't have to tell me, but the fact that you felt you had to say that says a lot about the women you run with."

"Sadly, it does. So, I'll see you around tenish in something that makes people go, 'Damn, that's hot.'"

"Do you have a color preference?"

"Red."

"No problem," she said happily because it gave her an excuse to go shopping for a hot red evening gown. "See you at ten. And, please, be on time."

"I will do my best," he said.

He ended the call even more impressed with Deneisha than he was before. And he was determined to have her, but he would take his time. Turning her head away from Dallas was gonna take time and patience, but Sherick was sure that she was worth it. Therefore, on Saturday night at exactly 9:55, Deneisha's phone rang.

"Good evening, Deneisha."

"Good evening, Sherick," she said, hoping that he wasn't calling to say he was going to be late.

"I am calling to say that I'll be there in five minutes," Sherick said, and Deneisha was impressed. "You see, I took your request to be on time seriously."

"If you hang around me long enough, you'll find that is one of my pet peeves."

"One that I will do my best to live up to."

"See that you do," she said, and it made him smile. None of the women that he'd been associating with for years had ever stood up to him and told him what their expectations of him were.

"Well, we're here. Our driver should be ringing your bell any second now," he said as the doorbell rang.

"See you in a few," she said, ending the call and opening the door when the bell rang.

"Miss Lewis?"

"Yes."

"I'm Denard. I'll be your driver this evening."

"Good evening, Denard. Let me get my purse, and I'll be right with you," she said, and went and got her mini crystal mesh shoulder bag, and they headed for the limo.

When Sherick saw Deneisha coming toward the limo on Denard's arm, he got out and was standing by the door when she arrived.

"I just have to say that you look amazing, Deneisha," Sherick said of the red sleeveless dress with the plunging V-neck neckline that she was wearing the shit out of.

"Thank you, Sherick." She accepted his hand. "You look very handsome too," Deneisha said, feeding him the compliment he was fishing for. He was wearing a midnight blue satin suit jacket, an open chest satin dress shirt, and flared trousers.

When they arrived at Venue 841, located on the south bank of the St. Johns River in downtown Jacksonville, Sherick had a question.

"This may seem like a stupid question, but are you armed?"

"Yes. I'm carrying a Sig Sauer P320 compact in my purse," she said as they approached the venue.

Something else she went shopping for when she found that her .380 was too big for her Stella McCartney bag. Preach wasn't available, so Yvette took her to somebody she knew and could trust.

"Why? Are they gonna try to take it away from me?"

"No," Sherick chuckled. "Half the muthafuckas in there are probably armed. I ask because you are my security for the evening."

"I did notice that Morris was conspicuous by his absence."

"You don't have a problem with that, do you?"

"No, but in the future, you need to let me know things like that in advance so I can plan accordingly. Is that understood?"

"Perfectly," Sherick said as he presented his invitation to the event, and they were escorted to a table. "There's Javon Coleman."

"Talking loudly at the center of the table?"

"That's him. Coleman likes to be at the center of attention." He laughed. "Even at the cost of upstaging his daughter's event."

"I see. That explains why she looks miserable at her own party."

"Honestly, she can't stand his ass, but she puts on a good front. Wouldn't wanna get cut out of the money." Sherick leaned closer to Deneisha. "A fate that befell the wife and his firstborn daughter."

"That's a story for another time. But that may be an angle I can exploit to get the job done." Deneisha smiled. "Without her knowledge, of course."

"Of course."

Shortly after, the evening meal was served. "I hope you don't mind, but I took the liberty of ordering for us."

"Something that I would prefer you didn't do."

"The choice was chicken, fish, or beef. But I promise that won't happen again."

"Not a problem, because it was just a choice of meats. What did you choose for us?"

"Chicken." He nodded. "I know I shouldn't stereotype you, but you *are* Black. I ain't met a nigga yet who wasn't raised on some barnyard pimp."

"True. The chicken is fine, but like I said, that needs to be the last time." Deneisha smiled. "We'll learn how to work with each other. It's about respecting boundaries."

"Absolutely," Sherick said as the servers set the plates in front of them.

While dinner was served, Joven Coleman chose that time to make a toast to his daughter. It was a long and cheesy speech, and from Deneisha's vantage point, it seemed the daughter felt the same way, as it was more about him than her birthday. When the toast was over, he took that opportunity to come around to each table to welcome his guests and brag about what an amazing event he had put on.

"Sherick!" Coleman shouted. Sherick stood up. "Glad you could make it," he said and shook hands with Sherick, but his eyes were on Deneisha.

"Glad to be invited. This is my guest, Deneisha Lewis."

Coleman bowed at the waist and planted a wet kiss on her hand.

"It is truly my pleasure to meet you, Miss Lewis."

"Good to meet you as well, Mr. Coleman," she said, fighting the urge to wipe her hand on something. "And, please, it's Deneisha."

"Well then, it has to be Javon," he said, grinning. "Thanks again for coming," he said to Sherick. Next, he turned to Deneisha. "I hope I'll see you again."

Deneisha looped her arm in Sherick's. "If you see Sherick, I'm sure you'll see me," she said, remembering that she was playing the role of somebody he was interested in. And as a matter of respect.

Now that they had accomplished their objective, Deneisha and Sherick gave the birthday girl the envelope they had brought for her, and they left the event. As they walked to the car, Deneisha had a question.

"Which car is Coleman's?"

Sherick looked around and pointed. "It's the white Lotus Emira," he said as Deneisha started walking toward it. "Where you goin'?"

"You hired me to do a job, right? Well, this is where it starts."

When Deneisha and Sherick arrived at the car, she looked around to see if anyone was watching, and then she attached a tracking device to the vehicle's bumper.

"What's that?" Sherick asked as they walked away from the car.

"It's a tracking system that will monitor his location and send the data to my phone. This way, I can track where he goes so I can see where the best place is to hit him."

"Smart."

"Thank you."

On the way back to Deneisha's condo, Sherick thought about saying something clever in an attempt to prolong their evening together, but he quickly dispelled that idea.

*Take it slow,* he thought as he glanced at Deneisha.

"I think that went well."

"I think so too. But let's get together sometime tomorrow, and you can give me more details about Coleman. And you can tell me the story about the wife and the firstborn daughter."

"We can do that. Have you ever been to a restaurant called Marker 32?"

"No, I haven't."

"It's a seafood restaurant in Jax Beach. I'll text you the address. What time is good for you?"

"I have an appointment in the morning," she lied. "So, let's say one o'clock?"

"One o'clock it is."

When they got to her condo, the driver got out to open Deneisha's door, and Sherick got out too. He politely walked her to her door and bid her good night. "See you for lunch tomorrow." Sherick started walking. "And I will be on time."

"Thank you," Deneisha said, and she went into the condo.

# Chapter Twenty-eight

Over the next two weeks, Deneisha tracked her prey. In addition to monitoring Coleman, Deneisha saw quite a bit of Sherick. They were both foodies, so they got together to share a meal and for Sherick to hear her report on her progress. That evening, they were dining at Restaurant Orsay, a French restaurant located on Park Street.

Over marinated calamari, Prince Edward Island mussels, pan-roasted duck breast, and Berkshire pork chops, they discussed the fact that Coleman was a creature of habit, so he followed a routine daily. The only difference in his daily agenda was which woman he saw and how many.

"This would be a good time to tell me about the wife and the firstborn daughter."

"The wife's name is Rosaland, and the firstborn daughter is Melviena. The story goes that Rosaland got tired of his philandering ways, and she got a lover. His name was Lucas, and he was a small-time dealer who sold for Coleman. He hears about the affair, and the next thing you know, Lucas's car gets blown up in front of his apartment." Sherick laughed. "So, as you can imagine, Lucas wants nothing else to do with Rosaland. But Coleman, he's a vindictive muthafucka, so instead of divorcing his cheating wife, he exiles her to Starke."

"Starke? What is that?"

"Not a what. It's a place. Starke is a small town in Florida with a population of approximately 5,000 people. Coleman bought her a four-bedroom, four-bath, 4,000-square-foot house for $700,000. Now, Rosaland carries it like she's some big-time socialite, so having to live in this one-horse town is killing her. But if she wants to keep her money and her access to it, she's behaving herself, hoping to make a comeback."

"Not gonna happen. He's getting too much stray pussy to go back to her," Deneisha added. "What about the daughter?"

"She objects to what daddy did to her mother, and she decides to make a stand, you know, on her mother's behalf. So, Melviena tells her father that she's quitting college. Mind you, the child is a brainiac, so she has a scholarship to the University of Miami, is on the dean's list, and the whole nine. She's driving a BMW M4, got a Miami Beach condo, and an AmEx Centurion Black Card. Daddy closed the account and had her evicted from the condo. Then she asked him what she was supposed to do."

"What did dear old dad say?"

"He told her to come home and get a job." Sherick paused. "Now she works as a customer service rep at some phone company, I'm not sure which one."

"Ouch."

"So you know the other daughter sees this and wants no parts of it. At that point, she became Daddy's favorite, and he showers her with all kinds of shit and makes sure the wife and other daughter know all about it. I heard they were at the birthday party, but I didn't see them there."

"So we know he's a vindictive, petty, muthafucka," Deneisha said, but knew that wasn't something that she planned to use. Was it good information?

*Perhaps*. But to Deneisha, it was just gossip.

"When do you think you'll be ready?" Sherick asked.

"I thought you didn't have a time frame."

"I don't," he said.

Although he wanted the work done, he was enjoying spending time with Deneisha, so he was in no hurry at all.

"Yes, you do." Deneisha sipped her cocktail. "But you'll be happy to hear that I'm ready. So the question is, and I do have a preference here, how much do you want to know?"

"Nothing."

"That would be my preference."

"I want to have as little accountability as possible," Sherick laughed. "If I hear about it on the news, that's fine with me."

"Nothing, it is." Deneisha raised her glass. "To Javon Coleman."

"May he rest in peace," Sherick said.

The following day, Deneisha put her plan in motion. Each day, Coleman visited different women. It was when he was most vulnerable. He had a bodyguard who walked him to the woman's place and then returned to the car, waiting until Coleman came out. He may have seen many women, but Nakeisha was his favorite.

Coleman went to see her every afternoon at the same time and was sure to leave at just about the same time. One day, while she was waiting for him to come out, Deneisha became curious about the pattern, so after Coleman left, she hung around for a while and was there when a car pulled into the driveway. A well-dressed man got out of the vehicle and went to the mailbox. Afterward, he walked to the house, sorted through the mail, and then unlocked the door and went inside.

"That answers *that* question," Deneisha said and started the car.

She thought about shooting Coleman as he came out of the house, but she moved away from that idea. There were too many potential eyes from so many windows on the block, not to mention Ring doorbell cameras. Fortunately, she had another spot in mind. Coleman didn't see her every day like he did with Nakeisha, but every Thursday afternoon, he had dinner with Naomi Burke. After dinner, they'd go back to her apartment, and he'd be in there for at least an hour and a half.

Naomi's apartment was on the second floor, right next to the stairwell. Deneisha waited until he returned to the apartment with her and noted the time. She waited for an hour before she went inside, walking right past his bodyguard. Deneisha took the stairs and waited for Coleman to emerge from the apartment. When she heard the door open, she came out of the stairwell and walked up behind Coleman.

Deneisha aimed her silencer-clad weapon and shot him in the back of the head. When his body dropped to the floor, she shot him once more in the back. She turned quickly, returned to the stairwell, and walked down the steps. She left the building, expecting to see Coleman's bodyguard at the door, but he wasn't there. When she arrived at her car, she saw him talking to a woman.

"Even better," Deneisha said as she drove away from the scene.

She left, thinking about what she had done and how it was easier than she had thought it would be, and questioned what that said about her.

# Chapter Twenty-nine

Sherick was at his house when his girlfriend, Trissa Winslow, informed him that his lieutenant, Taquan McClure, was there to see him.

"He says it's important," Trissa said.

"Take him to the den," Sherick said and got out of the Jacuzzi. Once he dried himself, he put on a robe and went to the den to see what was so important.

"Have you heard?" Taquan asked excitedly the second Sherick entered the room.

"Heard what?" Sherick asked as he went to the bar. He retrieved a bottle of water from the refrigerator and sat down.

"About Coleman?"

When Sherick heard Coleman's name, it immediately piqued his interest. "What about Coleman?"

Taquan chuckled. "He's dead. One of his hoes found him dead outside her apartment last night."

"That is good news," Sherick said, knowing that he now owed Deneisha $10,000, but it was money well spent. "With Coleman out of the way, we can move on the Brentwood Apartments."

"I'll make that happen," Taquan said and was about to leave the den to carry out his task, but Sherick stopped him.

"Don't fuck it up."

"I won't. I swear, that was a one-off," Taquan replied. He had made a mistake that cost Sherick a lot of money.

"Make sure it doesn't happen again."

"Yes, sir," he said and left the den.

As soon as Taquan was gone, Sherick picked up the phone and called Deneisha.

"Good afternoon, Sherick," Deneisha answered.

"How are you doing today, Deneisha?"

"I'm awesome. What about you?"

"I'm fine. I was wondering if you were free for dinner this evening."

"I believe I can fit you in."

"You can? That is so nice of you, Deneisha."

"Yes, it is," she giggled rather uncharacteristically. "Where and when would you like to get together?"

"Are you familiar with a rooftop steakhouse called Cowford Chophouse?"

"I am," she lied rather than tell him that she didn't go anywhere. She googled the spot. "It's a steak house on Bay Street downtown, right?"

"Exactly."

"What time?"

"I can send a car for you at five."

"That's fine."

"Great. See you tonight," Sherick said, and he ended the call with Deneisha as Trissa came into the den.

"Who was that?"

"My assassin," he replied, and drained the bottle of water.

"Do you always invite your assassin to dinner at one of the best restaurants in the city?"

"I do if the business is important enough. And in case you're wondering, it is. It is that important."

"Why do I get the feeling that your so-called assassin is a woman?"

"Because she is a woman."

"So this is a date and not a business meeting, am I right?"

"No," Sherick chuckled. "It is a business dinner. One that is gonna change the way we do business." He looked at the outfit Trissa was wearing. "How much that outfit cost you?"

"Excuse me?"

"I asked you how much I spent on that outfit you're wearing."

Trissa was wearing a Bottega Veneta Jacquard mini-dress and woven straw platform sandals.

"I don't know."

"Want me to tell you?"

Trissa frowned and shifted her weight to one leg. "Go ahead."

"That dress cost me seven grand, the shoes were another four hundred, and that Harlequin-hinged cuff bracelet you're wearing, it was only three hundred. We not even gonna clock the cost of all that jewelry you're rocking. That's got to cost at least, what, four, five grand?"

"Your point?"

"My point is that if you wanna keep dressing the way you do, you'll be all for this expansion and not worry about whether my assassin is a woman," he said in no uncertain terms.

"Okay, Sherick, you don't have to get all pissy about it," Trissa said, turning on her heels and walking out of the den.

Later that evening at the Cowford Chophouse, Deneisha and Sherick were enjoying tuna tartare and seared crab cake appetizers, as well as filet mignon with fried oysters, North Country bacon, crab meat, and asparagus.

"Do you remember Javon Coleman, the guy whose daughter's birthday party we went to?"

"I remember. What about him?"

"His body was found outside one of his girlfriends' apartments."

"Was he murdered?" Deneisha asked innocently.

"It seems so."

"That's terrible. Do the police have any suspects in the murder?"

"I don't know. But that is a good question," he said, and thought it might be a good idea if he checked with one of the cops he was paying off to see if the police were investigating the murder of a known drug dealer that they've been trying to arrest for years. And if they were, did they have a suspect? "I got some people I can ask about that."

"How is that inquiry gonna make you look?"

"I'll frame it in reference to how his murder affects my business."

"Naturally, my concern is that your inquiry be taken as an admission of some possible involvement on your part."

"And your concern is well-founded, but not necessary. The people I intend to make this inquiry are in my pocket. My self-interest is to their benefit."

"As long as there's a slice of pie for everybody?"

"Exactly."

"Let's talk about who's next."

"Kameron Martin. But let's enjoy this delicious filet mignon." He held up his glass. "And this wine, what is it?"

"I think he said it was a Crossfork Creek Merlot."

"Whatever. Let's just enjoy the meal, let me savor the sweet flavor of victory, and we'll talk about Kameron Martin tomorrow."

Deneisha smiled. "We can do that," she said, and there was no more discussion about business. So they talked, and somehow the topic of conversation turned to music. Deneisha mentioned that she would have loved to get tickets to see Salomé Warner in concert.

"But it's sold out," she said sadly.

Sherick smiled a devilish smile. "I just happened to have two tickets to tonight's show."

"You do?"

"I do."

"You wouldn't be interested in selling one of those tickets, would you?"

"No, I wouldn't be interested in selling one of them, but I would be more than happy to have you as my guest."

"Wait a minute. I'm not saying that I don't want to go because I do, but if you have tickets, I'm gonna assume you were going with somebody."

"And you would be correct," Sherick said, and now it was time to lie. "To be honest, I'm the Salomé Warner fan. The lady was just going because I wanted to go."

"If she's not into Salomé Warner—I mean, *really* into Salomé Warner," Deneisha smiled a devilish smile, "then it wouldn't be fair to make her sit through an entire concert."

"I don't think so either. So, what do you say?"

"I say I think you should take me to see Salomé Warner."

"I think that's only fair," Sherick replied.

After they left the Cowford Chophouse, Sherick had the limo take Deneisha home so she could change her outfit.

"I'd ask why you think you need to change your outfit. You look amazing, but I know better than to ask a woman about her wardrobe."

"A wise man," she said as they arrived at her condo. "Why don't you come back in an hour. I should be ready by then."

"One hour. I'm sure I don't have to tell you to please be on time," he said jokingly.

"I'll see what I can do," Deneisha said, and she got out of the limo.

Sherick told the driver to stay put, and he took out his phone to call and break the sad news to Trissa. Even though he had his eye on Deneisha, Sherick wasn't ready to let Trissa go just yet. Trissa was a huge Salomé Warner fan and had been looking forward to the concert for weeks. He told her a story about a friend in trouble who needed him to go over something and help resolve it.

"I understand," Trissa said sadly.

"Tell you what. Salomé Warner is gonna be in Miami on Saturday night. Why don't we fly down there and see the show? We can stay at the Mandarin Oriental. Would that make up for tonight?"

"Yes, yes, it would make up for tonight." Trissa paused to think. "Can we leave like the first thing in the morning? I'm gonna need to shop for a new outfit to wear to the concert in Miami."

"Of course you do," Sherick agreed. "Go ahead and make reservations for us, and I'll see you in a couple of hours."

"Okay. And make sure your friend knows what a sacrifice I'm making."

"I already told him, and he said to tell you that he appreciates you and your sacrifice. Gotta go, Trissa."

"I'll probably be asleep when you get home. So I'll see you in the morning."

"You sure you don't want me to wake you up when I get home?"

Trissa giggled. "You wanna wake me up, don't you?"

"I do. After spending my night with a bunch of men instead of my soft, sweet woman, yeah, I'm gonna wanna wake you up."

"You can try it and see what happens, but I'm not making any promises."

"Bye, Trissa," Sherick said, and he ended the call.

With Trissa taken care of, Sherick was free to enjoy his evening with Deneisha. In exactly one hour from the time she got out of the limo, her phone rang.

"I'm ready."

"I'm outside. I'll send Denard up to get you."

"No need. I'll be right down," Deneisha said, and she left her condo.

Her new outfit consisted entirely of Prada leather: a stretch Nappa jacket and a leather miniskirt that hugged her curves. To top it off, she wore Nappa leather boots and a thigh-length leather coat.

As she always did, Salomé Warner put on a fantastic show. Deneisha and Sherick enjoyed the performance and each other's company. When the night was over, Denard drove them back to Deneisha's condo, and Sherick escorted her to her door.

"Good night, Sherick. And thank your friend again for giving up her tickets so the real Salomé Warner fan could get their Salomé on," Deneisha said and shook her body the way she had seen Salomé shake hers.

"I'll be sure to tell her." Sherick looked Deneisha over from head to toe as she moved and shook his head. "Good night, Deneisha. I'm glad you enjoyed yourself." He started to walk away. "Oh yeah, what's your schedule look like for tomorrow?"

"Call me around one, and we'll get together for dinner or whatever," Deneisha said and unlocked her door. "Good night, Sherick."

"Talk to you tomorrow," he said as he walked down the hall, thinking about how well this was working out. But then he remembered that he was gonna be in Miami tomorrow with Trissa.

The following afternoon, at one o'clock, Sherick used the same excuse to get away from Trissa to call Deneisha and apologize for missing their appointment.

"I'm sorry, but I had to go out of town first thing this morning. It couldn't be helped."

"If it couldn't be helped, it couldn't be helped," Deneisha said and wondered what she was gonna do for dinner now that Sherick canceled on her. She had started looking forward to what she called their "foodie sessions." Sherick only ate in the finest restaurants in the city, and she was beginning to enjoy the time they shared.

*He's turning out to be a good friend,* she thought, because, to her, that's all it was. She was lonely without Dallas in her life, so she was glad for the company.

"I'll call you when I get back, and we'll get together," he promised.

"Talk to you then," Deneisha said.

She ended the call thinking that she didn't have to wait for Sherick to eat out. She called Yvette to see if she wanted to join her for dinner.

# Chapter Thirty

When Sherick returned to Jacksonville, he and Deneisha met for lunch at Mambos Cuban Café to discuss Kameron Martin, who was also having lunch at the same place. Sherick introduced Deneisha. However, Martin already knew who she was.

"Really?" Deneisha questioned.

"Javon Coleman." Martin crossed himself. "May God have mercy on his soul, mentioned you."

"I'm surprised," Deneisha said. "I only met Mr. Coleman once."

"Apparently, you made quite an impression."

"Deneisha is an impressive woman," Sherick finally said.

"Well, Deneisha, it was my pleasure to meet you in person."

"Same here," she said and sat down.

"Good to see you," Sherick said, shaking Martin's hand.

"Don't lie in front of the pretty lady, Mr. Powers. You know you're *not* glad to see me." Martin laughed. "You wouldn't mind at all if I were dead along with our friend Coleman." He looked at Deneisha. "Ain't that more like the truth?"

"It is. In fact, I would much rather have seen *you* dead than Coleman. Coleman was a weak-minded fool who thought pussy and personal vendettas were more important than his business."

Martin laughed loudly and heartily. "Now, you're telling the truth."

"I've never made a secret of the fact that I don't like you."

Sherick got in his face to say, "I respect you and the way you do business, so yeah, you dead and out of my hair would have been preferable to Coleman."

Martin nodded. "I'll take that as the backhanded compliment it was meant to be and keep it moving." He turned to Deneisha. "Once again, the honor in us meeting was all mine," he said, then snapped his fingers. The two men accompanying him got up and followed him out of Mambos.

Sherick sat down.

"I wonder if his knowing who I am is good or bad for us," Deneisha said.

"I don't think it concerns us. I'm sure, knowing Coleman, he mentioned you purely as somebody I'm fuckin' and his envy that I am and he's not."

Deneisha laughed. "You're probably right."

"Now that you've met him, what do you think?"

"I think his arrogance will make him an easier target than Coleman. He won't see it coming. He's counting on the goon squad to watch his back while he talks all the shit he wants."

"Good call. Those two goons are Anderson and Freeman. They've been protecting him for years. You're gonna have to get him away from them or kill them too."

"I'm gonna have to kill them. I can see that already," Deneisha said, watching from the window as Martin, Anderson, and Freeman got in a candy-apple red X3 BMW. "What else do I need to know about them?"

Sherick handed Deneisha a piece of paper. "That is all of his personal info. Address, cell number, his secret sidepiece's number, and her address. Also, you'll see the name, address, and number of his legitimate businesses."

Deneisha looked at the paper. “Titan Contractors and Cityscape Architects.” She nodded and put the paper in her purse. “How much time does he devote to his legit businesses?”

“Not much. Martin’s a pimp, a gambler, and a drug dealer. His half brother Zach runs the legit businesses and does his best to keep Martin out of his way.”

“Weak spot?”

“Maybe. But I’ll leave that up to you.” Deneisha nodded. “We never did talk about how to pay you for your services.”

Deneisha took a business card from her purse. “Transfer the funds to this account.”

Sherick took the card. “Consider that invoice paid in full.”

“I’ll consider it paid in full when it’s paid in full. Until then—” She stood up, “it’s an outstanding debt. I’ll be in touch,” she said and left Sherick at Mambos Cuban Café.

That afternoon, Deneisha went to the Enterprise rental counter at the airport and rented a Chevrolet Equinox. The following day, she was at the office of Titan Contractors. Call it a hunch, call it what you want, but Deneisha had a feeling that Martin would show up there.

By lunchtime, she started to think that there was nothing to her hunch and decided to pick Martin up at either his house or his sidepiece’s house when a candy-apple red X3 BMW pulled into the parking lot. Anderson and Freeman got out, and Anderson opened the door for Martin, who went inside, leaving Freeman to watch the car. Deneisha walked around to the blind side of the BMW and placed her tracker on the rear bumper before returning to her vehicle and driving away.

Her next stop was the home of Martin’s sidepiece, Carmen Pereira. Deneisha waited until she came out of the house and followed her as she set out to run errands. When she got to the dry cleaners, it was when Deneisha had her first opportunity to place her tracking device on Carmen's Ford F-150. By the end of the week, Deneisha had tracking devices on all of the vehicles she could attribute to Martin. They painted a picture of Martin's pattern, but Deneisha didn't see a clear-cut place to hit him like she did with Coleman.

*So much for easy,* she thought.

With the easy way off the table, Deneisha knew she would have to work to kill Kameron Martin. She returned to the airport and rented another car from Enterprise, just in case someone spotted the Chevy Equinox. This time, she rented a Toyota Corolla. With it being the most rented car in America, Deneisha thought she'd blend nicely into the background.

The data from the tracker, as well as her own surveillance, indicated that most of Martin's recent activity was centered on a construction project in Fleming Island. This unincorporated community sat twenty-one miles north of downtown Jacksonville. However, Deneisha had ruled that out because the Fleming Island location was isolated, which would make escape planning more difficult.

Deneisha was parked out of Martin's sidepiece's house when, suddenly, Martin came running out of the house, barking orders to his men. They dropped what they were doing and rushed to the BMW. All three piled into the vehicle and sped away. Deneisha started up the car and followed them as they sped north on I-95.

"Looks like they're headed for the construction site," she said aloud as she followed the BMW. As she suspected, they were heading for the Fleming Island construction site. Deneisha thought that this might be the opportunity she'd been waiting for.

When they arrived at the site, she watched as Martin got out of the BMW and ran into the construction office.

She sat wondering what the problem was, but soon realized that it wasn't her concern. Her only concern, at that point, was the fact that Anderson and Freeman were not with him.

After a while, Martin came out of the office with a man that Deneisha assumed was the project manager. When they started walking to the site, she took out her weapon and followed them. Since she knew it would come in handy one day to blend in with the rest of the workers, she had stolen a construction helmet and a vest. Deneisha followed them and was glad she had worn her Chelsea leather ankle boots instead of the Schutz knee-high boots she had initially planned to wear.

She had selected her spot, and now, it was just a matter of waiting for her prey to come into her sights, and then she could collect another easy ten grand. Deneisha took aim and was ready to shoot when Anderson and Freeman came running up to Martin.

"Great, just great," she moaned and lowered her weapon.

As the project manager walked away, Martin stood there, apparently explaining the problem to his men. When they started walking back to the BMW, Deneisha observed how they were walking with Anderson, who was leading the way, and Freeman followed behind Martin. Suddenly, she saw an opportunity. Deneisha raised her weapon, took a deep breath, and came out running from her position.

She fired.

Her first shot hit Anderson in the head.

Deneisha fired again as she ran.

Her second shot hit Martin in the chest.

By that time, Freeman was reaching for his gun.

However, before he could get it out, Deneisha hit him with a head shot. Then she walked up on her fallen prey and shot each one again. She shot Martin in the head. And then she shot Anderson and Freeman once each in the chest. Finished, she quickly walked back to her car and got in. Deneisha started the car and drove away, thinking that she had killed Anderson and Freeman for free, and thought seriously about telling Sherick that it was worth at least a grand or two apiece to kill them.

However, she quickly dismissed that idea because changing the terms of the deal would make her seem unprofessional in Sherick's eyes. Deneisha had to remember that it wasn't just *her* reputation on the line; it was also Dallas's reputation as well that she had to protect. She had made a deal with Sherick to kill three men, and she was going to stick by it. Anderson and Freeman were collateral damage who were killed to make her assassination of Martin easier.

"Okay, okay," Deneisha said aloud as she cruised down I-95, heading back to Jacksonville. She knew how important Dallas's reputation was and not to let her greed force her to make other choices.

As she drove, Deneisha wanted to call Sherick so badly and say, "Two down" before ending the call. But that too would speak to her professionalism, or lack thereof. She had agreed that she wouldn't tell Sherick it was done or send him an email or a text with a proof of death image of Martin and his bodyguards lying facedown in the dirt at this time.

*It would have made a great picture,* Deneisha thought as she passed the Jacksonville city limits.

# Chapter Thirty-one

Since Sherick was in Miami with Trissa, it was three days later when Deneisha got a call from him inviting her to join him for dinner at River & Post, a rooftop lounge on Riverside Avenue.

"Thank you for meeting me, Deneisha," Sherick said when she sat down at the table with him. He had only just heard about Martin's untimely death from Taquan when he returned to the city. Needless to say, it was welcome information, to say the least.

He told Deneisha that his trip out of the city was necessary to address a supply issue, but it wasn't a planned trip. He told her that it had him thinking about investing in automation and technology, as well as diversifying his suppliers to protect himself from risk.

Over their lobster Louis salad, dynamite shrimp, and seared sea scallops, Sherick took out his phone and transferred $10,000 to Deneisha's offshore account in Curaçao.

"Is it all right to talk about your third target, or did you want to savor the flavor of this too?"

"No," Sherick said and laughed.

He knew that if he didn't make his move on Deneisha soon, it would be too late. Once she killed Tyrell Young, there would be no need for these meetings, and he would lose his opportunity to get with her. Not only that, but the clock was also ticking; Dallas would eventually get released from prison.

"We can talk about Tyrell Young."

But Sherick could tell that there was something different about Deneisha that day. He wondered what it could be and, more importantly, how her mood would affect him and his agenda.

"Is everything all right?" he asked.

"Yes, everything is fine. Why do you ask?"

"I don't know. You just seem a little down today, and you're usually so, I don't know, upbeat."

Deneisha laughed. "Upbeat? I've never been described as being upbeat. No, Sherick, everything is great in my world. If it's anything, it's me missing Dallas."

That wasn't what he wanted to hear, but he went with it. "I completely understand."

Deneisha reached across the table and touched his hand. It sent chills all over his body.

"But you've been such a good friend, and I want you to know that I appreciate it."

*The friend zone. Shit,* he said to himself.

"No worries. You're good—what am I talking about? You're a great company, so it is truly my pleasure to hang out with you."

"Still," Deneisha said, finally letting go of Sherick's hand, "I just want you to know that I appreciate you."

It was at that point that their server chose to return to the table. "Is everything all right here?"

"Everything was delicious. You can go ahead and bring the check," Sherick said, and the server got their ticket and placed it on the table.

"I'll take that whenever you're ready," the server said, and she left the table.

"Do you have any plans for this evening?"

"Nothing I can't rearrange," Deneisha said because she had nothing to do and planned a quiet night in front of the television with some chips and a bottle of Mountain Dew.

"Come with me. There are some people I want you to meet," he said.

It was time to step things up and bring Deneisha into the fold before it was too late and Dallas was released from prison.

"Okay," Deneisha said and stood up.

She walked a little ahead of him as he paid the check. When he finished at the cash register, Sherick rushed to catch up with her.

"Where are we going?"

"I told you there are some people I want you to meet."

"Your people?"

"Yes. These are my people."

Deneisha smiled playfully. "I was starting to think I was some kind of secret, or you were ashamed of me, or something."

Sherick looked at her, and a look of pure terror washed across his face. "No, no, nothing like that."

Deneisha laughed. "I was just trippin', Sherick. That was just me trying to act like a jealous female."

Sherick laughed. "You had me for a minute. I was like, where is this coming from?" he said, glad to know that she had a sense of humor.

"Believe me, that is *not* who I am," Deneisha laughed as they got to the parking lot. Morris saw him coming and got out of the car. "Hey, Morris."

He bowed slightly. "Pleasure to see you, as always, Deneisha."

Morris opened the door to an Alfa Romeo Giulia.

"Is this new?"

"No, it's not."

"The last time I saw you—never mind."

"What?"

"The last time I saw you, you were driving a Ferrari, but you can have more than one car. My bad."

"No worries. Why don't you ride with us? Your car will be safe here, and Morris will be more than happy to bring you back to it."

"Okay," Deneisha agreed, and Morris opened the back door. When she started to get into the backseat, he stopped her.

"Beautiful women sit in the front seat," Morris said as Sherick got into the backseat.

"Thank you, Morris," Deneisha said, accepting his hand and the gesture.

Morris then drove them to the house where his people hung out. Since he rarely came to the house, they were surprised when they saw Morris pull up in the Alfa Romeo.

"Who's that he got with him?" Davenport asked.

Taquan came to the window. "Never seen her before. But we're about to find out," he said, and went to the door and opened it as Sherick and Deneisha got there.

"What's up, Sherick?" Taquan said and allowed them into the house.

"Deneisha Lewis, these are my lieutenants. That is Taquan McClure, that's Hugh Davenport, and that's Julian Barker, but we call him Jules."

"Nice to meet all of you," Deneisha said politely.

"Come on, Deneisha," Sherick said, and he led her out on the deck. "Can I get you anything?"

"No, I'm fine," she said and sat down. Now that she had met "*his people,*" Deneisha wondered what came next. Sherick sat across from her.

"So, let's talk about Tyrell Young," he said, taking out his phone and handing it to Deneisha.

"That him?"

"Yes. Naturally, I'll introduce you to him."

"In the meantime, why don't you tell me what his deal is?"

From there, Sherick told Deneisha more about Tyrell Young than he did about the other two targets. As he described Young's operation in detail, it left her with the impression that Tyrell Young was the main one that Sherick needed out of his way.

"I don't mean to insult you, but are you dressed appropriately to go to the club and have a drink?"

That night, Deneisha was dressed in a Brunello Cucinelli silk dress and Christian Louboutin leather boots.

"Not really. Why?"

"Young owes a club called Mais. That's where we're going. So, does Morris need to take you home so you can change?"

"Yes, he does," Deneisha said excitedly because she hadn't been to a club since she'd been in Jacksonville. Dallas wasn't into the club scene. Therefore, like playing video games, Dallas saw it as a waste of time and would have no parts of it.

Sherick got up and called for Morris to take Deneisha home to change her outfit and then come back and get him. When she returned, she was wearing a Tom Ford draped cocktail minidress and Schutz leather stiletto pumps.

"You look amazing, but you always do," he said, and they left the house.

When they arrived at Mais, which meant "More" in Portuguese, they were escorted to the VIP room by a member of Young's security staff.

"Is Mr. Young available?" Sherick asked.

"He's in the club," the young man said. "I'll check if he's available to see you."

"Thank you," Sherick said and handed the security guard a twenty-dollar bill.

"Thank you, sir."

"Please send a server over here."

"Right away, sir," he said and walked away happy.

After that, it didn't take long for word to spread that Sherick Powers was in the club, and he was tipping.

"Twenty dollars for taking them to a table," he said, holding up the bill. "Is Young in the house?"

"He is," Rita, one of the servers, said, grabbing her tray. "I'm going to make some of that money."

"Go on and get it, girl. I ain't mad at you," the young security officer shouted as Rita left the room to go make that money. Once she had taken their order, she got the drinks and returned to the table with them.

"Is Mr. Young in the club tonight?"

"Yes, he is. Would you like me to tell him that you wanna speak with him?"

"Yes. Please tell Mr. Young that Sherick Powers would like a moment of his time," Sherick said and placed a hundred-dollar bill on Rita's tray.

"Not a problem. I'll be back with your change."

"You can keep the change," Sherick said.

A few minutes later, Rita returned to the VIP room, and she went straight to Sherick's table.

"I spoke with Mr. Young and told him that you wanted to speak with him."

"Thank you," Sherick said, and the server went on about her business.

"So, why do you want to see him?" Deneisha asked.

"No reason in particular. I wanted you to lay eyes on him, and besides, I just like showing you off," he said as Tyrell Young came into the VIP room. "There he is."

He spotted Sherick, and then he laid eyes on Deneisha. And after talking to a few people, Young came to their table. Sherick stood up when he saw him coming.

"Sherick," Young shouted as he approached the table. "How's it going?"

"Doing fine." Sherick turned to Deneisha. "I'd like to introduce you to Deneisha Lewis." She stood up and extended her hand.

"It's an honor to meet you, Mr. Young."

"Please, Miss Lewis, call me Tyrell."

"Well then, you have to call me Deneisha."

"It would be my pleasure, Deneisha." Young bowed at the waist and kissed her hand. "It was nice meeting you."

"What is it with your friends and kissing my hand?" Deneisha asked when Young left the VIP room. With their purpose for being at Mais accomplished, the two of them finished their drinks and left.

"That's Young's ride over there," Sherick said, pointing to an Audi A8 Founder's Edition.

"Thank you," Deneisha said, and she approached the car and placed her tracking device on the bumper. "Let's go."

The following morning and over the next few weeks, Deneisha tracked Young's movements. He wasn't as easy to track as the other two targets. He had no consistent pattern to follow, and he wasn't addicted to the pleasures of women.

During that time, Deneisha and Sherick had become practically inseparable. They met for lunch or dinner just about every day. And when they weren't sharing a meal in the finest restaurants in the city, they were going to parties and openings, or they were on the phone talking. Their phone conversations weren't long, and one could say that they weren't really about anything.

However, they were different conversations for Deneisha than they were for Sherick. He saw it as the relationship he wished to develop, one that was beginning to take shape, whereas Deneisha saw their relationship as more like that of a girlfriend. The type of relationship that she had with Court or Breezy. Deneisha was lonely without Dallas and needed a friend. Sherick saw that need and exploited it to suit his purpose.

But each night, no matter where they were or what they were doing, at eight o'clock sharp, Deneisha's phone would ring.

"Excuse me, Sherick, I need to take this," she would say, and she would go talk to Dallas until the guard made him get off the phone.

It took Yvette, who was not a fan of Sherick's, to get her back on track and let her know that something else was going on. They were having lunch one day, and Deneisha called Sherick.

"I'm at Singleton's Seafood Shack, and I ordered their New England clam chowder, and it is some of the best clam chowder I've ever had," she called Sherick to say.

Yvette couldn't hear what Sherick said in response, but she knew what she was gonna say as soon as Deneisha hung up the phone.

"Okay, Sherick, I'm having lunch with Yvette, so I'll talk to you later," she said and ended the call.

"I wonder what Trissa thinks of you being on the phone with her man all the time?"

"Who is Trissa?"

"Sherick's girlfriend."

Deneisha sat back. "I didn't know he had a girlfriend. What's her name?"

"Trissa, Trissa Winslow."

"You know her?"

"Of course, I know her," Yvette laughed. "Me and her used to be friends, but we fell out because I called him out for being the cheating ho that he truly is."

"I didn't know that about him," Deneisha said and sipped her wine. "Of course, he's not gonna say, 'Hey, Deneisha, I'm a ho.'"

"But that's exactly who that muthafucka is. A ho."

"How do you know?"

"'Cause I know him, Deneisha. Why are you so ready to defend him?"

"'Cause that is not the guy *I* know."

"Deneisha," Yvette said, pleadingly, "you don't know him like I do."

"How do you know him?"

"I'll give you an example." Yvette was getting frustrated with Deneisha. "You remember a couple of months ago, Salomé Warner was in town?"

When Deneisha heard Salomé Warner, she was all ears.

"I remember."

"He had tickets to see Salomé Warner, and he called her at the last minute and gave her some bullshit story about needing to 'help a friend.'" Yvette finished her drink and signaled for a waiter to bring her another round. "I know he took some other woman. Trissa's into Salomé Warner, like you're into Salomé Warner, so you know the woman was heartbroken. But she didn't believe his lies. So, you know what she did?"

"What did she do?"

"She made him fly her to Miami. They stayed in her favorite hotel, and she made him take her shopping for a new outfit for the show. I think she made him spend at least $10,000 on the outfit he bought her."

"What show?"

"Salomé Warner."

Deneisha was stunned, but she tried her best not to show it.

"She had a concert in Miami the same weekend she was here," Yvette told Deneisha. "She was here on Thursday; she was in Miami on Saturday."

It was all Deneisha could do to finish her meal. Sherick had lied to her more than once, and she was forced to wonder why. He told her that the woman to whom the ticket belonged wasn't as big a Salomé Warner fan as she was. Then he lied again when he told her about being in Miami to address supply chain issues in his legitimate business, and that's why he was there for three days.

Now, Deneisha was faced with a dilemma. Should she call Sherick on his bullshit, or was the smart play to complete her "assignment," as Sherick liked to call it, get paid, and not fuck with him ever again in life? She decided to do both.

Deneisha would complete the assignment, and then, "I'll call Sherick's lying ass on his bullshit," she vowed. But first things first. She had to kill Tyrell Young.

She had been a little too picky trying to find the perfect place and time to kill and complete the assignment. Deneisha just needed to decide when and where she was going to make the kill and be done with it, *and* Sherick.

"But he lied to me. He's been lying to me all along," she told Dallas during their nightly phone call. "I just wanna know why."

"Have you looked at yourself in the mirror lately?" Dallas asked.

"What do you mean?" Deneisha asked innocently.

"Show me a man who don't wanna fuck you, and I'll show you a gay man."

"You think that's all it is?"

"I'm sure of it. I know Sherick. I don't wanna believe that about somebody I called a friend, but like I said, I know him, and Yvette's right; he's a ho."

"You know Trissa?"

"Sure, I do. She's been with him, bought and paid for, for years. He owns her and any thoughts she might think she has. She might know all about you and know, in her position, it's best not to say anything about it for fear of losing that position."

"What should I do?"

"Make that money. Do what you need to do because that's business. After that, it's up to you how you play him. If you're convinced that it has to be something else, play out the string and see where it leads."

"Okay."

First things first, Tyrell Young had to die.

The only place Young was consistently at was Mais. The problem with killing him there was that he was best protected there. The night Sherick brought her up there to meet him, and Young came in, two men accompanied him. She didn't count, but Deneisha was sure that he had more men in the club. Her surveillance of their operation revealed that they conducted the bulk of their activities from that location. So, even if she were to be able to kill Young there, how was she gonna get out?

With few options available to her, Deneisha resolved herself to follow Young and wait for her opportunity.

# Chapter Thirty-two

Deneisha didn't see Sherick for the rest of the week, and she came up with several creative excuses as to why she suddenly had so much to do.

"And besides," she told him, "I have a job to do, remember?"

"Yes, you do, and I'm keeping you from it."

"You actually are. So we'll talk later," she said and rushed off the phone.

Sherick was no fool. He felt Deneisha was slipping away, and he knew the reason had to be Yvette. The day Deneisha called him while she was having lunch with Yvette was the day everything changed, so he backed off.

"No matter," Sherick told Morris. "As long as she takes care of Young for us, it's all good," he said, now thinking that he should have taken his own advice and not invested all that time and money trying to catch a train that may never come.

"That *is* what you brought her in for," Morris said.

He'd had a front-row seat to watch Sherick's pursuit of Deneisha. Morris thought that he shouldn't have thrown all that time and money at somebody else's woman and thought it was funny watching Sherick try, and, more importantly . . . fail.

Deneisha had been following Young for a week, waiting for her best opportunity to complete the assignment. That was how she now referred to it. "Completing the assignment."

She had already come to grips with the fact that she would have to kill his bodyguards to get to Young. Between Holloway, Abbott, Carver, Ingram, and Gaines, Young was always protected by at least two of them, and, at times, all five. She needed to thin that herd to her advantage.

The question was . . . where and how to get them out of the way?

Deneisha knew where each one lived, whether they were married or single, who had kids, and she knew that Carver still lived with his mother. Ingram and Gaines were the best, so she needed them out of the way first. On the day she would make her move, she needed Holloway and Abbott to be protecting Young.

The next night, Young spent the night at the apartment of his sidepiece, Kimberley Swanson. When Deneisha went home for the night, Ingram was sitting in the car parked outside. In the morning, when she returned to pick up surveillance, it was Holloway and Abbott sitting in the car parked outside the apartment.

"This must be my lucky day," she said and waited for Young to come out of the apartment. It was almost noon when Holloway got out of the car and went to the door. When he returned, Young was with him, barking orders as they made their way to the car.

Now, if they stayed true to form, they were going to take Young somewhere to eat. Young wasn't the foodie that Sherick was, but there were a few spots that he frequented. Therefore, Deneisha was surprised when they stopped at Hawkers Asian Street Food.

"Not his usual spot" was what Deneisha was saying when she heard Young yelling, "What the fuck you bring me to this place for?"

"Kimberley said she wanted Bibimbap from here," Abbott said.

"Since when do you work for fuckin' Kimberly?"

"I don't, Boss, I work for you."

Deneisha must have thought that the sun, moon, and stars were in perfect alignment when both Holloway and Abbott got out of the car and left Young alone.

"This is going to be too easy," she said aloud as she watched them go into the trendy Asian restaurant and approach the counter to order. Deneisha looked around for witnesses, and, not seeing any, she got out of her car and casually walked up to the Founder's Edition Audi A8.

"Good morning, Mr. Young. Sherick Powers sends his regards," she said and boldly raised her silencer-clad weapon. She shot Tyrell Young six times. Two head shots and the rest were to the chest.

# Chapter Thirty-three

With her contract complete, and despite what Dallas and Yvette said, Deneisha was not convinced that all Sherick wanted was to fuck her. A big part of that was her own self-worth. Deneisha saw herself as more than just an object for men's pleasure.

It took a couple of days for word of Tyrell Young's death to get back to Sherick, and when it did, he immediately picked up the phone and called Deneisha.

"Good afternoon, Deneisha."

"How are you, Sherick?"

"I'm doing fine, Deneisha, thank you for asking. How are you?"

"I'm awesome."

"Great." He paused. "I was wondering if you didn't have any plans, that you'd consider having dinner with me?"

"Tell me where and when."

"I always choose the restaurant. You choose."

"Are you familiar with Rue Saint-Marc? It's in San Marco. They serve French cuisine."

"I am."

"Of course you are. Five o'clock work for you?"

"Works fine. See you there," Sherick said, and he ended the call, trying, but not succeeding, in gauging her mood. "Well, Morris, time to see how strong my game is."

"Indeed, we will, Boss," Morris said and led the way to the car.

At five o'clock, when Deneisha walked in Rue Saint-Marc, Sherick and Morris were seated at a table. Morris got up when he saw her come in and approach the table.

"How are you, Deneisha?" he asked as they passed each other.

"I'm awesome, Morris. How are you doing?"

"I'm well," he said, taking a seat at a nearby table where he could see them as Deneisha sat down with Sherick.

"Hi, Sherick," Deneisha said.

"How are you doing today?"

"Like I just told Morris, I'm awesome; couldn't be better if I had written the script myself. I'm serious. Lately, it's been as if the sun, moon, and stars are in perfect alignment for me because everything is going my way."

"That's great. I have something for you."

"And what might that be?"

Sherick took out his phone and held it up so Deneisha could see it. Next, he made a small production of transferring the final $10,000 to her offshore account in Curaçao, and she made just as big a production of verifying that she received it. With that out of the way, they enjoyed pommes paillasson, oysters, Mediterranean sea bass, and roasted lamb loin, and they talked like they usually did before Dallas and Yvette opened her eyes.

"When you first offered me this job, you hinted at a more long-term position inside your organization. I believe you said something about the forest for the trees and your wholehearted belief that you were in desperate need of my skills and your services."

"And I meant it when I said it, and I still wholeheartedly believe that." Sherick leaned forward and tried to salvage the game he was running. "In the last few months, you have challenged me in ways that nobody has. You've made me see things in ways that I never imagined."

"So, what would I be doing?" Deneisha asked.

"You'd be my advisor. And what you'd be doing is what you've been doing."

"Challenging you in ways that nobody has and making you see things in ways that you never imagined."

"Yes."

"What does this position pay?"

"How does a thousand dollars a day sound?"

"Sounds like you just hired an advisor," Deneisha said with her hand extended across the table. To Sherick, it represented the successful continuation of the game he was trying to run to win Deneisha's affection and make her his. Deneisha saw it as validation that she was more than just an object for men's pleasure.

Therefore, the next day, Deneisha started her new position as Sherick's advisor and immediately made an enemy of Taquan. He had gotten back in Sherick's good graces after fucking up a deal that cost Sherick an enormous amount of money. Now, here comes Deneisha . . . and she had his ear.

"Where the fuck did she come from, and how did she get so much influence over him so fast?" was the question Taquan asked anyone who'd listen. That list included Trissa.

"I asked and was told to shut up and deal with it," she told Taquan, so she was no help.

"Yeah, well, I ain't goin' out like that," Taquan vowed.

"What are you gonna do, kill her?" Trissa asked.

"I just might," he said and left Trissa's condo.

"I didn't hear you say that," Trissa remarked as he walked to the door.

Things only got worse when Taquan informed Sherick that Sean Collins, who controlled a substantial piece of the market in Northeast Florida and South Georgia, had invited him to a meeting.

"Did he say what the meeting was about?"

"No. But his people said it would be in our best interest to attend with an open mind."

"What the fuck does that even mean?" Sherick turned to Deneisha and asked.

"I think it means—" Taquan began, but Sherick held up his hand.

"I wasn't asking you," Sherick said, and Taquan was embarrassed because Davenport and Jules were in the room when it happened.

"Sounds like a trap to me," Deneisha said. "I wouldn't go unless Collins could guarantee your security."

"That's not how it works," Taquan protested.

"Maybe," Sherick said. "But that's how it's gonna be." He turned to Davenport. "Make sure Collins's people understand that."

"I'll make it happen the way you want, or it's not happening, Boss," Davenport said, and he left the room, giving Taquan the side-eye.

"Jules."

"Yes, Boss?"

"I need you to find out everything you can about this meeting. I need to know when and where it's supposed to go down."

"On it, Boss." Jules looked at Taquan. "I won't let you down," he said and rushed to leave the room.

"Why you do that?" Taquan asked without looking in Sherick's direction.

"Do what?"

"Front on me like that?"

"What the fuck are you talking about?"

There was complete silence in the room, and then Taquan looked at Sherick.

"If you don't know, I can't even begin to make you see it," he said and left the room with his pride in shambles.

"What was that about?" Sherick asked Deneisha when the door closed.

"I can't be sure, but I think it was about you totally emasculating that man."

Deneisha stood up and began looking around the floor.

"What are you doing?"

"Looking for that man's balls."

"Oh, you got jokes, huh?"

"No joke," she said, and she was sure that she had just made an enemy in Taquan. "I'm gonna get Morris to take me to my car. I need to go home and handle some business. But if you like, I'll come back when I'm done, and we can talk about where we go from here with this meeting."

"Yes, Deneisha. I need you to come back when you finish talking to Dallas," Sherick said as he stood up. "And we can talk about the next steps."

When Deneisha left the house, Morris drove her to her car, and she went home to make her call with Dallas.

"What did you decide?" was the first question out of Dallas's mouth.

"I told him that he hinted at a job inside his organization. And he hired me to be his personal advisor."

Dallas laughed. "What the fuck is a personal advisor?"

"Somebody to tell him when he's fuckin' up." Deneisha laughed along with Dallas. "But seriously, do you know a player named Sean Collins?"

"Yeah, he's the big boy on the block. Rumor is that he inherited Oscar Pennington's connections to the Sinaloa Cartel."

"That does make him the big boy on the block," Deneisha said. "So, tell me why he would call for a meeting that will be in our best interest to 'attend with an open mind.'"

"My guess is that it's about the product."

Deneisha laughed. "No shit, Sherlock."

"My advice for you as his personal advisor is to advise him not to go anywhere near the meeting until he knows what it's all about."

"He's got Jules on that," she informed him.

"Another weak muthafucka who doesn't deserve to breathe the same air the rest of us breathe."

"Why don't you tell me how you *really* feel about him?"

"I believe I just did," Dallas laughed.

"Wrap it up, Goodwin," Deneisha heard the guard shout.

"Gotta go?" Deneisha asked sadly.

"I do. I love you, Deneisha."

"I love you more, Dallas," she said and ended the call.

She changed into a Pucci stretch jumpsuit and headed back to Sherick's house. It was after ten o'clock when she arrived, but Deneisha was just in time to see Trissa, dressed in an Oscar de la Renta minidress that Deneisha knew cost almost $7,000 because she had priced the dress and thought it was outrageous. And so were the Tom Ford, crocodile-embossed leather pumps she wore with it.

*But if outrageous is the look you're going for, that is the dress . . .* she thought as the women passed each other in the foyer when Morris let her in.

"Have a good night," Deneisha said to her.

"Fuck you, Assassin," was what Trissa had to say as they passed.

Trissa got into a Range Rover and gave her the finger as she drove away.

"Where she going?"

"To the club."

As Morris escorted her to the den where Sherick was waiting, Deneisha looked at the outfit she was wearing and thought it was a little outrageous, but she wasn't going to the club. She was a bit surprised that Trissa was permitted to go out without any security.

*But she's not my woman,* Deneisha thought as Morris opened the door.

When she went into the den, Jules was in there telling Sherick what he had found out about the meeting, but all Deneisha could think of was Dallas saying that he was another weak muthafucka who didn't deserve to breathe the same air as the rest of them.

"What's funny?" Sherick asked.

"Nothing," she said, but she was still laughing. She looked at Jules, and just like that, Deneisha knew she had made another enemy.

"The word on the street is that he's connected with the Sinaloa Cartel, and he wants to buy serious weight," Jules told Sherick.

"That's what my source says as well," Deneisha added.

"Is that move good or bad for us?" Sherick questioned.

"I think it would be a good move," Jules offered.

"Nobody asked you." Sherick turned to Deneisha. Now, she was sure, based on the way Jules looked at her, that she had indeed made another enemy.

"I agree. Especially with the moves you've made, I think making that move puts us in a superior position."

"What moves?" Jules asked, and Sherick ignored the question instead of admitting that he had Deneisha kill Young, Coleman, and Martin.

"I'd bring along extra security, but yeah, that is a shindig we definitely need to be at," Deneisha said.

"What's a 'shindig'?" Jules asked, and Sherick laughed at him.

"It's a large party, celebrating something big."

"Don't feel bad," Deneisha said, but she was still laughing. "It's a term from the sixties."

"But somehow, you seem to know it and used it to make me look stupid."

Sherick laughed and thought this was a good time to quote Forest Gump. "Well, you know what they say . . . Stupid is as stupid does."

Deneisha laughed so hard her cheeks hurt, and Jules left the den with his head hanging low.

"I just wanna thank you for making another of your lieutenants hate me."

Sherick laughed. "Sorry, but I couldn't resist. And besides, you know what they say . . . Stupid is as stupid does."

"You are so wrong for that."

"I know. But the truth hurts."

"If he's stupid, why does he work for you?" Deneisha needed to know.

"That nigga is loyal as a puppy."

"But if he's so stupid, I imagine that when you do let him think for himself, he fucks up, a lot."

"He does." Sherick laughed. "That nigga fucks up more than that other fuckup."

Deneisha shook her head. "You're right, you do wholeheartedly need me," she said. "Good night, Sherick. I'll see you in the morning."

"Morris will see you out. And, Deneisha," he stood up and walked her to the door. "It's true, I do desperately need your help. And I'm glad you're here."

"We'll get things straightened out. But I am sure that this meeting with Sean Collins is exactly what we need. Good night, Sherick."

# Chapter Thirty-four

When Deneisha arrived at Sherick's house the following morning, he and his men, Morris, Taquan, Jules, and Davenport, were ready to go.

"Where are we going?" Deneisha asked.

"My sources got it a little different from yours," Taquan said.

"In what way?"

"They say the meet is to weed out the muthafuckin' snitches and rats before the *real* meeting in a couple of weeks. So we're going to talk to him."

"Who's your source?" Deneisha asked.

"Anton Moore. Niggas call him Ton," Taquan said as they left the house.

"So he's your source?" she questioned.

"Yeah, he's my source. You got a problem with that?"

"Not at all, as long as he's credible."

"Trust me, me and this nigga go way back. I can trust him."

"That's good to know, Taquan," Sherick said.

When they were on the way to the car, Morris was in the front, followed by Sherick and Deneisha. Taquan and Jules were behind them, and Davenport brought up the rear. Sherick leaned close to Deneisha.

"When we meet with Collins, I want you with me to feel him out."

"What?" Taquan questioned. "You bringing her to the sit-down over me?"

"Yes." Sherick stopped and got in Taquan's face. "Your recent decisions make her the more reliable and, honestly, stable choice."

"That is so fucked up on so many levels," Taquan said as a single shot rang out.

Deneisha, Morris, Taquan, Jules, and Davenport all pulled their guns and looked around for the shooter, but he was invisible. That single shot blew off half of Sherick's head. He lay there with his brains hanging out of what remained of his head.

"Oh shit!" Morris shouted when he saw him lying there.

"Somebody call 911," Jules shouted and dropped to his knees next to the body.

"Already on it," Deneisha said. But she knew there was nothing they could do for him.

Sherick was dead.

It was confirmed when the first responders arrived on the scene, and Sherick Powers was pronounced dead. The damage from that single shot to the head was too extensive.

"I'm sorry, but there was nothing we could do for him," the paramedic said when she spoke to Deneisha.

"Thank you. I know you did your best to save him," she said.

"How you know she did her best?" Taquan asked angrily and walked away from the scene, got in his car, and drove away.

Trissa was hysterical at the loss of her man and had to be taken to the hospital to be sedated. Her doctor kept her in the hospital overnight for observation. Morris, Jules, Davenport, and Deneisha went inside Sherick's house. The question on everyone's mind was who would want Sherick dead. As far as Jules and Davenport were concerned, he was running a nice, quiet program and wasn't having the kind of problems that would get him murdered.

However, Deneisha and Morris knew differently. They knew of at least three people who had reason to retaliate against Sherick. The people who worked for Kameron Martin, Javon Coleman, and Tyrell Young all had reason to kill him.

*But how would they know it was him?* was the question Deneisha asked herself.

She had no answer.

As she sat there, Deneisha reviewed each of the hits in her mind. There were no witnesses to see her do it, no cameras to capture her image and leave a digital trail to follow. And if that *were* the case, where were the police? They were the ones most likely to follow a digital trail back to her.

So who?

Just then, Taquan burst into the house.

"I know who killed Sherick," he announced.

Jules and Davenport bounced to their feet. "Who?" they both questioned. Deneisha and Morris looked at each other.

"It was Big Psych that had Sherick killed."

"You sure?" Davenport questioned. Like everybody else, he had lost confidence in Taquan because, like Sherick said, his recent decisions made him unreliable.

"I don't wanna ride on the wrong muthafuckas," Jules said.

"Yeah, nigga, I'm sure it was Psych or some niggas who was down with him," Taquan insisted.

Davenport threw up his hands. "Now, it's Psych or some niggas who was down with him. Which is it?"

"It's one or the other. You know, if it was some niggas that's down with him, Psych had to know about it."

"That's true," Jules agreed, but he looked at Deneisha for validation.

"I wanna know why you think it was Psych—" Deneisha finally began.

"Or some niggas who was down with him," Davenport threw in sarcastically.

"Or some niggas who were down with him," she nodded at Davenport. "Why are you so sure it was Psych?"

"Because Sherick told me about the argument they had," Taquan said.

"I don't think he's involved." Deneisha shook her head. "Not over that shit."

"How you know?"

"First of all, I was there."

"You were?" Taquan questioned.

"I was," Deneisha said, and Morris nodded his head, confirming that she was there. She turned to Davenport and Jules. "We were at a record release party for—" She snapped her fingers and looked at Morris. "What was his name?"

"Dee Fame," Morris said, laughing. "Psych was there because he got money tied up in the boy. He put money behind the boy because he was counting on the murder case giving him some street cred."

"What was the argument about?" Davenport asked.

Deneisha laughed. "Sherick told somebody Dee Fame couldn't rap, and the only fame he was gonna have was for the murder case the cops were sweating him about, and Psych heard him."

"Psych did get mad and wanted to go to blows over that shit," Morris said, seemingly confirming Taquan's point. But then he laughed. "You know, Sherick's fool, right? He threw up his hands, and they boxed around each other for a minute until Psych's fat ass got tired."

"They ended up laughing that shit off, and Psych ended up agreeing with Sherick." Deneisha laughed. "Fact is, the boy can't rap, and he's going to jail."

Jules looked at Taquan. "What Sherick tell you happened?"

"He told me the next day, Psych was back on that shit because Sherick punking him was the talk."

"I ain't buying that, Taquan," Jules said.

"You taking her side now?"

"It ain't about whose side I'm taking," Davenport stood up to say. "Both people who were there say there wasn't nothing to it. But you say different."

"No," Deneisha said, and everybody stopped talking and looked at her. "It's possible that shit did change. He might be involved."

"What you think we should do, Deneisha?" Morris asked, and the question seemed to anger Taquan. With Sherick dead, he saw himself taking over Sherick's organization. But now, he saw Deneisha as a threat to his taking control.

"I think we need to go talk to Ton and see what he has to say about the meeting. But then I think we need to be patient and see what happens after I meet with Collins."

Taquan stood up and took a step toward Deneisha. "What makes you think you're going to meet with Collins?" he demanded.

"Sherick wanted her there," Davenport replied, standing between him and Deneisha. Taquan stopped moving when Morris stood up too.

"This how it's gonna be?"

"It's how it is," Morris said, and he stepped toward Taquan, who took a few steps backward before he turned and went toward the door. Then he stopped, turned, and faced them.

"This ain't over," he said and left the house, slamming the door on the way out.

"Do you really think we need to talk to Anton Moore?" Jules asked.

"Where would we even find him if we wanted to?" Davenport asked.

"The bigger question is, do we really think Big Psych had Sherick killed?" Morris asked.

"I don't think we should rule him out. Psych might have had him killed," Deneisha said. "But like I said, let's be patient, go to the meeting, see what Sean Collins has to say, and we make decisions about what we're going to do after that."

"I can go for that," Morris said, and Davenport and Jules nodded in agreement. "What now?"

Deneisha stood up. "Now, I'm going home," she said and grabbed her purse. "I'm gonna take a long, hot bath and clear my head. It's been a long few days."

"You need me to come with you?" Morris asked.

"I don't think so, Morris, but thank you for offering. I should be all right. I don't think anybody wants to kill me." She smiled. "At least, not yet."

"At least let me walk you to your car," he said. As far as he was concerned, he was Deneisha's bodyguard now.

"Thank you, Morris." Deneisha left the den and walked out the front door. "Why don't you come get me tomorrow early, and we can talk about this meeting?"

"What time?"

"Not too early, Morris. Say ten, eleven o'clock?"

"Sounds good." Morris opened her car door, and Deneisha got in. "See you in the morning," he said and shut her door.

When Deneisha got to her condo and went inside, she was surprised to see that Taquan had broken in. He was sitting on the couch in her living room with his gun pointed at her.

"Why am I not surprised to see you?" Deneisha said, even though she was entirely caught off guard. Had she had the slightest idea that Taquan would be there, she would have had Morris bring her home.

"All the same, why don't you reach in the bag and pull out that .380 you carry?" Taquan ordered.

Deneisha sat down, went into her purse, and took out her gun. She laid it on the coffee table in front of her.

"What now?"

"What happens now is I kill you, and I take back what you were trying to take from me."

Deneisha had never been so scared in her life. She had faced death more times than she could count at this point in the robberies she committed with Dallas. But this was different. She crossed her legs, folded her hands in her lap, and tried not to show her fear.

"And just what am I trying to take from you?"

"Sherick's organization!" he shouted and pointed the gun at her. "I don't know where you came from or how you got his ear so fast, but me and Sherick go back years."

"That's true. He told me that he was loyal to you for all the shit you two went through together. But you've been fuckin' up lately, haven't you, Taquan?"

"He told you about that?"

"About the Dominicans?" Deneisha nodded solemnly. "He did." She shook her head. "How did you let that get so far out of your control?"

"It *wasn't* out of my control!" he shouted.

"Not that it matters now, but tell me what really happened. Not that bullshit you tried to run on Sherick. That's how you blew it with him. You know that, right? You tried to lie your way out of it, instead of telling him the truth."

"You're right, it doesn't matter now." He pointed his gun at her. "You're gonna die."

"Anything I can do to change your mind about this?"

Taquan laughed. "What? You think I'ma let you get up so you can get to your other gun?"

"The thought had crossed my mind."

"You mean this?" Taquan held up Brianna's nine. "I had enough time to search the place and found that."

"What now?" Deneisha asked again and tried to think of a way out of this or think of some way to get to Dallas's .44 Magnum. He hadn't found that, or he'd be waving it around like he was with Brianna's gun. But it was in the bedroom on a shelf in the closet.

"Stand up and strip."

Deneisha shook her head. "I knew it was gonna come to this."

She bounced up and started angrily removing her clothes. It was the only chance she had.

"I've seen how you look at me. You've wanted me since the first time you saw me. You know this is only a weak-bitch muthafucka like you could ever imagine seeing something like this," Deneisha said when she was standing in front of him naked. "Well, come on. Let's get this over with," she said and started for the bedroom. "And it better be good," she said, walking quickly.

"You don't have to worry. It will be the best you'll ever have. It'll definitely be your last, I promise you that," Taquan said, taking his time getting to the bedroom.

When he came into the room, Deneisha had Dallas's gun and fired one shot. The recoil knocked her off her feet, but Taquan was dead.

# Chapter Thirty-five

Deneisha got dressed, and then she called Preach.

"Hey, Deneisha. It's been a minute. How you been doing?"

"I need your help."

"What you need?"

"I need you to come to the condo as soon as you can."

"I'm into something right about now."

"No problem." She looked at Taquan's dead body. "I'm sure it will keep until you get here," she said, and hoped that none of her neighbors heard the single gunshot from Dallas's cannon and called the police.

"I'll be there as soon as I can," he promised. It was an hour and a half later when he arrived with Yvette.

"Hey, girl," Yvette said when she walked in . . . and then she saw Taquan's body on her living room floor. "Oh."

"Where's Preach?"

"Parking the car," Yvette said as Preach entered the condo.

"Hey, Deneisha. What's up?" he asked, and that's when he saw the body. "Oh. That's what's up." He sat down and took out his phone.

"Yeah, that's what's up," Deneisha said.

"That's Sherick's boy, Taquan, right?" Yvette asked.

"Yes. Sherick is dead."

"Did you kill him too?" Yvette asked.

"No. We don't know who killed him or why. But there's a meeting tomorrow with Sean Collins, and Sherick wanted me to go with him, but Taquan thought he should be the one going."

"First of all, what were you doing with Sherick Powers in the first place?" Preach asked when he ended his call.

"I was doing some work for him."

"What kind of work?" he asked.

"Sherick paid me to kill Kameron Martin, Javon Coleman, and Tyrell Young for him."

Preach laughed, but he was impressed. "That was you?"

Deneisha nodded proudly. "He was consolidating power."

"In a big way," Yvette laughed.

"Well, I just called a cleaner."

"What's a cleaner?" Deneisha asked.

"Somebody who will make all this shit go away," Yvette said with a wave of her hand.

"He'll be here in about an hour. But in the meantime, you need to go somewhere."

"Where?"

"Doesn't matter, just outta here. I'll wait here for the cleaner. Take Yvette with you."

Yvette stood up and went to the door. "Trying to get rid of me as usual, huh? That's okay, I'm used to it. Come on, Deneisha."

"Where are we going?" she asked.

"Does it matter?" Yvette asked, and they left Preach alone in the condo to wait for the cleaner to arrive.

When they returned to the condo later that afternoon, there were no signs that a murder had been committed there. The visible blood stains that Deneisha had seen on her way out of the condo were nowhere in sight.

"Cleaner did a good job," Yvette said as she looked around the living room.

"He did," Deneisha said. "What happens now?"

Yvette took out her phone. “That’s up to you.” She sat down. “I don’t know if I could live somewhere where I killed somebody.”

“I know what you mean. I can hardly look at the spot,” Deneisha said, and plopped down in a chair in front of the spot where his body dropped.

“Hey, babe, we’re back,” Yvette told Preach when he answered.

“I’m on my way,” he promised and ended the call.

“Now, it’s just us girls here. What was really up with you and Sherick?”

“Exactly what I said happened. He hired me to kill his competition.” Deneisha smiled.

“What, girl? Give it up.”

“But he was trying to be slick.”

“*That* sounds more like the Sherick *I* know.”

“Truth was, I missed Dallas, and I, like a lonely fool, I thought he understood that and was trying to be a friend.” Deneisha shook her head and looked at Yvette. “It was me that he took to see Salomé Warner that night,” she sadly admitted.

“Noooo,” Yvette said in disbelief.

“Yes, girl, it was me. He used to take me to eat in the best restaurants in the city, and we went to record release parties and art gallery openings until you hipped me to what was really going on,” Deneisha laughed.

“What’s funny?”

“When I told Dallas about it, he asked me if I had looked at myself in the mirror lately. And then he said to show him a man who don’t wanna fuck me, and he’ll show me a gay man,” Deneisha said, and Yvette laughed.

“He’s right. That nigga wasn’t nothing but a pussy hound. I don’t know why Trissa puts up with his ass,” Yvette laughed. “Yes, I do. He paid for the privilege of dogging her a long time ago.”

"I felt like such a fool. But I turned it around on him. He was gonna pay me a grand a day to be his advisor," Deneisha said as the doorbell rang.

Yvette stood up. "That's Preach," she said and started toward the door.

"Thanks for hanging out with me," Deneisha said, walking her to the door.

She opened the door and let in Preach. He looked around. "Cleaner did a good job," he said. "Try to stay out of trouble, Deneisha."

"I'll do my best," she promised and showed them out. "What now?" she asked aloud. "One thing is for sure," Deneisha said, looking at the spot where she had dropped Taquan's body. "I can't stay here," she said, grabbing her purse and getting out of there.

She spent the night at The Lodge and Club at Ponte Vedra Beach and was back at the condo in the morning when Morris, Davenport, and Jules arrived to take her to the meeting with Sean Collins at The Riverfront Hyatt Regency.

"I haven't seen or heard from Taquan since he left the house yesterday," Jules reported.

"When I see him, he's a dead man," Davenport promised Deneisha.

"Thank you. I hope I can count on you all to have my back," she said instead of telling them that she killed Taquan. "I know I don't know everything about this business, but if you all stay with me and have my back, I promise to do the best I can."

"They know, Deneisha," Morris said.

"They know what?"

"They know that you killed Martin, Coleman, and Young." Davenport and Jules nodded. "They know you earned that spot and the power you're carrying."

"Best that there not be any secrets between us. Agreed?"

"Agreed," what were now her men said in unison.

Deneisha smiled. "Well, I guess this would be as good a time as any to tell you that Taquan is dead." She walked to the spot. "I shot him." She pointed to the floor. "And his body dropped right here."

"Damn," Morris said and looked at the spot. "Not even a trace of blood."

"I called a cleaner," Deneisha admitted. "Give me a few minutes to change my clothes, and we can go to the Hyatt," she said, and her men made themselves comfortable.

When she came out of her bedroom, she was wearing a black cashmere dress by Givenchy and a pair of white Jimmy Choo pearl-embellished sandals with a four-inch stiletto heel, that she'd been saving for just the right occasion.

"Ready," she said, and her men rose to their feet.

When they went outside, Deneisha was looking for one of Sherick's many cars but didn't see any that she recognized.

"What are we riding to the meeting in?" she asked, and Morris raised his hand to unlock the doors to a red BMW 7 Series sedan.

"I picked it up this morning. Out with the old, in with the new," Morris laughed. "I got a good deal. I traded the Ferrari and threw in the Alfa for good measure. The man said I could pick any car on the lot."

Deneisha laughed. "That was a good deal," she said and got into the backseat of her new BMW.

Morris drove her to the Hyatt for the meeting with Sean Collins and the other major players in the city. As she sat there, waiting for the meeting to start, Deneisha was surprised when Imani Mosley and Alexis Fox walked in and took seats. Dallas told her about them and said that Mosley's family had been doing business with the Sinaloa Cartel for years. She and Fox just recently became partners. Deneisha wondered if this was a meeting to form a buying group, as she had been led to believe, what were they doing there? When Sean Collins entered the space, everyone fell quiet.

"I wanna thank all of you for taking time out of your busy day to come here and hear what I have to say." He looked around the room and noticed that neither Sherick nor Taquan was there. However, he did recognize Morris sitting beside Deneisha.

"Where's Sherick?" Collins asked.

"Sherick is dead," Deneisha said.

"Did you kill him?"

"No." Deneisha looked at Psych. "He was killed by a coward who wasn't man enough to face him."

"What about Taquan?"

"Him, I killed when he tried to kill me."

"Who do you think killed Sherick?" Collins asked.

"Honestly, I believe it was somebody in this room." Deneisha pointed at the people sitting around the room. "But in the interest of peace, I will forgo seeking revenge and retribution for his murder."

"That's mighty nice of you, sister," Collins laughed loud and heartily. "But you don't have to worry about that because if I find the coward before you do, *I'll* kill him."

Deneisha laughed. "I was just kidding. When I find out who did it, I'm gonna get medieval on that person."

The crowd of assembled drug dealers laughed.

"What's your name?" Collins asked.

"Deneisha Lewis."

"Well, Deneisha, Sherick being murdered by cowards is why I asked you all to come here." He looked around the room. "Every one of us has been touched by violence. Now, some of y'all are sitting here thinking, 'Yo, Sean, violence is a part of the game.' And it is. But I propose that it doesn't have to be."

He paused to allow that statement to sink in.

"Let me tell you why I asked you all to join me today. We are all in the same business, competing for the same market. And that has led to some of us doing a lot of senseless killing to protect what we see as 'our' market. What I'm proposing is that we stop the killing because I'm sure we can all agree that it's bad for business," he said, and heads around the room nodded in agreement. "We need to work together, and more importantly, buy product together. Now, except for Deneisha, who we all just met, I've known everybody in this room for a long time, and I know I can work with all of you to make this work."

"Who's gonna be at the head of this group?" Barney Rowe asked. "You?"

"That's up to the group to agree on."

"I think you would make a good leader," Imani Mosley said, and Alexis Fox nodded in agreement. "If the floor is open for nominations, I'd like to nominate Sean Collins to be the first chairman of the board."

"I second that motion," Alexis Fox said, and now, Deneisha knew why Imani and Alexis were there. They did business with the Sinaloa Cartel, just like Collins. They were there to validate his position as the first chairman of the board by pushing the vote in his direction. It was a smart move.

With the motion carried, the remainder of the meeting was devoted to appointing board members, and then the meeting was adjourned. When Deneisha walked out of the meeting, she realized that she was now in control of Sherick's house.

She was at the condo the following day, looking online for a new condo to buy, when her phone rang. She didn't recognize the number, but she decided to answer it anyway.

"Hello."

"Hello, Deneisha. It's Sean Collins. Am I catching you at a good time?"

"Yes, Sean. What can I do for you?"

"I wanted to let you know that I have some information that you might be interested in. I was hoping we could get together and talk about it."

Since that was how Sherick came at her, she was a little reluctant to agree to meet him.

"Where and when?"

"I'm outside. Why don't you come out?"

"I'll be out in a minute," Deneisha said. She grabbed her gun and left the condo. When she got outside, she saw a Mercedes sedan and walked to it with her weapon in hand. As she got closer, Collins rolled down the window.

"What you got for me?" she asked.

"Get in."

Once she got inside the car with Collins, Deneisha asked her question again. "What you got for me?"

"I saw how you were looking at Psych and, more importantly, how he was looking at you. I did a little checking with some of Psych's *less* loyal people, and they tell me that it was Psych personally who shot Sherick." Collins shook his head. "I didn't know fat boy could shoot like that, but they say he was some type of sharpshooter in the army when he was young." Collins chuckled. "Who knew?"

"Well, thank you for letting me know."

"No problem. I'm having a few friends over at my house tonight. I hope you can attend."

"I will be happy to come. Just text me the address and time."

"Great. I'll be in touch," he said, and Deneisha got out of the car.

She went back into the condo and sat in her chair. She looked at the spot on the floor where she dropped Taquan's body. Instead of feeling fear or any regret for what she had done, Deneisha now felt powerful. She picked up the phone and called Morris.

"What can I do for you, Boss?"

"I need you to come get me. We've got something we need to take care of."

"I'm on my way."

When Morris arrived, Deneisha told him what she had learned about Psych from Collins.

"What you wanna do?"

"Let's go kill him." She got both of her guns and put them in her purse. "Then we have a party to go to at Sean Collins's house tonight."

Morris fist-bumped Deneisha. "You in there now."

She smiled. "Let's go."

Morris drove Deneisha to Psych's house. They got out, walked up to the door, and rang the bell. When Psych opened the door, he was surprised to see her and Morris standing there, but he tried to play it off.

"Hey, Deneisha. What's up?"

"Hey, Psych." Deneisha smiled. "Sorry to just show up here like this. But there's a lot of talk going around that you know something about who killed Sherick, and I wanted to talk to you myself, and see if we can clear the air."

"I've been hearing that talk too. I'm glad you're here." Psych stepped aside. "Come on in."

"Thank you," she said and followed Psych into the living room, where four of his boys were waiting. She leaned close to Morris.

"You ready?"

"For what?" he whispered.

When Deneisha stepped into the room, she had both guns out and opened fire. She hit Psych with a shot to the back of his head with her first shot, and then she shot another man. Morris very quickly retrieved his gun and shot one of Psych's men.

Another of his men got out his gun and fired a couple of shots in Deneisha's direction as he tried to run, but she caught him with a shot to the back, and he went down. The last of Psych's men fired at Deneisha and Morris before she killed him with two shots to the chest.

When the shooting was over, Morris looked at Deneisha in a combination of awe and disbelief.

"Who the fuck *are* you? I mean, that was some John Wick-type'a shit there," he said as they walked out together.

"Come on," she said. "We got a party to go to."

Morris escorted Deneisha to the BMW, and he drove her away from Psych's house. She looked out the window and thought about how far she'd come. Deneisha had gone from shoplifter to stickup girl, to assassin, and now, she was firmly ensconced in Sherick's organization.